Finch Bo

Single Books
Speech and Debacles

SPEECH AND DEBACLES

HEATHER DIANGELIS

Speech and Debacles
ISBN # 978-1-80250-952-6
©Copyright Heather DiAngelis 2022
Cover Art by Kelly Martin ©Copyright May 2022
Interior text design by Claire Siemaszkiewicz
Finch Books

SPEECH AND DEBACLES

Dedication

To Dad, who always said I could do anything I
dreamed. I wish you were here to watch this
one come true.

Acknowledgements

It goes without saying that it takes a village to create a book, and mine is no exception. Thanks first and foremost to my amazing agent, Jessica Reino — thank you for finding the joy and meaning in *Speech and Debacles* and for championing it every step of the way. Thank you to my editor, Anna Olson, for just *getting* this story; your suggestions have helped mold it into something better than I ever could have imagined. Thank you so much to my cover artist, Kelly Martin — I've spent more time than I can count ogling your beautiful work. And thank you to Finch Books and the Totally Entwined Group, particularly my publisher Rebecca Scott, for giving me the opportunity to join this amazing club. I'm pinching myself every day over how lucky I am to be here.

To Mossy, Bollas and the rest of the Speech and Debate crew — and especially to Bollas, whose stage light extinguished too soon. Through an eternal array of never-ending Saturdays and early morning bus trips, I learned, I loved, I lost, and I learned again. You all encouraged me to dust off my knees and persist, no matter how bleak the outlook. I hope you'll forgive the liberties I took on the timeline of the Speech and Debate season throughout this book.

To Laura Brown and Kari Mahara, my constant confidantes who've read almost every word I've ever written and are always available for bouncing around ideas; I would be nowhere without you. To Maria Ann Green, for being my critique partner and cheerleader and just getting me. To Nikkie Pacuk, for encouraging my passion for writing, editing and reading all the way back in those days of Glee-inspired fanfiction. And thanks a million to the #22Debuts bunch, who never ceased to keep my spirits up when our debut year got tough.

Thanks to my best friend in the entire world, Carolyn "K" Corzine, for co-creating all those handmade books for our second-grade teacher and every issue of our teenybop magazine with the painfully low subscriber list. More than twenty-five years into this friendship, you still inspire me.

To Jan Abbott, my phone date buddy who never ceases to warm my heart with her encouragement and love.

Thanks forever to Dad, who kindled my love of reading and told me I could do whatever I set out to do. I miss you every day.

To Sydney, my sweet toddler who ran around the living room while I added the finishing touches to this novel, and who had the audacity to be born at the start of a pandemic.

To Junior, the energetic light of my life who shows me love in his own special ways and had no complaints about watching an extra episode so Mommy could "write her story."

And finally, thank you to Tony—my love, my partner, my world. You've encouraged my writing from the beginning and always acted as a reliable sounding board. There's no one else with whom I'd rather spend quarantine.

Chapter One

Taryn

Taryn Platt had dragged herself to school today, but the logic behind the gesture escaped her—besides the obvious fact that Grandma had made her. Even her mom hadn't said more than, *"You should probably get moving."*

Taryn powerwalked through the crowd toward the Arts Wing, her backpack bouncing on her shoulders with each overextended step. Because Grandma wouldn't accept any excuses to stay home.

Grandmas were unreasonable like that.

Yesterday, Taryn's arrival at a new school on her first day of junior year had been a miserable mess of trudging through hallways and forgetting names. Now here she was on day two, unprepared for a second round of suffering but required to endure it all the same. A different set of classes than yesterday, a new set of people to remember. Block scheduling was a royal pain in her jean-clad butt. And, good lord, this gigantic school hadn't made it easy.

Taryn's previous school hadn't come close to the square footage — acreage — of this place, even if the student population had been larger. Apparently, that's what happened when you switched from an inner-city school to the rich suburbs...from Mom's foreclosed-on house downtown to Grandma's detached home, complete with paved driveway and pruned flowerbeds.

A boy whizzed past, grazing Taryn's shoulder and leaving a cough-worthy draft of cologne in his wake. A girl two paces ahead skidded and caught herself before weaving onward, as if passing cars in traffic via squeaky-clean tennis shoes. Everyone in this deep sea of backpacks had mastered the fine art of arriving to class on time.

She turned the final corner to the Arts Wing and slowed. The crowd was considerably thinner here. Hell, maybe she was early for the first time since starting at Fir Grove High School.

Yeah, right.

Now if she could only find her damn Drama class.

Taryn retreated to the wall and tapped her phone to life to check her schedule, like she hadn't already memorized it. There it was in plain letters — Drama III, Auditorium 1B. Surely this school couldn't have more than one auditorium, let alone enough auditoriums to break them down into sublevels "A" and "B." Her old school had shared the "auditorium" with the gymnasium, which meant there was definitely no room for a Drama class — let alone Drama I, II, III and IV, one level for each grade.

A gold placard above the double doors in front of her said "Auditorium 1." No "B" in sight. With a deep breath, she climbed the five steps to the main entrance. Then she pulled open one of the large red doors. Inside the auditorium, the lights were dim — not a single student.

Day two and I'm lost again. Typical.

Maybe there was another door around the corner. Taryn's lack of experience aside, she was pretty sure auditoriums had multiple entrances.

She pattered down the steps, turned to the right and sped down the hall and around the corner. The damn bell was going to ring soon.

Halfway down the hall, she came across another door that, judging by its position, must have been a side entrance to the auditorium. She tugged on it and peered in but was met once again with a dimly lit empty room.

Fudge nuggets.

Another door down the hall led to a dark backstage area. Definitely no classes going on in there. Just a quiet area with shadow-filled corners, the kind of place she'd love to escape to and catch her breath.

But no time for that. She turned another corner at the end of the hall, sped past several closed doors with no windows that apparently didn't lead to classrooms. At least by now she had a shallow understanding of how the wings were dispersed across the campus — the sciences just past the registration desk, the humanities near the main entrance and so on. As such, she'd intended her first day in the Arts Wing to go much smoother than this.

Only two more corners before she was back where she started. Based on her luck, the next hall sure as hell wouldn't have the room she was looking for. Then she'd be stuck going to the office with a desperate plea for help. "I found an auditorium but apparently not the right one?" *Pathetic.*

On the next turn, something sharp jabbed into her shoulder.

"Ow! What the—"

"Holy—" came a voice several inches above her.

Her hand flew to her shoulder as she took in the victim of her rush. She'd somehow managed to run into a freaking elbow, of all things. A very pale elbow connected to a very pale arm speckled with blond hair.

"I'm *so* sorry," the voice said.

Right. Elbows were typically attached to human beings. Taryn looked up to find a boy a head taller than herself. He had the widest cheekbones she'd ever seen, despite his frown. Freckles dotted his face, and on top of his head was a swooped-up arrangement of whitish-blond hair.

She blinked hard, struggling to recall where she'd been headed before her shoulder had rammed into the cutest freaking elbow she'd ever seen—a thought she'd never expected to pop into her head.

"That's okay. It only hurt a little." *Or maybe more than a little.*

One side of his mouth crooked into a smile. "I've been told I have sharp elbows, so you know, I'm a walking hazard."

She laughed as he stepped aside. He splayed his hands out to give her the full go-ahead.

Above them, the bell rang. Taryn looked up at it, as if that would make her hear it better. At least she wasn't the only person still in the halls. Being late didn't feel nearly as bad when someone else was late, too.

"Shit. I have to go." She stepped past him. "Thanks for the elbow warning. I'll watch out for them next time."

Jesus H., stop embarrassing yourself.

"Noted!" he called after her as she sped down the hall. She glanced over her sore shoulder for a quick smile to acknowledge his remark, but he'd already disappeared. It was only then that she realized she should've asked for directions. Too late now. And probably for the best, since stumbling through an awkward question to a cute boy would have been slightly more humiliating than showing up late for class. Or so she assumed.

She heard the correct auditorium before she saw it, a jumble of words wafting toward her. When she reached the door, almost a full hallway circle from where she started, it was wide open, with "Auditorium 1B" above it. She slipped inside and halted.

The teacher was already at the front of the room. Instead of assembling the students, though, he was lost in conversation with a tall boy who was clutching a tan satchel slung across his torso. Neither seemed to notice her.

She took a step forward, unsure where to sit. A couple dozen students were scattered throughout the room in the most casual classroom setting she'd ever seen. The red padded seats of the auditorium angled to the back of the room in an upward slant. While two walls were made of concrete, the other two were flimsy wooden partitions that extended from floor to ceiling. They wrapped around two sides of the room like a curtain, blocking the students into a makeshift room with theater seats but no stage.

There were far more rows of seats than necessary. The students in the room could sit two to a row with room to spare. And for the moment, that seemed approximately how they were spread out. Was the teacher just supposed to shout across the room?

She found a bare spot halfway up the rows and slunk over. It was probably a rule against nature to be shy in a Drama class, but to hell with that. People could come to her if they wanted to talk.

Not that they would. But that wasn't the point.

If the teacher had noticed that it was time for class, he gave no indication. In fact, no one in the room seemed to give a flying flip about the clock or the bell or whatever schedule all the other teachers cared about at this fancy, multi-auditorium school. Come to think of it, that guy in the hall with the elbow spears hadn't been in a hurry to get to class. For his sake, she hoped his teacher cared as little about punctuality as hers did.

The door to the room closed. Her ears perked up at the sound.

But the teacher hadn't been the one to close it. No, a pale arm was retreating from the doorknob. The guy from the hall, showing up late as if he knew the teacher wouldn't care, in stark contrast to her desperation to find the room.

He walked up the stairs at the edge of the auditorium, passing rows of seats. Then he glanced her way.

She swallowed hard and darted her gaze to the front of the classroom, where the teacher was continuing his side conversation. Cute though he might be, Elbow Guy was not her type. Not only had he been late for class, but he'd been walking in the opposite direction of the classroom when the bell rang.

Still, her hand found its way to her shoulder, rubbing the sore spot. There'd probably be a bruise by bedtime.

Satchel Guy at the front took his seat, and the teacher glanced at the clock. The students in the auditorium phased out their conversations, as if they knew the time had finally come.

The teacher cleared his throat. "Welcome, welcome, welcome. This is Drama III, the class for juniors where none of your dreams will come true, but at least you'll have fun. If you didn't sign up for Drama III, or if you have some weird agenda against fun, then now's your chance to split."

Chuckles bubbled around the room as the teacher looked around expectantly. No one stood.

"Good. Welp, I'm Mr. Banley-Zimmerman. Most of you probably know that, and if you didn't, then I probably don't know you yet. Rest assured, we'll get acquainted. Sorry in advance for that."

More chuckles. Okay, so this guy was a bit...eccentric. Maybe that came with the territory for Drama teachers. At her old school, the few people actually paying attention would've rolled their eyes at a guy like this. Here, though, the students just went with it.

And hey, maybe that was a good thing. Maybe she was in good company for once.

Because yeah, she'd always had a thing for acting, even if she'd never done it. She had no clue if she'd be any good at it, no idea if she'd one-hundred-percent freeze the moment she was on a stage.

Except...

Except this was where she wanted to be. Just like the characters on *Timbre!*, also known as the greatest TV show of all time, period, where a group of teenage misfits formed a musical theater club. The show was also known for its power ballads, shocking revelations and super intense kissing.

Hells yes to all the kissing. Girls kissing girls, boys kissing boys, boys kissing girls. Enough to give Taryn's bisexual heart all the feels. Which might or might not be why she ran a fan account with more followers than there were students in her school.

Not that she would ever admit that to a single soul inside Fir Grove. Announcing she was a super fan probably wasn't the way to make new friends fast.

Unlike the characters on *Timbre!*, Taryn couldn't sing — of that much she was sure. But if going to a new school meant new beginnings, then now was the time — the only time — to take a leap and get on a stage. To show up for a fine art she loved but had never practiced beyond observing her favorite television show.

Maybe she'd suck at acting, maybe not. Either way, no backing out now.

"Taryn Platt?"

Taryn blinked. Did someone just call her name? She looked left, then right. A few people watched her, and others looked around the room like they were also confused.

With a glimpse at the front of the room, her heart stuttered. Mr. Banley-Zimmerman stared directly at her, a goofy smile on his face.

"Are you Taryn Platt?" he asked. His voice was gentle, neither mocking nor unamused.

She blinked again. *Speak! Tell him it's you!*

"Yeah," she croaked.

Wow, way to go, Ms. Hidden Talent Actress.

"Thank you kindly, Taryn." Mr. Banley-Zimmerman tapped at the tablet resting on the podium in front of him. "Gavin Varns?"

The attention now off her, Taryn closed her eyes as the teacher continued taking attendance. How long had she been lost in television fantasies? What else had she missed the teacher saying?

If she'd been paying attention, would she have caught Elbow Guy's name? Not that she needed it or anything. Because, again, he was most assuredly not her type. Though, one more look couldn't hurt...

She opened her eyes and glanced down the row. Elbow Guy leaned back in his seat, one ankle crossed over the opposite knee. And his eyes were already on her.

She blinked twice on reflex and looked back to Mr. Banley-Zimmerman—a much safer focal point. He cleared his throat and moved to the first row with a stack of papers, likely syllabi. She could do this. She could gather her nerves and be awesome at Drama class. Definitely.

No one would find out she didn't belong.

Chapter Two

Riker

Riker Lucas was rife with ridiculous ideas. Terrible, even.

Like showing up for every single inane class on the second day of junior year. Or wearing the tennis shoes that scratched the skin off his heels just because they matched his shirt.

Or checking his damn email.

Yeah, peeking at that inbox was by far the most senseless thing he'd done in the past seven hours. Because his emails—much like life in the Lucas household—contained nothing but crickets and rejection these days.

He reread the message, double-checking that it was as bad as he'd originally thought.

Dear Mr. Lucas,

Thank you for your interest in voice acting for Seasons of Dust. *We have listened to your demo with interest, but ultimately, we found it is not the right fit for our needs.*

We will keep your demo on file for ninety days. After that
time, you may submit work to us for new casting calls.
Sincerely,
Goldblarg Entertainment

So yeah, that happened. Another attempt at voice
acting shot down like a waterfowl in *Duck Hunt*. Riker
leaned over in the metal classroom chair and shoved his
phone into the backpack by his suffering feet. Maybe
the message would disappear if he couldn't see the
screen. Then he could proceed like nothing happened,
could resort to scouring the *Voice Venture* website for
the meager voiceover gigs he and thousands of other
account holders fought over.

This email would *not* disappoint him.

Disappointment was for people who cared. People
who needed to prove themselves.

It was just that…well…he'd been banking on that
part in *Seasons of Dust* for weeks. After an entire six
months of recording voiceover crumbs for pennies
through his *Voice Venture* account, he'd finally —
finally! — been personally invited to send an audio demo.
Goldblarg Entertainment didn't say how many people
they'd chosen to submit scripted samples, but still, it was
the best opportunity he'd obtained to date. Riker had
spent the rest of that night recording and rerecording,
bringing to life three distinct character voices for the
company's script. Then he'd sent off the sample and
cleared his mind by playing his favorite video game,
Timescale, on his laptop for the rest of the night.

And now, three weeks later, digital proof of wasted
effort.

Of course, *of course*, he had to get this news right as
calculus class was about to start. He could've survived
without listening to another teacher today.

Never mind that it was the second day of junior year and attendance was mandatory without a doctor's note. Forget that Riker had a whole new set of classes to attend and syllabi to skim, thanks to the bulky block scheduling at Fir Grove High School. Because despite the legal and rational reasons to make an appearance on this overcast Tuesday, Riker wanted nothing more than to put his pajama pants back on and play his video game next to a bowl of cereal.

Anything to make him forget that terrible idea to check his inbox.

Not that school wasn't…an adequate way to take his mind off his failure to get a voice acting gig. There were just way more sensible things to do than sit through his fourth—and final—period class. Like learning real-world skills instead of that integral and derivative crap his calculus teacher, Mr. Robin, would undoubtedly spew at him by the end of the hour-and-a-half period. Riker had already had Mr. Robin for sophomore year, so he knew the guy was about as enthralling as a turtle.

Even *Timescale* was more educational than high school. Riker would wager his lunch money for a month that his calculus teacher didn't possess the logic to simultaneously build an impenetrable fort against eighteenth-century reanimated corpses and invest in an appropriate ratio of defense spending and tactical training.

And some day, Riker would even be the person who voiced some of those video game characters. He was hella sure of it.

It just wouldn't be now. *Thanks a lot, Goldblarg Entertainment.*

At the front of the room, Mr. Robin cleared his throat. With a tablet in hand, he began reading the rollcall. Riker stared through his calculus teacher's head, eyes focused on nothing.

Keep doing every little voiceover gig I can get, he said to himself. *Try like hell to get a bigger and better one. Be such a badass at it that I can support myself after I graduate from this futile place of learning.*

"Riker Lucas?" came Mr. Robin's voice. "Yep, you're here."

Riker nodded on autopilot. No matter how far afield his thoughts traveled, the sound of his name would for sure bring him back to the moment. Bonus points that he didn't even have to raise his hand for this teacher.

With any luck, he could get through the whole class zoned out like this. It wouldn't be the first time.

He reached down and scratched the back of each heel, trying to put space between the uncomfortable shoes and each sock. He'd have to burn these shoes to prevent the temptation to ever wear them again.

Calculus class was unlikely to be the highlight of his afternoon. So far there had only been two positives from the entire span of the first two days of school, both related and on the same day. One—his familiar and trusty Drama class, where he could actually practice the useful skills of talking in front of people and testing out character voices (the chill teacher was an additional perk), and two—the girl with the rapidly blinking green eyes who'd rammed into his elbow by mistake and was already in his Drama class by the time he'd arrived. If he'd known she would be in the auditorium, he would've cut his hallway detour short for once.

He lifted a hand to his elbow, as if just the thought of her made it ache.

Pull yourself together, Rike.

He dragged his hand up his arm, then scratched his neck, as if he'd intended to do so all along. Just then, a syllabus landed on his desk, courtesy of Mr. Robin. Riker took this as a cue to look down at the paper and pretend to read it while his thoughts continued to wander.

Knockout green eyes or not, Elbow-Ram Girl, otherwise known as Taryn, hadn't shown an ounce of interest in him. Her eyeballs might as well have been flung from a trebuchet for how fast she looked away every time he'd tried to catch her eye. Then she'd bolted out of Drama class at the sound of the bell as if she'd signed up for a sprinting contest between classes.

Just my luck.

Somewhere near the front of the room, Mr. Robin said, "Great. If you could all flip to the third page, and..."

Riker obeyed. Still, he couldn't understand why every teacher found it necessary to walk through the syllabus on the first day of class. Most everyone would forget all this stuff right after they left the building, and they'd only look at it again when they needed to know what came next. That was how Riker worked, at any rate. Reading the syllabus today was mere busywork.

God, this place sucks.

He glanced down at his backpack. Maybe he could pull out his phone and slide it behind a book when Mr. Robin wasn't looking. He could check his email again, see if maybe he'd been invited to submit a sample to some other company. It wasn't impossible.

Stop. No more crappy ideas today.

The fumes of a dry-erase marker pulled Riker from his reverie. At the front of the room, Mr. Robin had begun to write a list below the underlined phrase "Today's Goals." Riker's fingertips absentmindedly stroked his left elbow.

Another day, another class. Another hour and—he glanced up at the clock—twenty minutes before the final bell would ring and he'd zip his way to the bus. After fifteen minutes of a bumpy ride, Riker would be in his happy place, *Timescale* in front of him, rejection email and green eyes and inattentive parents far from his mind. If he was lucky.

Chapter Three

Taryn

Mr. Banley-Zimmerman pushed a whiteboard to the front of the sectioned-off auditorium, the wheels squeaking like a tinman in need of oil.

Sitting halfway toward the back of the room with no one in arm's reach, Taryn blinked hard. On the third day of Drama class — the sixth day of school — she hadn't planned on listening to a lecture. So far, the class wasn't living up to her expectations.

Because Drama was nothing like the show *Timbre!*

For one thing, no one so far had stood on their chair and belted out a song while gesticulating dramatically. Second, there wasn't nearly as much kissing. No kissing at all, actually.

There was about as little drama in this Drama class as there was in the turkey sandwich Grandma had made her for lunch.

But some things were similar. Her teacher was hokey in an almost-charming way, no seating chart existed, and there were at least two boys and three girls with superb amounts of hotness.

Speaking of which…

Down at the end of her otherwise-empty row sat the guy with the sharp elbows, in the same seat as last time with his familiar high cheekbones, matching outfit and meticulously spiked-up hair.

As far out of Taryn's league as most people she found attractive. He was the type who could probably tell at a glance that she only stood in front of the bathroom mirror long enough to brush her hair and teeth.

The kind of guy who never wondered whether he belonged in this class — her polar opposite. Sure, she'd signed up for a class that involved acting, but that didn't mean she was ready to jump up on a stage yet.

Good God, Taryn. He's too hot to touch — don't even try it.

Plus he's not punctual, so…

Mr. Banley-Zimmerman scrawled "Monologue" across the whiteboard in red.

"So!" he said, capping the marker and tossing it onto the silver tray below the whiteboard. "Monologues. Anyone want to tell me what those are?"

Even as a newbie, the answer to that one was pretty obvious. Not that she'd raise her hand or anything.

Her thousands of *Timbre!* account followers would drop their jaws if they could see her now. If they discovered that she wasn't nearly as outgoing in real life as she was online, that she possessed nothing close to the tenacity of the characters on the show. But of course, her fan account was only digital words and images — no eye contact or vocalization involved.

For some reason, replying to a question in class felt ten times more daunting than getting on a stage and projecting her voice.

The latter would have a script. It involved the expectation of pretending to be someone she wasn't.

As for the former, well…real life didn't have a script.

A girl near the front of the room raised her hand and answered, though Taryn couldn't quite hear.

"Perfect," the teacher replied. "Take notes, everyone. A monologue is a lengthy speech by a single character."

Take notes? Taryn's memory of the syllabus was fuzzy, but she'd assumed the whole point of this class was acting, not note-taking. Would the teacher test them on this? At the end of her row, Elbow Guy stretched his arm across the back of the seat beside him, making no effort to lift a pen. Maybe he knew something she didn't. Or maybe he was just a bad student.

Better safe than sorry. She pulled a notebook from her backpack and jotted down as much of the definition of "monologue" as she remembered.

"The type you've probably all heard of is called the 'dramatic monologue'…"

* * * *

For the next fifteen minutes, Mr. Banley-Zimmerman lectured about different types of monologues, writing out their names on the whiteboard and adding famous examples in dark-blue dry-erase.

"So! Any questions?" he asked from the front of the room, eyebrows raised. Around Taryn, shoulders shrugged and heads shook.

A guy near the front with slicked-back hair said, "Nope!"

"Good. Because now we get to the fun part."

More fun than taking notes, I hope.

"Now that you're all experts on monologues — which you obviously are after listening to me — you'll get to put that into practice for your first assignment. This is on the syllabus, so hopefully some of you saw it coming."

Taryn's mouth twitched. *Oops.*

Her teacher walked up to the whiteboard and underlined the word "Monologue" twice. "You all need to find a monologue, memorize it and act it out! And don't worry, it only has to be two minutes long. One-hundred-and-twenty seconds."

Oh God. Was it good or bad that her first acting assignment was solo? At least she wouldn't have to consult with anyone while she figured out what to do. She could do trial and error in the privacy of her own — well, her grandma's — home.

The teacher continued. "I brought a few dozen scripts from my office with monologues in them, so you're all welcome to poke through to find one that speaks to you. But there are a lot of other places you could look, too. The internet, of course. Or movies. Even a novel if you're feeling fancy. Just as long as it's one person talking for two minutes."

He looked around with his arms spread out. Taryn blinked back at him. No one in the room said anything, though most seemed to be paying attention.

"So. Questions?"

Again the room was silent. Taryn saw a couple of people in front shake their heads. They'd probably done assignments like this a dozen times before.

"Good. Great. Grand. Wonderful. We've got twenty minutes left, plenty of time for you to think about what you want to do. You can use next class to work on perfecting them, so try to pick out your piece before that and bring it with you. You'll perform the class after that!"

Wow. This guy wasn't messing around. They were diving right in, with only one full class period to prepare. Taryn foresaw many long evenings of memorization ahead. Not to mention the time she'd spend freaking out about giving a monologue in front of a bunch of people she didn't know — in a class where she already had trouble participating.

But.

Despite all that, a nagging feeling in the back of her brain reminded her that she wanted to do this. She hadn't watched three seasons of her favorite show because she hated the idea of the stage. Quite the opposite.

"Hey. Earth to class."

Taryn looked up. Mr. Banley-Zimmerman was still standing there, now with his hands on his hips. A few students chuckled.

"I didn't lug these scripts over here from my office just because they look pretty. Come rifle through them. If you find one you like, you can take it home. Just let me know which one you take."

Taryn put her hands on the armrests, ready to lift herself to standing and peruse the scripts. She hesitated, waiting for someone else to move first.

Down at the end of her row, Elbow Guy stood, the only indicator that he'd been paying attention. As if he'd done so a thousand times, his elongated legs carried him so quickly down the steps that she'd barely stood to imitate him before he had his hand on the stack of scripts. Likewise, others in the room stood and made their way forward.

Jeez, she wished Mr. Banley-Zimmerman didn't have everyone's names memorized so she could give Elbow Guy the rightful nomenclature in her head. The teacher hadn't done a rollcall since she'd zoned out on the first day of class.

"And if you lose one, I expect you to sign over your firstborn!" Mr. Banley-Zimmerman called over their heads.

As Taryn and a few others approached the table at the front of the room, the as-yet-unnamed Elbow Guy fanned out the scripts. His fingers, long and lean like the rest of him, with knuckles as bony as his sharp elbows, skirted over the covers, grazing each as though his simple touch would bring them to life.

Should I say something? I want to say something.

I could make a joke about his stabby elbows.

No, definitely not.

Act natural. He probably doesn't remember you anyway.

She reached for the closest script at the same time that he extended his arm for the one next to it.

Her heart stuttered as the skin of their fingers brushed for a fraction of a second. Taryn averted her eyes. Did he do the same?

She picked up the script, pulling her hand away from his. This contact was much softer than the elbow-ram of a few days previous, but it still made her neck pulsate.

Hm. Taryn was sure he wasn't her type, especially after he showed up late for a third Drama class in a row. Almost like he did it on purpose. How on earth could she be attracted to someone — guy or girl — who didn't respect the rules?

But holy cow, he did unnatural things to her heart rate.

Okay, Taryn. Focus. Don't look at him. Monologue time.

She took a small step away from the table as she examined the cover of her chosen script, *Fences*. She'd never heard of it. She flipped it over to scan the back cover and gathered that it was a story about crushed dreams in the 1950s. Not her cup of tea.

Gaze still pointed downward, Taryn set the script back on the table and picked up one with no one else's hands nearby. This script had a warped heart on the cover, something about AIDS in the 1980s. Also not her thing, but at least the presence of queer characters made her feel a little more at home. She ran her fingers across the top of the pages, where several sticky notes poked out. Mr. Banley-Zimmerman must've marked them. Flipping to a tab at random, she found a lengthy monologue, all about death, death and more death.

Yikes. Not the story for her.

At this rate, she might as well pick a monologue from a *Timbre!* episode. She had most of the lines memorized at this point, anyway. Then again, it was doubtful the show contained any two-minute stretches of dialogue from one character, and songs didn't count.

Taryn looked up at the others who'd gathered around to look at scripts, purposely avoiding a glance in *his* direction. Two classmates were engrossed in tabbed pages. Lucky them.

Then she let herself look where she wanted. Elbow Guy flipped quickly through the pages of the script in his hand, so fast there was no way he could have read three words. He tossed it down and picked up another, doing the same flip-through. Either he hadn't found anything interesting or he had no intention to. His eyes gave no impression of concentration, his eyebrows straight lines. But then why bother coming to the table?

He tossed the next script onto the stack and raised his eyes.

To hers.

She flinched. On impulse, she lowered her head and picked up the first script her fingers bumped. Out of the corner of her eye, she saw Elbow Guy's feet depart. Presumably back to his seat, though she didn't dare look that far from the script to verify.

* * * *

Taryn moved her shoulders up and down as she stared at the computer monitor. How on earth did Grandma survive with this clunky desktop instead of a laptop or tablet? The thing was fancy and newish, sure, but she couldn't relax on the couch with it, let alone take it to her room.

Taryn could tick off a list of all the things that sucked about living with Grandma. There was nothing wrong with the woman herself, but the transition to Wealthy Town left much to be desired.

Case in point—the desktop computer chilling in a makeshift office, screen facing the door for all passing eyes to see. Always the chance of someone reading over her shoulder from the doorway. Not that she did anything *bad* on the internet…still, fangirling over television kisses would take too much explaining.

For another thing, Grandma apparently didn't know anything about entertainment, unless she counted the shelves upon shelves of books positioned throughout the house. Bonus points for internet, but streaming services were apparently frivolous non-necessities.

Rich people had the strangest sense of how to spend their money.

Hell, even Taryn's mom had paid for streaming before her house was taken away. She only canceled it after the foreclosure, as if that fourteen dollars per month would save her now.

As for the foreclosure, well...

Switching to Fir Grove High School was great, but suffice it to say that leaving behind her old house for Grandma's almost-clinical one wasn't thrilling. Even the giant brown and red flower patterns on her bedspread made her new bedroom feel more like a hotel room.

Taryn was now resigned to free — and dubiously legal — *Timbre!* clips on the internet, at least until she had streaming access to all the episodes again. On the plus side, the next season would soon air on primetime television, no extensive cable package required. For now, she could survive on distorted online clips.

Probably. Maybe. Hopefully.

Taryn had spent the better part of an hour adding an update to her fan account and subsequently replying to comments left by some of her followers. Without the ability to rewatch episodes in full, she'd had to search for GIFs to find the exact dialogue from the season finale when Molly kissed Valerie, Taryn's all-time favorite character. All this so she could post her own moony-eyed throwback about it. The season had ended months ago, but Taryn had to keep her updates fresh, keep her followers engaged so they wouldn't jump ship before the start of next season.

And yeah, she could lose herself in her fan account, could let time pass by unnoticed, but that didn't make up for the complete lack of other things to do in this house. Four times bigger than her foreclosed-on home but somehow quieter and entertainment-deficient.

She leaned back in the leather office chair, looking left, right. Nothing but a desktop computer and books in her field of vision.

Books.

She blinked twice. Mr. Banley-Zimmerman had mentioned they could use novels for their monologue assignment. She seriously did not feel like doing homework now, but this assignment was more exciting than real homework, and she'd been unable to find a script she liked during class. Maybe one of these shelves housed a book she could use...

Better to do this quickly while she had the motivation.

The first spine that spoke to her had a gray matte finish. She pulled it off the shelf and ran her fingers over the gold-embossed lettering — *Sense and Sensibility*. A red bookmark ribbon poked out from the top of the pages, looped and knotted to attach to the binding. The hunk of long-gone tree in her hand shouted *classic literature*. She wasn't a big reader, but something as pretty as this book begged to be touched.

She opened to a random page and read. Then she did the same to another page.

Lots of formal language. Not so much in the way of monologues.

Lovely for sure, but not exactly light reading.

Next.

The second book she pulled from the shelf had a glossy paper cover over the hardback. *Gone with the Wind*. She'd at least heard of this one but knew next-to-nothing about it.

Once again, the random pages she skimmed seemed irrelevant for the assignment at hand. Not to mention racist.

The third book contained raised bubble letters on the cover, a worn but sturdy paperback titled *Catch-22*. After three randomly selected pages, though, Taryn was sure it wouldn't serve her purposes either.

This exercise was pointless. She might as well search the internet for "famous monologues" and resign herself to being a cliché drone doing the minimum she could get away with.

She sighed and plopped onto the floor, legs crisscrossed.

She seriously had to have a conversation with Grandma about streaming services. Except Grandma would tell her to read a book instead—less brain rotting that way. It seemed impossible that her mother had grown up in this house.

Taryn looked back to the bookshelf with a final desperate glimmer of hope. One more book. She'd pick up one more and hope it had a monologue somewhere.

Squeezed between two tall hardcovers was a tiny white book with plain black lettering on the spine. *The Catcher in the Rye,* by J. D. Salinger. She nodded at the spine. This one she'd heard of, even though she didn't know much about it. Hell, if there weren't a monologue in it, she could at least hope for amusement.

The white cover might have been pristine in a bygone day, but now it was covered in finger smudges, as if it were too delicate to handle the touch of a lowly casual reader. Whoever had read this before—Grandma?—apparently hadn't bothered with delicacy.

Taryn opened to a random page and read.

Oh.

The very first sentence she caught was about someone watching girls in a lobby. This one was in first-person, like the whole book was a monologue. Taryn had no context, but she pictured a girl like herself leaning back on a leather couch, waiting for someone, her eyes raking over women as they passed.

Well damn, sounds like a book I can relate to.

The narrator continued with observations of heaps of girls waiting for their dates, commenting on their legs in turn.

Uhhh. Is this about me?

A bark of a laugh escaped her lips. Yeah, right. Like Grandma would have queer books on her shelves. But it was still fun to think about.

By the time she got to the end of the page, she'd concluded two things. One—unfortunately, this was probably not from a girl's point of view, owing to the character's male roommate at school, and two—the book must be old, unless words like "swell," "dopey" and "get sore" had become hip without her notice. Who knew, maybe they had.

Either way, a lot of what this character said, the way this character talked, wasn't far off from herself. Examining girls, being cynical, adding "way" and "just."

It was almost like she could...

The corners of her mouth quirked up.

Like she could talk as a present-day girl and give the book a whole new meaning for her monologue assignment, without changing a word.

She lay on her stomach and flipped to the beginning.

Chapter Four

Riker

The girl practicing in front of Riker had said some form of "um" or "uh" seventeen times in the last sixty seconds of her monologue. That was with a script in front of her face. But hey, at least she pushed through. She had some serious stamina, if not stage presence.

He clapped three times as she finished and bowed to her audience of one. "That was good," he said.

"Thanks!" she squealed. "Now I just have to memorize it."

"Always the hard part." At least, he assumed most people thought it was the hard part. Memorizing lines had always come easy to him. It seemed like the right thing to say to the classmate who'd asked if she could practice in front of him after Beezy — otherwise known as Mr. Banley-Zimmerman, who doubled as his Drama teacher and Speech and Debate coach — gave everyone class time to work on their monologues.

She flipped her hair over one shoulder and smiled. "Your turn to practice. I'm all ears."

"Thanks, but I'm still trying to figure out what to do." He hoped she wouldn't question the piece of paper already in his hands — if she looked closely, she'd notice it contained an entire two-minute monologue.

"Oh, okay, no worries! I'll leave you to it, then."

He nodded as she sauntered back to her auditorium seat. Riker adjusted in his own seat and tilted his head back. Around him, the sound of practicing classmates chimed in his ears.

He hadn't come to class prepared to show anyone his monologue, least of all a classmate he hardly knew. He was sure that girl had been in his Drama class the past two years, but no way could his brain dig her name out of his hippocampus, stellar memorization skills or not.

From the moment Beezy had announced the assignment, Riker knew he'd perform an Oscar Madison monologue from *The Odd Couple*. He'd been on the Speech side of the Speech and Debate team for two years, going on three, so if anything, this assignment felt like a free pass from Beezy. Riker practically had *The Odd Couple* memorized — it was a script he'd considered for last year's Speech season before he'd chosen something with a little more flash and originality.

Thanks to this Drama class assignment, though, an Oscar Madison monologue gave Riker the opportunity to channel one of the greatest actors who'd ever played the part — Walter Matthau. Knowing the script so well gave Riker leeway to play with the voice, to hone his Walter Matthau imitation while adding his own twist.

Just the kind of character voice he could use for a new *Voice Venture* demo.

But rehearsing in front of other people — even for his Speech coach — really wasn't his thing. He'd rather act to a wall a thousand times. Few things were worse than the humiliation of a shitty practice performance in front of other people.

The only reason he'd looked at scripts last Drama class was to get the ball rolling for everyone else. Beezy had appeared so hopeful his students would dive into the scripts he'd hauled in from his office, but no one seemed willing to budge. As far as teachers went, Beezy was about the most laid-back of them all, even if he was just a predictable middle-aged guy. Riker couldn't leave him hanging.

And if going up front to look at scripts prompted Riker to accidentally brush hands with Taryn Platt, then damn, that was a bonus. Maybe Beezy was a matchmaker in disguise.

He chuckled out loud at the thought. Beezy was clever, but surely he didn't get paid enough to perform matchmaking duties on top of teaching Drama and coaching Speech and Debate.

Hopefully, if anyone in class heard Riker laugh, they'd assume it had to do with his monologue practice. More likely, no one had heard him over the noise in the room.

Riker crossed his right ankle over his left knee, the paper on his lap shifting. He used this as an opportunity to steal a look at Taryn, who'd been sitting in his row the last he saw.

Yep, still there.

Still pulling his gaze in like an asteroid brought into orbit.

Taryn had both feet flat on the floor, a single photocopied piece of paper in front of her. Her lips moved quickly. From Riker's vantage point, it seemed like no sound was coming out. Taryn had either chosen to practice alone or hadn't found anyone to practice with.

He extended his arm over the back of the seat beside him. If it were the latter situation, he could offer to practice with her. Maybe he'd even get to examine her eyes up close.

If the former, he'd be best off staying far away, leaving her to do her own thing.

He looked back down to the monologue in his lap. He didn't want anyone interrupting him, so he'd give her the same courtesy.

Though if *she* were the one to offer help, he wouldn't pass up the chance, even if actual help wasn't on his wish list.

None of it mattered. He couldn't focus with all the noise in the room anyway. Gaze still down, he perked up his ears to the trio two rows in front of him. One guy powered through his monologue, stuttering over words but persevering without hesitation, while two girls interjected with "good!" and "I like that!" They had more energy than Riker could honestly give. Maybe they weren't being honest either.

With a mind of their own, his eyes drifted back to Taryn. She sat more stiffly now, as if afraid to move. Or *unable* to move.

Her lips no longer mimicked words. Though he was a dozen chairs away, he sensed she was looking through the paper instead of at it.

Taryn's jaw clenched.

Was she in pain? Or maybe she had trouble hiding her emotions about something. Hell, if Riker's emotions showed on his face during class, he'd probably look much the same as Taryn right now.

In a flash, her face paled and she clenched a hand around the armrest. It happened so quickly that his gut told him he'd imagined it. But no, she was still pale, still appeared to be in pain. Her fingers tightened, exposing white knuckles.

He stood. With six large steps, he crossed the row until he reached her. Peering down, he said, "Hey."

She raised her eyes to his, her head unmoving. "Hi."

He swallowed his spit, unsure where to go from here. He should've asked, "Are you okay?" He should have knelt next to her and discreetly said, "Do you need help?" But somehow, it seemed too late for that already.

Taryn let out a breath as her body relaxed. A contrived smile spread across her face. Whatever had been going on—something with her body? with her mind?—had passed.

Halle-freaking-lujah.

But.

He shifted his feet. Now he stood looking down at her like a loser. Not even at her level, as if he'd assumed some protector role she hadn't requested. How rash of him to imagine she needed help. If something were actually wrong, someone else would have noticed. She would have said something, at least to Beezy. He'd been too hasty.

Always coming up with outlandish ideas.

Follow through, Rike. You can't walk away now that you said hi. He cleared his throat. "Can I sit?"

Taryn nodded. "Sure."

He pulled down the flap of the auditorium seat and sat at an angle to face her. There was nothing to do now but dive in with purpose. Retreat at this point would be a more shameful fate. "Do you want help practicing? I could, um, I could listen to your monologue if you want."

"Oh. I think I need more time before I do that. I'm not..." She tucked a strand of hair behind her right ear. "I'm not ready to show anyone."

"Sure, okay. I'll leave you to it, then." He stood abruptly, the auditorium seat springing up. *Smooth move, Rike.*

He strode back down the aisle and plopped into his seat. It was then that he realized he'd probably only spent ten seconds in Taryn's presence. An unworthy attempt. If he hadn't been so flustered thinking she was in pain, he could've gathered the nerve to stick around for more than four sentences. As it was, maybe he'd just invented her discomfort as an excuse to get close.

Stop being a total screw-up!

If there were a schoolwide award for Most Likely to Misread a Situation, he'd have top honors. In no way had this gone as well as the time they'd run into each other in the hall, and that had involved ramming his elbow into her shoulder so hard she'd yelped.

Even worse, he loathed that he couldn't stop hating himself for messing everything up. Nothing ever went his way, and the bitter voice in the back of his head never let him forget it.

He didn't dare look back in Taryn's direction at this point. If she were watching him now, it was probably with annoyance. So much for making a good second impression.

Chapter Five

Taryn

As the girl on the stage took a bow, Taryn lifted her hands to clap along with everyone else.

Taryn had paid enough attention to her classmate's *Chicago* monologue to know the girl was rocking it and had definitely been in Drama class before this year. The rest of the minute and forty seconds had been spent internally freaking out.

Taryn had never taken a Drama class. She'd never been on a stage. And soon, everyone in the class would know it. She'd get laughed out of the auditorium, first off the stage — which was now visible to the room after Mr. Banley-Zimmerman had moved the wall partitions — then out of Auditorium 1B.

"Great job, Monroe!" Mr. Banley-Zimmerman said from an auditorium seat in the back center of the room, a clipboard on his lap. "Good, good, good. Okay, who's next? Taryn?"

Taryn swallowed. Was he volunteering her or was she actually next on his list? Regardless, it wasn't like she could say no.

She stood and made her way to the side of the stage, where she climbed the five stairs. As her feet propelled her toward center stage, the corners of her vision blurred. The only thing in her line of sight was the movement of her feet.

This was such *a bad idea.*

She faced the audience and lifted her chin. In the rows below, most of her classmates blinked up at her, suspiciously polite. But the guy who'd bumped into her in the hall all those days ago — the same one who'd offered to help her practice last class during the most inconveniently timed menstrual cramps ever — stared past her head as if determined to only half listen. Disappointing, but probably for the best. If he looked like this now, she couldn't imagine how bored he would've been if she'd taken him up on his offer to practice together. She'd dodged the humiliation bullet.

Her eyes landed on Mr. Banley-Zimmerman, whose smile was so large she could see a glint from one of his crooked front teeth. He gave a slight nod, encouragement to begin.

She nodded back.

You got this. Channel your inner Timbre!

She licked her lips once, popped a hip out to the side with a hand on top and began.

As she talked about watching girls from a lobby, she raised her eyebrows and nodded knowingly. At another point, she rolled her eyes and flicked her wrist as if shooing away the thought of girls waiting for their dates.

She continued, her voice high-pitched and overly feminine, a cynical femme droning on about ogling girls. She took turns focusing her gaze at different parts of the air in mock eye contact, smirking at one spot, raising her eyebrows at another. She pulled an imaginary phone out of her back pocket and pretended to text one of her lines. When she caught Mr. Banley-Zimmerman's eyes, she gave an in-character gasp, then belted out her next line. Her teacher's eyes crinkled with laughter, his hand writing furiously though he didn't look down.

Yes!

She dared a single glance at Elbow Guy. To her surprise — delight? — he was no longer staring past her. Instead, his eyes were firmly on her, shining bright. One shoulder shifted, but he was otherwise still.

Please let him realize I'm interested in guys, too…

She finished with a wave of one hand. The final word rang out across the auditorium as she stood motionless, a trick she'd picked up from *Timbre!*

Moments later, applause burst out from her classmates and teacher. She exhaled.

Yes, yes, yes!

She wanted a giant smile to spread across her face, but it was somehow blocked now that her monologue was over. Instead, all she could manage was a meek blink, a modest shrug of the shoulders.

God, how nice it was to hear a room of people clap for her. For *her*. Like she was a freaking actress. It was just a classroom's worth of clappers, but still…hot damn.

A smile still wouldn't come. With her assignment finished, the confident character she'd channeled disappeared into a wisp of smoke.

Her own confidence had floated away with the character.

She ducked her head and scurried off the stage, down the steps. Within a fraction of a second, she was back in her seat. She swiped her fingers across the back of the opposite hand, catching them on the dryness forming around her knuckles. The clapping had ended, of that much she was sure.

"Taryn, thank you."

She swallowed. Nothing in the room seemed stable or even solid. Still, she forced herself to turn in her seat to face the teacher.

"Good job," he said. "Can you see me after class, please?"

"Uhh." *Crap, did I say that out loud?* "Yes?" she croaked.

"Great. All right, who's next?"

Taryn didn't catch the next name he called. It didn't matter — teachers never asked to see people after class for good reasons, so there was about an eighty-eight percent chance she wouldn't be in this class long enough to need to know anyone's name.

He knows I'm a fraud. They all do.

Then, as if pushing its way through the black hole of her thoughts, she heard a familiar voice.

A gentle voice with a hint of roughness at the edges. A voice she'd thought she had down pat after hearing it only twice, but now something was vastly different about it.

Elbow Guy.

His specific words didn't make a difference — her ability to concentrate on them flew upward and past the rafters.

She was more focused on the *who* than the content.

There was no question about his talent. He performed with ease, stressing the right words, inserting passion at the right parts. She had no clue what the monologue was from, but it felt old-timey and classic. Elbow Guy's voice was skewed, lilted, like a performer from a period long forgotten—an era of cigar rooms and olive-green armchairs.

She didn't need the name of the source to know he enjoyed being on a stage. His tone was conversational, his body relaxed, as if this obscure character voice came as naturally as taking a shower on autopilot. If anyone had asked—not that anyone would—she'd guess Elbow Guy had performed for people dozens of times.

Everything about this guy, from the tip of his swooped-up hair to the bottom of his shirt-matching sneakers, reminded her why she represented the "B" in "LGBT."

Ohmygod. I can't believe I'm going to miss out on staring at this guy.

Fudge, I still haven't caught his name!

Mr. Banley-Zimmerman was definitely going to kick her out of class, tell her she wasn't ready for the big leagues of Drama III. Compared to Elbow Guy, Taryn was a toddler rushing to take off the training wheels. Maybe she'd get to see him in a school play sometime. Watching from the audience was all she was destined to do. It would suck not having the chance to get to know him, but…well, such was life.

* * * *

Taryn clutched the straps of her backpack, digging her fingernails into the purple nylon. Whatever Mr. Banley-Zimmerman had to say to her, there was no way it would be good. She'd been too damn mortified after her monologue to be enthusiastic about anyone else who'd performed. Unless the sheepish smile she accidentally gave after Elbow Guy's performance counted. Not only was she a terrible performer, she was a terrible audience member.

In front of Mr. Banley-Zimmerman was one of her classmates—the one who always seemed to be talking to the teacher before and after class. With one hand on his hip and the other flailing in the air as he spoke, his words came out rapid-fire and his tan satchel swayed at his side.

"I seriously thought this was going to be totally useless, you know? But, like, I kept reading, and ohmygod, you were so right. I have to chop it up and stuff, but that shouldn't take too long. At least, I hope not. Do you think it will?"

The teacher shook his head and said, "No," but the guy continued talking as if he hadn't been waiting for a response. What on earth was he talking about? They hadn't received another Drama class assignment yet. Then again, she hadn't exactly looked ahead on the syllabus...

"Easy-peasy, Coach. I'm so excited. Like, so so so excited. It'll be dope. You're going to love it!"

Coach?

Mr. Banley-Zimmerman nodded and smiled. "I'm sure I will."

Taryn's fingernail clutch tightened. This guy's personality was so beyond anything Taryn could ever be.

"Taryn, hi."

She raised her gaze and found her Drama teacher staring at her with a warm smile, her nameless classmate gone. She forced her feet forward. But when her left foot hit the floor, pain shot through the left side of her abdomen. Taryn steeled her jaw to prevent a wince. Then the pain disappeared as quickly as it had begun.

Well, that's new.

Her teacher blinked at her — oblivious, she hoped.

"Yes. Hi. You wanted to see me?"

Her teacher's cheeks were blush-red, his lips shockingly maroon, though he didn't wear lipstick as far as she could tell. He bobbed his head as he spoke. "Yes. There's something I want to talk to you about."

Here comes the reprimand. Bring it on, Mr. Drama Teacher, so I can go sulk over this at home with sappy Timbre! *clips.*

"You might've heard that I'm not just the Drama teacher. I'm the Speech and Debate coach, too."

Wait — what? What does that have to do with anything? Her hands relaxed as she lowered them to her sides.

"No, I didn't know."

"Well, surprise! I am!"

She held her tongue from releasing a sarcastic "Congratulations?" Instead, she settled on, "Oh, okay."

He continued. "I loved the way you interpreted that scene today. Holden Caulfield as a female? And you meant it to be in the present, right? You beefed up that character in a way I've never seen. Fascinating."

So...I'm not getting the boot? "Thanks."

"You're welcome. So, I wonder if you might be interested in joining the Speech and Debate team. Or at least considering it. We're always looking for talent, and I think you really have the type of acting skills that'll shine in competition."

"I'm...uh. I'm confused. No offense, but what does acting have to do with Speech and Debate?"

"Oh! Right. It's not just giving speeches and debating policy, though you can go into one of those events if you like. There are all sorts of acting events — giving dramatic monologues and interpreting poetry, all that jazz."

Her eyes widened as she processed this. *Holy shit. He thinks I could* compete *in those events?*

"Think about it, okay? Our first meeting is Monday after next, in this section of the auditorium. Meeting starts at four, should last about forty-five minutes. And if you come to the first meeting, you're not obligated to sign up. If you like what you hear, you can stay longer to talk about what event you want to do."

"Gotcha. That might be okay."

He smiled. "I hope so. Like I said, I really think you have a shot at doing well. We'd love to have you."

She swallowed, taking it in. His request was a far cry from kicking her out of class.

What would be the harm in showing up for a meeting? She could at least find out what being on the team would entail, and what kind of other people would be there. If everyone on the team was as outgoing as that guy with the satchel, she'd know off the bat that it wasn't a good fit, and she could run far away before feeling the sting of not fitting in.

"Okay. Yes. I'll come to the meeting."

Chapter Six

Riker

Nine dollars and seventy-three cents.

That was the balance on Riker's *Voice Venture* account.

Did he want to request a bank transfer? His account page wanted to know.

Riker sighed. An extra nine-almost-ten bucks in his pocket would be nice, but it wouldn't even cover a trip to Chipotle. Not that he *needed* the money, per se. If he texted his mom that he wanted to grab food after school the next day, a twenty would be waiting for him on the kitchen table in the morning.

Still. The ability to buy something himself would be nice. Especially the microphone he'd been eyeing online for a while now. Hard to say whether it'd make a difference in the quality of his voice recordings, but at this point he'd try anything to get better gigs. Anything except ask his mom to buy it for him.

"Riker? Honey?"

Speaking of which…

He looked up from his low earnings balance. His mom stood at the threshold of his bedroom, fingers closing the clasp of her small purse. A sure sign she was on her way out. Again.

"Yeah?"

"I'll be back later. Don't forget to unload the dishwasher."

"Sure, Mom."

She slipped her purse onto one shoulder. "Thanks, honey."

And with that, she turned and retreated down the hall. He didn't let the dual use of "honey" sway him. While he wished the endearment had a greater meaning, he knew it rolled off her tongue without thought. She'd been using the term on him and his five adult sisters for as long as he could remember, no matter the scenario.

His mom's destination was a mystery, as always. Ever since Dad had moved out months ago, Riker was lucky if Mom didn't leave before dinnertime. At least she trusted him to make his own food, but it would've been nice if he didn't have to eat it alone. Not even his dad or his two local sisters, who sometimes popped in after Mom had left, could be bothered to eat with him. His three out-of-state sisters put in far less effort. Their check-in texts were about as mundane as the weather forecast.

So he alternated between *Timescale* and *Voice Venture*. Almost like a compulsion. Except it wasn't. He could quit either one if he wanted.

Only he didn't want to.

There was always another level to beat, another couple of dollars to earn, so why stop?

He heard the closing click of the back door leading to the garage, evidence of Mom's departure. And with that, the silence of the evening commenced. Five years ago, he never would've imagined the house could feel so empty when he had two parents and so many sisters.

But alas.

He clicked over to the "Jobs" page of *Voice Venture*. At the top of the list, organized by most recent, were a few he hadn't seen. He scrolled, checking them quickly to not miss any he was actually qualified for.

There!

Voice actor needed for online video about bridge engineering.

Must be able to speak clearly and pronounce technical terms with confidence.

Many postings had "Hire me!" buttons next to them, but this one had an "add name to list" button instead. He clicked it quickly to throw his hat in the ring before the list inevitably filled up. This would invite the hirer to listen to his public samples on the site. Regardless, the chances of his name being chosen from the list were close to zilch. Not that he had any statistics backing that up.

Now if someone would invite me *instead of the other way around.*

Back on the "Jobs" page, he scrolled down, down, down, until he hit postings he'd already seen—ones that had lingered for days or weeks, not picked up yet because of their outlandish requirements that, he assumed, few users on the site met.

Required — English-speaking 55+ female with natural-born Croatian accent.

Riker might've been able to pull off a Croatian accent with enough research — he'd done it before with French — but sounding like a native speaker? Hardly.

Riker refreshed.

Nothing new. He scratched the back of his neck.

He refreshed again.

A new posting had been added, shining brightly for him right on top of the list.

Voice actor needed for 45-second social media spot.
Script provided. $4 payable upon completion.
Required: Ability to speak as two distinct male characters.

No time to debate it. Riker clicked on "Hire me!" as fast as his skinny fingers would go.

Ninety percent of the times he did this, he ended up on a page that said, "Sorry, this job has already been claimed." Ninety percent of the time, he'd lose out on another chance to get experience, low pay or not.

This time, however, he was rewarded with a rarer message. "Congratulations! You have now claimed this job. Please read on for further instructions."

As if he'd done something to earn it besides being the fastest clicker. But hey, no complaints.

Now that he safely had the tiny gig, he pulled his hands away from his laptop. His heart twittered like a snare drum in his chest. He took one deep breath, then another. The act of recording was what he always looked forward to, but for some reason he couldn't understand, the feel of the chase — the combination of incessant refreshing, anticlimactic failures and final success — sent a thrill through him.

Like it was a game.

An obsessive, never-ending game he could always play, even if he was alone or feeling like life had taken a giant dump on him.

Which wasn't unusual these days.

He opened the script for the task and read through it to get a sense of the tone. It was a conversation between two males about premature ejaculation and what they could do to prevent it. Far from character acting and not exactly thrilling material — definitely not something that would give Riker his big break — but it wasn't so bad. And, thank God, it was highly unlikely anyone at school would ever hear it.

He read it again, this time forming the voices in his head. After a third read-through, he was ready for his first recording attempt.

First step was to get in the right position for recording, which meant no slouching in bed. He relocated to the kitchen and set up his laptop at the table. It sucked that his mom always left, but hey, at least it meant he had the kitchen table to himself.

He opened his recording program and sat up straight in the high-backed kitchen chair with his feet flat on the floor. After opening and closing his mouth and moving his lower jaw from side to side, he hit "record."

A minute later, he played back the recording for review. Not bad, but one of the characters needed better enunciation while the other had at least two robotic lines...

After four more recordings, Riker sat back in his chair and hit "Play." He nodded along as the audio progressed. Yes, he'd definitely improved with each attempt. This latest version, if he could be so self-congratulatory, was clear, concise and believable.

This is the one.

He submitted it.

One more completed project on his repertoire, another ounce of experience added to his voice-acting career. Four more dollars toward that fancy microphone he'd been pining over.

Reason told him to step away from the online world, to close the browser before he could check it again and snap the laptop closed before he opened *Timescale* instead.

He went back to the "Jobs" page to check for new postings. *Just one more look...*

But nothing new. Why did he bother? He didn't *feel* like doing another recording. He didn't *feel* like scouring postings right now.

He refreshed anyway.

Again, nothing.

Riker pushed his chair away from the kitchen table and stood quickly. He couldn't bring himself to close his laptop, but at least he could step away for a minute. Dinner. Yes, he needed dinner.

He added a pot of water to the stove and pulled out a box of macaroni and cheese—his go-to meal that Mom kept well-stocked in the pantry. Leaning his back against the counter, he closed his eyes. Maybe he could stop himself from glancing at his computer, from trying to squeeze in two minutes of his game while the water boiled.

There was no *need* to check his computer during every spare second. But for some reason, the urge was ridiculously strong.

Focus, Rike. Think of something else. Something happier.

Taryn popped into his mind. Green-eyed Taryn who'd gotten up on that stage during Drama class and acted the hell out of *The Catcher in the Rye* once she'd overcome the urge to scrutinize her feet.

Then Beezy had asked to talk to her after class. *God*, Riker hoped that meant Beezy was trying to recruit her for the Speech and Debate team. His teacher-slash-coach would jump at the chance to bring someone like her into their ranks. Riker could sure as hell use the excitement—her presence would be something to actually look forward to.

She might be the reason he needed to drag himself to practice.

He liked Speech and Debate—really—but for some reason, getting to practice and tournaments took an inconceivable amount of effort. He was always okay once he got there, but that mental hurdle ahead of time was a beast.

Sigh.

He opened his eyes. These thoughts were pointless. Even if Taryn joined the team, even if he got to see her a few extra hours a week outside of class time, it didn't mean she'd talk to him. He'd already made a fool of himself when he rushed to her side that day in class. As if she were a damsel in distress and his mere presence would make all her troubles—or whatever troubles he imagined she had—go away.

Always full of ridiculous ideas.

Besides, he didn't even know if she liked boys. Especially after she portrayed a female Holden Caulfield admiring girls' legs. Taryn had given no other indication of her sexual orientation during Drama class, and why would she?

That'd be just my luck. Find a girl I'm interested in, then misread the signs in every way possible.

As far as he was concerned, a girl like Taryn could have anyone she wanted, and chances were, it wouldn't be Riker. Maybe someday he'd stop being a failure. Not today.

He turned to the stove, where the water had reached a rapid boil. As he'd done a hundred times before, he opened the box of macaroni and cheese, set aside the powdered cheese packet and poured the pasta into the pot.

Always macaroni and cheese alone, never to share — not with his mother, his father or the whole grouping of five siblings, who, these days, lumped together in his mind as one solid unit instead of adults with separate lives. Two years ago, his house had been much more active. Mom and Dad had been living in the same space — maybe not on the greatest of terms, but cordial enough — and his youngest older sister had still lived there too. The four older sisters had stopped by often, going so far as coordinating times to show up together.

Not anymore. It was as if the entire family had abandoned Riker in a house built for eight. And it only served to pull him further into whatever darkness swirled around his brain, whatever madness consumed him at any given point.

He needed to play *Timescale*. Anything to get this crap off his mind.

The noodles weren't quite soft enough yet, but whatever. He drained them in the sink and returned them to the pot to mix in butter, milk and bright orange powdered cheese. Then he spooned it all into a bowl and returned to his laptop.

The video game took a frustrating five seconds to open. But then he was in.

The familiar menu appeared, containing images of fantastical places in various time periods. As he clicked into his game, he imitated the voice that replied to him. He said the same words more clearly, then tried them again with an accent.

He'd last left his character near the edge of a cliff in Madagascar, sometime in the nineteenth century. The ghostly red river hogs had been a bear to deal with, but the French soldiers were far worse. He dove in.

* * * *

Riker jumped when he heard the front door open.

He dropped his chin to his chest. There was no point getting up to figure out which family member had just let themselves in. They'd make their presence known.

"Hey, bud."

Ah. The tell-tale voice of Dad, the deep resonance easily distinguishable from all other family members.

Riker turned in his chair. "Hey."

"You eating dinner this late?"

The microwave clock read 10:12, and the macaroni and cheese beside Riker's laptop was halfway gone and had started to harden. Well damn, he must've stopped eating a while ago and hadn't even realized. "Yep."

His dad leaned against the counter, shoes still on. Making no attempt to get comfortable, it seemed. Five months ago he'd lived here, and now they'd fallen to this.

Dad crossed his arms. "Your mom out tonight?"

Riker shrugged. "I guess."

"Can you tell her I paid the mortgage through the end of next month? She'll see it if she checks the bank account, but..." He paused, scratched his head. "I just thought she should know so she won't have to worry about it."

"Okay."

Is that it? Did he come here to say something he could've texted straight to Mom? Or even to me?

"And hey, Jaclyn called and told me she stopped by last week."

Yes, his sister Jaclyn had stopped by when he was in the middle of a *Timescale* binge. This wasn't exactly newsworthy. "Yeah."

Riker looked back to his laptop, where his video game character waited patiently for its next move. He clicked to continue playing. With any luck, he could bore his dad into leaving. It would be better for both of them. For *all* of them.

Chapter Seven

Taryn

The fluorescents gave the sectioned-off auditorium a fake glow that Taryn had never noticed during Drama class. The layout of the room hadn't changed, but it was suddenly too bright for indoors now that the final bell had rung, an insufficient mockery of the sunlight outside.

A dozen other high school kids had scattered themselves across the twenty-or-so rows of auditorium seats, babbling away under the harsh lighting. Though separated into groups of twos and threes, many talked to each other—loudly—across the room, each voice drowning out the next.

Taryn stood in the entryway at the back of the auditorium, unsure where to sit. Reflex told her to go for the same seat she occupied during Drama class, right near where she was standing but far from the other students. Logic begged her to make a new friend in a different seat. She scanned for potentials.

Far away near the front, a girl with a gray exposed-shoulder T-shirt and a brown and pink knit cap sat with her back to Taryn, currently talking to no one. Maybe she needed a friend, too. Maybe she wasn't talking to anyone because she was waiting for someone to approach her. Taryn took a step forward.

The girl turned to Taryn as if sensing her watching from across the room, then tucked a strand of layered blonde hair behind an ear, exposing cartilage lined with glinting earrings. Heat rose to Taryn's cheeks as she quickly looked away.

Shit. Too attractive. Abort, abort.

She scanned the room further, hoping for something to click. Then—finally—someone from her Drama class. The overexcited guy with the tan satchel sat a few rows in front of where she stood, his arm flinging through the air to the tune of his words. The dark curls covering his head bobbed as he spoke to someone— who?—in a different row. He caught sight of Taryn as he finished a sentence, and a grin spread across his face.

"Hey! I know you!"

Several other students turned to look at her as she shifted her feet. She forced a smile at Satchel Guy. *Please, dear God, don't tell me everyone here is as outgoing as this guy.* "Yes. Hi."

"What's your name? Terry, right?"

Not quite. But closer than "Gesticulating Satchel Guy," which was about the best guess she had for *his* name.

"Taryn. Like 'Karen.' But not in a bad way." Was it too soon to bolt out of the door? Too late?

"Ah! That's an awesome name, Taryn-Like-Karen. Welcome to our humble abode." He swung his arm outward, presenting the auditorium seats to her as if she hadn't taken Drama class in here every other school day for three weeks. Two girls across the room gave a small wave with just their fingers, and a boy three seats to their right smiled and nodded.

"Um. Thanks. Hi."

With this guy's pretend spotlight blinding her worse than the overhead lights, leaving might make things even more awkward. She lowered her backpack to the floor and slid into the aisle seat she always sat in during Drama class—the easiest choice. After a deep breath, she stared at the front of the room and internally counted to three. The others continued talking around her.

Needing a distraction pronto, she leaned down to her backpack and unzipped it.

Her planner wasn't the most enticing diversion ever, but it would have to do. She heard students entering as she attempted to scan her class due dates for the upcoming two weeks.

When she'd exhausted that route, she flipped to the back of the planner and let her eyes gloss over the measurement conversion table. Definitely not pressing information, but it beat lugging out a textbook to start a homework assignment that would be interrupted by the start of the meeting.

Speaking of which...

She turned her head to check out the face clock on the far side of the wall—3:58. Two minutes to go.

She dragged her eyes down from the clock, suddenly curious. And yep—Elbow Guy from her Drama class was now in the same seat as usual, same row as her. That made two people she recognized—neither of whom she actually knew.

He sat alone but looked nowhere as uncomfortable in his solitude as she felt. With exposed plaid socks matching the checks on his shirt, he leaned back in his auditorium seat, the elbow closest to Taryn propped on the back of the empty seat beside him. Elbow Guy stared ahead, nodding slowly as if listening to a conversation across the room. Perhaps he was.

Through a door on the other side of the sectioned-off auditorium, two men entered. One was Mr. Banley-Zimmerman, her Drama teacher. The other, taller and wider, maybe a little older, with thick corduroy pants and dark brown shoes, loomed over the room like his head might graze the impossibly high ceiling. Taryn didn't recognize him.

Mr. Banley-Zimmerman settled himself behind the podium while the other man passed out a stack of papers, starting at the front of the room and working his way back. The number of students in the room had expanded since Taryn had last looked—far more people than she'd been expecting for a Speech and Debate team. When the man reached Taryn, he smiled so large his teeth drowned out the rest of his face. She took the two packets he handed her, then stood to pass the spare to the only other person in her row.

Deep breaths. Act natural. He's hot but just human.

Elbow Guy continued staring at the front of the room as she walked toward him. Maybe he hadn't noticed her. Maybe he wanted to ignore her. Maybe she'd have to wave to get his attention.

Maybe, maybe, maybe.

She stopped just out of arm's reach. Then, like he'd timed it, he turned to face her. He uncrossed his legs and raised his eyes to her, his hand palm-upward for the packet.

"Thanks," he said, almost too quiet to hear.

"Welcome."

She walked back down the row to her seat, scrunching her eyes shut for a second before releasing them. Could she get more awkward? Who just said "Welcome" with no other words? What if he thought she'd been welcoming him to the room or something? As if *she* were the one who belonged here, not him.

Faaaail.

She sat back down and clenched and unclenched a fist. Hopefully he didn't notice.

Stop it. He isn't thinking twice about you.

She dared a glance at him and, sure enough, his face was buried in the packet of papers.

Probably something she should've been doing as well. She looked down at her own packet, which displayed "Fir Grove High School Speech and Debate" in large, bold letters at the top.

The rest of the first page was a tournament schedule, various dates followed by the names of the host schools. At least fifteen tournaments, all Saturdays, some at schools she didn't recognize. Her old school, lacking a team, wasn't on the list.

The first tournament was in only three weeks.

Holy hell. This is a huge commitment.

She flipped to the second page — details on an overnight weekend tournament, all the way out in Pennsylvania. Was this required? Jesus, did she have to pay for it? Her heart rate picked up. She didn't even know if she *wanted* to do Speech and Debate, had no clue if she'd be any good at it, and she was already expected to go on a trip that involved a hotel? Would

Grandma pay for this if she asked? Mom sure as hell wouldn't.

The third page was titled "List of Events," beginning with debate categories and stretching into page four with the speech ones. Her eyes glossed over as she read the event names, full of words she couldn't define — Policy Debate, Lincoln-Douglas Debate, Humorous Interpretation, Declamation, Domestic Extemporaneous...

On and on the packet went, each phrase just as confusing as the last. Underlined words here, italicization there, bold or highlighting elsewhere. So much to remember, so many important points.

Shit. I shouldn't be here.

Had she missed her chance to leave? She glanced around the room. Her Drama teacher was still at the podium, looking around at everyone like he was about to begin. The other man stood a few feet away from him, also looking at the students spread out across the auditorium seats.

Mr. Banley-Zimmerman cleared his throat. "Hey, everyone, let's get started."

Dammit. Too late. If she left now, people would notice. Best to sit it out to the end of the meeting then run away without looking back.

"So — welcome, welcome! Glad to see you all here. If you've been here before, I'm happy you're back. Thanks for sticking it out." A large smile crossed his face. "And if this is your first time, we'll try our best to not scare you away. I promise we're not as terrifying as we look."

Laughter reverberated around the room. Taryn took the chance to scan some of the people who'd taken up seats around her since she arrived. At a quick glance, at least four of them were noticeably younger than her — frosh? At least she wasn't alone in her newness, for however much that was worth.

Her eyes wandered over to Elbow Guy. He — the opposite of her, she was sure — looked anything but nervous. He'd rolled his packet of papers into a scroll and was currently tapping it on the arm of the seat next to him. His eyes stayed on Mr. Banley-Zimmerman, but, for some odd reason, Taryn sensed he was looking past the coach instead of at him.

Maybe he'd heard this all before.

Maybe —

Maybe he could guide her through what she needed to know.

She swallowed hard and turned her focus back to the front of the room. *Don't be ridiculous.*

"I'm Mr. Banley-Zimmerman, but you can call me 'Mr. B.-Z.' I think you all know me. And this" — he pointed to the man to his right — "is Mr. Zimmerman-Banley, a.k.a. 'Mr. Z.-B.' Most of you know him, but if you don't, he generally handles the Debate events, while I oversee Speech."

The overly large Mr. Zimmerman-Banley, his hands on his hips, nodded and smiled. Taryn cocked her head at the inversion of their surnames. Did that mean the two coaches were…married?

"If you don't know him yet, you will soon. And — important note — you can come to either of us for anything, about Speech or Debate or anything else. I can't tell you that enough."

He nodded once, twice, as if letting the message sink in. Taryn looked back to Mr. Z.-B., who seemed perfectly at ease in his stance next to the podium. Like he'd stood in that position for countless meetings.

Mr. B.-Z. continued. "Mr. Z.-B. gave you all a pack of papers, so let's go through that. First of all, the schedule! Right there on page one! Folks, I'm not kidding this year — give page one to your parents, and I'll email it too. Put it on your fridge. Run a big highlighter across all the dates. Draw pink and purple hearts all over it. I don't care, just make sure your parents see it, and don't forget the dates.

"If you can't come to a tournament, I need at least eight days' notice. *Eight!* Notice I didn't say 'seven.' Which means don't come up to me during a Saturday tournament saying, 'Hey, by the way, I won't be here next week.' If you do that, I will not remember. Seriously. Don't be that person."

Several people around the room chuckled while others groaned. Okay, so just like in Drama class, Mr. B.-Z. was strict but at least had a sense of humor.

"Everybody flip to the second page."

A ruffle of papers sounded around the room as Taryn glanced again at Elbow Guy, who hadn't bothered to open his scroll. A few rows in front of him, the far-too-gorgeous-for-comfort girl with the blonde hair and knit cap sat hunched over her packet, slashing a green highlighter across the topmost page.

"Page two is about — you guessed it — the weekend tournament! If you don't give me a permission slip two weeks before the tournament, you will not go. Seriously, everyone. Two weeks in advance, I need a piece of paper in my hands signed by Mom, Dad, Grandma, Grandpa, Uncle Joe — I need a legit signature from whoever pays your electric bill and tucks you in at night. There is no such thing as too early, folks. Okay?"

A couple people in the front row nodded.

"*Okay?*" he repeated. "Out loud this time."

A chorus of "okays" came from around the room.

"Good, good. So if you're new here, don't be scared about the weekend trip. All you have to pay for is food, so don't worry too much about costs! And if you need help with buying food, *please* let me know. I'm discreet, promise."

Taryn gulped as Mr. B.-Z. gave a stern look to the room at large. Okay, so not having to pay for a hotel was good. Very good. Her mom could probably pitch in for two days of food, as long as Taryn was frugal. Maybe this wouldn't be that bad. She'd have to run it by Mom and Grandma, but there didn't seem to be a clear reason they'd say no...

"Right. So. The next two pages are a list of event categories. Let's save that for last, 'cause that's a long discussion. The fifth page is everyone's favorite part—selling ads!"

More groans erupted around the room. Taryn swallowed hard. Selling ads meant money, and that was *not* something she could spare.

"Ads are simple, everyone. Really. To be on the team, you're required to sell one hundred dollars' worth of ads, which will go into the back of the program at the end-of-season showcase. I don't care how you do it, folks. Go door to door at businesses downtown. Team up with your friends and beg the manager at McDonald's. Or, if you're beyond lazy, just ask your parents to write a one-hundred-dollar check. Not gonna say that hasn't happened."

Taryn refrained from scoffing. That *definitely* wouldn't be her course of action. But she had to give Mr. B.-Z. credit. He seemed to totally grasp the fact that not everyone here had money, even if it felt like they did. And despite the zillion rules she had to follow to be on this team, she figured Mr. B.-Z. would make sure she didn't miss a beat of what was expected.

"If you run into any fundraising problems, let me know. Those ads are due in a little over two months if you decide to join the team. Which, obviously, you should."

"Don't worry, Beezy. You're stuck with us!" Satchel Guy piped up. Light laughs fluttered around the auditorium.

Beezy? Had she heard him right?

"We've been trying to get rid of you for two years now, Gavin," Mr. Z.-B. cut in. "Thought we were treating you like crap, but you just keep coming back."

"Sorry for your luck, Zeb," Gavin replied.

This time several students burst into laughter, like they were all in on a friendly joke, and even Taryn felt the corners of her mouth rise. Without thinking, she glanced at her row mate for his reaction. He laughed along with the others, a giant toothy smile lighting up his face. He caught her eye for a split second, and she blinked hard and diverted her focus back to the coaches.

"Bad luck, indeed," Mr. B.-Z. continued. "Okay, everyone. Next page. Adult help! Yes, we're putting your family to work. To make this Speech and Debate season run as smoothly as always, we need everyone to trick one adult into helping out at one tournament. They get a tiny stipend for the day that pretty much covers their lunch and gas money, but hey, we do what we can.

"I don't care who you recruit, as long as they're over eighteen and not a high school student. We need judges for every single tournament, so they can pick whichever Saturday works for them. *Or* if they're interested in working the concession stand or tallying scores when we host our own tournament in November, all the better! I'll shoot an email to all your parents, since I know how much you all love to not relay messages to your folks. And don't forget to give whoever you find a huge thank you and a bouquet of roses."

Taryn uncrossed her legs and recrossed them the opposite way. If Mr. B.-Z. had presented this requirement at the beginning of the meeting, it might've been enough to make her pick up her backpack and scram before she got in too deep. There was no way her mom would do this, and it would be too much to ask Grandma after all she'd done for them.

"Now that the boring stuff is out of the way, let's split up to talk about the events. I'll lead a discussion down the hall to talk about speech events, and Mr. Z.-B. will talk to the rest of you about debate. We'll start in, say, twenty minutes, and I can take questions before that."

Taryn leaned back in her seat. Presumably she'd have until at least next week to choose an event, then two weeks to memorize and polish. If she joined. Which was still a massive if because there was a ridiculous number of hurdles she'd have to leap over to get this to work.

And yet, the whole idea of Speech and Debate sent a thrill through her. The performance, the competition, being part of a team. *This* team. Living up to the *Timbre!* dream in a way she never would've foreseen on her own before Mr. B.-Z. swooped in and asked her to come to a meeting for a club she hadn't known existed.

There had to be a way to make it work.

Chapter Eight

Riker

Paperback spines slid under Riker's fingertips, a soft whoosh flapping in his hand's wake. To hell with mind-numbing homework and overeducated teachers — all he needed in his life was a bookshelf stuffed full of stage scripts. There were more plays here in Beezy's office than he could possibly read, but that wasn't the point — the hope of reading them all, of acting them all out, made his stomach somersault with glee in ways little else did.

And now he was tasked with finding a script to perform for this year's Speech season.

He tugged one from the shelf and flipped to the summary page, leaning his butt against Beezy's desk. Formally, this was Beezy's workspace. Informally, everyone on the Speech and Debate team used it at their whim.

The summary page boasted of soldiers, trenches and brotherhood — not his go-to genre. The second book he pulled contained talking mice, an over-eager cat and a woman with a broom. He put it back on the shelf with a non-committal shrug. He mentally tagged it as a "someday" read, far down on his wish list.

The third script he pulled from the shelf was thinner than the first two. Its yellow cover was rough under his fingertips, the texture unyielding. He flipped to the summary page. Within ten seconds, a smile crossed his face. Yes, this was a good place to start. He snapped it shut, curled the book into an almost-fold and shoved it into his back pocket. Then he reached for another.

Knuckles rapped on the office door, so lightly he was surprised he'd heard them. When he looked up, he found the girl from Drama class — Taryn — with her tiny tan fist raised to the door.

"Mr. Ban — I mean, Mr. B.-Z. said all the scripts are in here."

His fingers dropped from the spines. God, he was ridiculously happy Beezy had asked her to come today. Predictable, that man — always recruiting the best talent from his Drama class. "They are. You looking for one?"

Her dark brown hair swayed as she nodded. "There's a line to talk to him one-on-one, but he said I could look at the scripts while I wait. I, um — I don't know where to start."

He smiled. This was something he could help with. With any luck, he'd redeem himself from looking like a fool that time in Drama class when he'd thought she was in pain. "What event are you doing? We can narrow it down from there."

Taryn shifted from one foot to the other, her gaze darting between the wall and the floor. "I'm not sure? I know the packet has that list of events, but I've never…" She trailed off.

God, if only he could get a better look at those eyes. He tilted his head, trying to examine them from a different angle. No luck.

"So you weren't on the team at your old school?"

There. There were those eyes, the dark lashes framing them. He swallowed, returning her gaze, unsure whether to break it or hold on.

"No." She pulled away from the eye contact—a tragedy. "I don't think we had a Speech and Debate team. At least I never heard about one."

"You're starting from scratch, then." He inspected the scripts—much safer scenery that didn't cause his pulse to pound like a rabbit's foot. "Welp. To start, no need for 'Mr. B.-Z.' now that you're on the team. No 'Mr. Z.-B.' either. You'll run yourself in circles trying to keep their names straight. From now on, it's just 'Beezy' and 'Zeb,' the miraculous coaching duo. As for the events…" He scratched his chin, debating whether to take a leap with his next words. She might bolt and call him a creep if he didn't play his cards right. "I always kind of thought your category depended on your personality."

She chuckled, a soft tinkling that filled the room.

A chuckle wasn't a reply. It was distinctly a non-reply. And God, how he wanted words from her.

"So what kind of personality would that be?" he prodded.

She blinked and shrugged.

"Quiet. Gotcha."

Taryn laughed, more loudly this time. Her shoulders relaxed. "I guess sometimes quiet, yeah."

"Now we're getting somewhere." Riker directed his attention to the bookshelf and ran his fingertips over the spines once more. Under any other circumstances, he would've stopped there. But Taryn seemed worth the untangling effort. "Quiet personality, but"—he glanced her way—"able to dazzle the audience once you're on stage. The debate events are probably out if you don't like confrontation on the spot, but there's a Speech event where you give a speech that someone else already wrote. Or there's an event where you write your own speech, if you're into that."

He felt more than saw when she lowered her backpack to the floor and stepped toward him. The hair at the back of his neck tingled. He'd already given a bold compliment. Now it was time to take a bold guess.

"But something tells me boring old speeches aren't your style. Not after that monologue you gave in class."

"Oh."

Her voice came from inches away, so close her breath brushed his cheek. Jesus, could he get away with kissing someone in Beezy's office right here and now? He cleared his throat.

"There's the dramatic acting event, and then the humorous acting one."

"Maybe…"

"But I think I know exactly what would suit you." He zipped his fingertips across the scripts in one rapid motion like a rock 'n' roll pianist. Then he raised his hand to a higher shelf and pulled down a thick, purple-spined volume. He dropped it onto Beezy's desk with a thud. "This."

She examined the cover. "Short stories?"

"Yep. The Prose and Poetry event. You pick a short story, weave in some poems that have the same theme, and bam — you're ready for competition."

Her gaze remained on the book. "The whole event is just reading stories?"

He nodded. "And poems. But you have to, you know, use voices and stuff to be any good. The people who win this event kind of act it out as they read."

"Hm. I see." She opened the book to the table of contents, then ran her fingers down the ink, a faint whisper following their path. The visual alone matched the sense of ease and comfort he always felt when touching script covers. He gulped.

"Would I have to pick a story from *this* book?"

"Oh, no way. Pick whatever story you want. Take excerpts from a novel if that's your thing. This is just what Beezy gives people who don't know where to start."

"So you've been on the team before, then?"

He smiled. "This ain't my first rodeo."

"Hells no, it ain't!"

Riker looked up for the source of the words. Gavin held one hand against the doorframe and leaned into it. Riker pulled his mouth into a toothy grin — polite, but not as genuine as the smile Taryn had just caused.

Gavin pulled off his satchel and slid it to the ground next to Beezy's desk. "I don't know if he told you, Taryn-Like-Karen, but Riker here is our reigning champion in Humorous Interpretation. Speech kids the world over dream of juggling as many characters as he can."

"The world over?" she pressed, one side of her mouth quirking upward.

"Damn, I like this girl." Gavin clapped a hand on Taryn's shoulder. "Okay, maybe not 'the world over.' Speech kids the country over."

Riker rolled his eyes. Leave it to Gavin to find the best in everyone. "I won *two* tournaments, then got tenth at State. That definitely doesn't make me a national champion."

"*Only* two tournament wins," Gavin stage-whispered to Taryn. "And he was just a sophomore!"

She chuckled. "And what about you?"

Gavin flapped his hand as though waving away her question. "Oh, hell. I do okay at Dramatic Interp. Not great, not terrible. I got a kick-ass script in mind for this year, though."

"Yeah?" she asked.

Okay, so this was Riker's time to zip out. The last thing he wanted to do was overstay his welcome with Taryn.

He liked Gavin as well as anyone, but he'd already heard the guy's over-the-top-exciting idea to act out *The Normal Heart* for competition. He wanted to look back at Taryn, to catch a glimpse of those inquisitive eyes and dark eyelashes, but he forced himself to turn away and slip out as Gavin continued talking.

Several of his Speech and Debate teammates were in the hall, and he strode past them with a smile but no verbal communication. When he returned to the auditorium, he found more people talking, spread out across the rows of seats. Beezy and Zeb stood at the front of the room, each of them speaking with a different student.

Riker headed for his favorite seat under the clock. Before sitting, he pulled the folded script and a pencil out of his back pocket. Back here, he'd have the chance to read through it in private, with little chance of someone peeking over his shoulder.

He flattened the script across his lap and ran his fingers over the cover. The title — *Robin Hood* — stood out in barely raised letters, a green as deep as the spare chalkboards peppered throughout the school.

He underlined and made notes in the margins as he read, his mind swirling with possibilities for how to condense the story to an eight-to-ten-minute performance, which unnecessary characters to cut for brevity and which voices he might try. He nodded and smiled as he underlined a whammy of a line three-quarters of the way through the script.

I can definitely work with this.

Last year's tournaments had gone well, but this year he needed to be *great*. As a junior, his placement at competitions needed to go *up*, not down. His work had only just begun.

* * * *

By the time Riker stood, most of the auditorium had cleared out, with the exception of two girls scribbling wildly into notebooks. He strode down the stairs, careful to not interrupt their concentration, and headed into the hallway. He slowed his pace past a classroom brimming with noise — Beezy's attempt to brainstorm with the Speech kids, mostly first-years, about which events and pieces they wanted to do. A typical exercise after the first meeting of the year, but one he didn't need to partake in. He was perfectly capable of figuring it out himself now.

He peered into the room and caught sight of Taryn, sitting in the middle row but off to the edge, not

opening her mouth. She was blinking hard as Gavin —
why the hell was he in there when he'd already chosen
his piece? — gestured wildly in front of her.

Zeb stood at the front of the classroom next door,
speaking to a more focused group of kids with
notebooks. The debaters.

Back inside the cramped space of Beezy's office, one
of Riker's teammates leaned back in the office chair
with his feet on the desk, a script in hand. Another
pressed their hands into the bland metal of the desk as
they leaned on it. They looked up as Riker approached.

"Hey, man. What's up?"

He smiled. "Not much. Just here to grab another
script."

They nodded and resumed talking. On any other
day, he might've joined their conversation to distract
himself. But today he was in script mode, and not much
could sidetrack him.

With *Robin Hood* still in his back pocket, he scanned
the spines for his next victim. The fourth he pulled from
the shelf sounded promising. Book in hand, he made
his way back to the auditorium for more quiet reading
time.

Chapter Nine

Taryn

Gavin, who Taryn apparently couldn't lose if she tried, plopped into a classroom chair in front of her, dropping his tan satchel to the ground. The room was almost full of would-be Speech competitors, all waiting to hear from Beezy. Gavin twisted his upper body around to speak.

"Hi! What's up?"

She blinked twice, forcing herself to not let the strain of her efforts show. After three weeks of Drama class with him that hadn't entailed a single exchanged word, this situation oozed strangeness. She'd talked to him about competition events ten minutes ago in the coach's office after Riker (she had finally learned Elbow Guy's name!) had vanished, but she thought Gavin was just being nice. Less of a friendly thing and more of a you're-here-so-I'll-talk-to-you thing. Maybe she'd underestimated him. And now here they were, conversing in a classroom after school and waiting for their Speech coach.

"Not much since ten minutes ago. You?"

"Not much, not much. Super stoked for this season. You think you're going to join, then?"

"I think so."

His lips pulled back to reveal a large smile. "Good! We always need fresh blood. Seriously, if you have any questions, just let me know."

"Thanks."

"I really liked that monologue you did in Drama class, by the way. The one where you were Holden Caulfield but a twenty-first-century girl? So freaking original. I laughed out loud when you pretended to text."

Unable to make eye contact, Taryn stared at his forehead. The fact that someone from her class had remembered her *Catcher in the Rye* monologue was more than she could've hoped for. And now here was Gavin, describing something specific from it.

People don't notice me. That's not what they do.

"I'm, uh...I'm glad you liked it."

"Oh my God, I just realized. What if you used *Catcher in the Rye* as a Prose piece and performed it like you did in Drama class? You'd just have to add some poetry to it to qualify. It would be so good."

She cocked her head. Well, damn, the guy had a point.

"Not sure what poem you'd do with it. Poetry kind of goes over my head, so I'm definitely not the person to ask."

"I think you're on to something."

Gavin smiled. "Hell, I'm not on to anything. You're the one who came up with it for class! Keep pulling those tricks out of your sleeve and you'll be golden."

An hour ago, she would've scoffed at the idea of satchel-wielding Gavin being kind, perhaps even genuine. Yet here he was, complimenting her, encouraging her to run with her own ideas.

"You know what? I think I might."

His smile grew. "Now we're talking! Beezy's going to give you a standing O when you do that character again. Guaranteed."

Heat rose to her cheeks. She crossed her legs. "Thank you" was on the tip of her tongue, but for some reason that sounded too formal. She smiled and blinked.

"That would be...that would be pretty cool."

"Damn straight!" Gavin flashed his teeth and turned to face the front of the room. Not a second passed before he'd begun talking to the person in front of him.

So much for that.

The chair next to Taryn creaked. She looked up to find the blonde girl with the open-shouldered shirt plopping down. Her dark red lips were unusually full, covered in flawless matte lipstick. She scribbled something onto her Speech and Debate packet, as if determined to jot down a note before it flitted from memory.

Taryn fidgeted in her seat and diverted her eyes to her own hands resting on the otherwise-empty desk. She ran her fingers down the top page of her packet. Maybe if she pretended to read, she could push Super-Attractive-and-Totally-Unapproachable Girl from her mind. Words whirled in her vision, one bold letter running into the italicization of another.

One more look couldn't hurt...

Another glance revealed the girl scribbling away, flipping pages as she went. Her entire packet seemed covered in loopy handwriting and color-coded highlights. How could she discern anything in that messy jumble? As if Mr. B.-Z.—*err, "Beezy"*—hadn't already riddled the packet with too many types of emphasis.

The sound of a cleared throat came from the front of the room. Beezy stood at the whiteboard, his hands clasped together palm-to-palm.

How long had he been standing there?

The students quieted quickly. For being so casual, the guy sure had a way with a room. Taryn folded her hands in her lap, ready to dive into whatever else Beezy was about to throw her way. She'd already been overloaded with information since the start of the Speech and Debate meeting today. Jamming more into her already-full brain wouldn't make much difference at this point.

"Hey, everyone. This is the room for talking about Speech events. Glad you made it! I saw a couple students make a run for the parking lot after the meeting, so thanks for not being one of *those* people."

Laughter bubbled around the room.

"Also...Mr. Z.-B. is in the room next door talking about Debate events. If you want to do Debate instead of Speech, you should head over there. If you're not sure whether you're more suited for a Speech event or a Debate event and you just want to see what's up, that's okay. You can chill with us until you figure it out. We'll be happy to convert you to the dark side.

"Now, if I could get you all to flip to page three, you'll find the 'List of Events' section. And then ignore page three, because that's all about Debate. Move on to page four."

Taryn did as instructed. Despite Gavin and Riker's explanations and encouragement, the whole concept of

Speech events was still foreign. Anything to help her comprehend *why* she should do the Prose event would be great.

"So, when most of you think of Speech, you probably think of the classic events that involve giving a speech. For Original Oratory, you write an eight-to-ten-minute speech ahead of time and memorize it, then give the speech. For Declamation, you memorize a speech that someone else wrote. Simple enough."

Okay, this was sounding much more down-to-earth now. If only her algebra teacher could make everything seem so straightforward, she might actually have a shot at an A.

"The extemporaneous events are similar, but shorter and more on-the-spot. They'll give you a topic and thirty minutes to prep some ideas, and then you give the speech. There's Domestic Extemp for US policy issues and International Extemp for foreign policy issues, familiarity with politics recommended. Those of you on the fence between Speech events and Debate events might find yourself right at home with the extemporaneous categories. Everyone with me so far?"

Taryn nodded. In front of her, Gavin nodded as well. The girl beside her continued to scrawl words across her packet.

"Good. Now for the acting-based Speech events. Our most popular ones are Dramatic Interpretation and Humorous Interpretation. I'll leave it to you to figure out which one's serious and which one's funny. In a nutshell, you act out a script as multiple characters, and you stand in the same spot the whole time."

Taryn swallowed at the thought of that. Those two events sounded super advanced, perhaps something she could aspire to as she got more comfortable in Drama class. She was nowhere near Riker's level.

"Then there's Duo Interpretation, which involves two people. Choose your partner wisely, because you'll both have to go to all the events together, and you'll want a back-up plan in case one of you can't make it."

This time she resisted an out-loud groan. Being tied to someone for every tournament sounded like the opposite of a fun time.

"And that brings us to..." He paused and ran his finger down the page. "Oral Interpretation. We call it 'Prose and Poetry' around here, just an old habit. For this, you piece together a story and some poetry with a similar theme, and then you read it out of a book. It's the only Speech event you don't have to memorize, but trust me, you'll memorize it faster than you expect. If you just want to get your feet wet in the Speech world, this might be the path for you."

Hmm. She hadn't realized the event didn't involve memorization. That almost seemed like a cop-out, especially if she wanted to prove she could excel in Drama class.

Either way, this Speech team—no matter which event she picked—presented an opportunity she hadn't had at her other school. It was like her very own *Timbre!* episode, except with (hopefully) way fewer crises and (likely) way less dating. For her, at any rate.

She peeked at the girl next to her as Beezy wrapped up his spiel. One of the girl's exposed shoulders hunched upward as she wrote, her neck stretched forward like an elegant swan. A strand of hair hugged the curve of her cheek, following the route of her jawline.

"Gorgeous" wasn't a strong enough word.

The girl's eyes flicked upward at Taryn.

It took everything in Taryn to hold the gaze, if only for a second. The amber brown stared back at her, the eyelashes above them fluttering. The girl could've posed as a telepath with a stare that intense.

Taryn stared at the back of Gavin's head and held her breath. Tingles ran the lengths of her arms, the thin hairs standing on end. Whoever this girl was, she was far out of Taryn's league. But then again, so was Riker. What did it even matter who she crushed on?

And yeah, this had definitely turned into crush at first sight.

So what if Riker and this girl held an equal stature in Taryn's mind? Eggs in baskets and all that.

"Hey there."

Taryn startled. The voice had come from close to her ear. Too close. When she turned toward the noise, she realized the girl next to her had leaned in. Beezy had stopped talking and the rest of the students were no longer so quiet. How much time had passed in what she'd thought was a split second?

She resisted a gulp. People didn't talk to her. Least of all beautiful people with bare shoulders.

"Hi," Taryn replied.

The blonde girl smiled, displaying two rows of straight glimmering white teeth. The word "privilege" surfaced in the back of Taryn's mind, but she quickly squashed it.

"I didn't catch your name," the girl said, her gaze unwavering, every eyelash immaculate.

"Um, Taryn."

The girl held out her hand with an odd formality, like a kindergartener playing grown-up. Taryn shook it. "It's nice to meet you, Taryn. I'm Quinn. Are you a frosh or just a late joiner?"

"A junior. So a late joiner, I guess."

Quinn slid her hand away slowly, her fingertips brushing against Taryn's palm and sending a quiver through it. "Well, we always need people. The team's big, but the more the merrier. Do you know what you're going to do?"

"Like, which event?"

Quinn nodded.

"I'm not sure. I thought maybe…Prose and Poetry."

"Ah. Well, yeah, it's a good event if you don't have experience. I did Declamation last year, but this year I'm writing my own speech to see if I can place in Original Oratory too. I'm only here because I have to talk to Beezy about my ideas."

Taryn couldn't help but let her face fall slightly at Quinn's words. Gavin and Riker had been so confident in her ability to do Prose and Poetry, but Quinn and Beezy made it sound like an event for beginners. Which she was, but still.

"Seriously, it's cool you're here. I know *I'm* excited you're not running off." At this, Quinn held Taryn's gaze. As if there were a deeper meaning between the lines.

All thoughts of disappointment from a second ago flitted away.

Quinn raised one eyebrow.

Unable to hold still, Taryn licked her lips for the mere sake of movement. Then she broke Quinn's eye contact and looked down at her hands.

Whatever moment they had—or whatever moment Taryn hoped they had—was gone.

Quinn giggled. "Well, I hope I'll see you at next week's meeting. Or maybe later this week, if we practice on the same day."

"I'll probably be around."

"Good."

Quinn gathered her packet, pen and highlighters, shoving them into her backpack so haphazardly that the action clashed with Taryn's perception of Quinn's meticulous color-coded organization.

Quinn sent one more look in Taryn's direction. "See you around, then, Taryn."

Taryn nodded, though Quinn's back was already turned as she headed toward Beezy.

Smooth.

With the super-beautiful out-of-her-league girl gone from her vicinity, Taryn took a moment to examine her surroundings. Half the students had already cleared out, Gavin included. Others were writing down ideas in notebooks or had pulled out their phones. A student walked away from Beezy, giving Quinn the opening she needed. Taryn raked her eyes over the arch of Quinn's shoulders, down the curve of her lower back, at her pink shirt bringing out the highlights of her hat, then...

She pulled her gaze away. The last thing she needed was for someone to catch her staring. Instead, she scanned her packet until Quinn left the Drama-teacher-turned-Speech-coach wide open.

Beezy time.

With a deep breath, she tossed her backpack over her shoulders and clutched the packet between her hands.

One step, two, then three. No one had claimed the coach's attention yet. Good.

His lips curled into a grin as Taryn approached. Did he ever stop grinning? This guy had more energy than a squirrel on caffeine.

"Ms. Platt! Just the person I wanted to see. Not that I'm playing favorites or anything. I'm happy to see everyone, and that's my official answer in case anyone asks."

He winked at her, hokey and exaggerated. She couldn't resist a smile in return, her fingers loosening their grip on the packet.

"Hi."

"So, what do you think? Do you want to join? We could really use you."

"Yeah, I was thinking I might. I have some questions, though."

"Bring it on. That's what I'm here for."

One of the oddest things about Beezy was that Taryn had no doubt he meant it.

"Well, I was wondering about Prose and Poetry. It sounds like the kind of thing I want to do, but I'm not sure if it's a good idea."

"Ah. Let me jump in right here. I find that the event you want to do is often the event that's right for you. Don't choose something you don't want—you'll end up bored with it. And you really don't want to be bored with something you perform multiple times a week."

"I guess I just…I don't want to take the easy way out. If that makes sense."

Beezy *hmm*ed. "It does make sense. But here's the thing, Taryn. From the simple fact that you're afraid to take the easy route, you're revealing you're not the kind of person to do that. So what if some people do this event because they want it to be easy? You don't have to make it easy. You can make it as challenging as you want. And that's a pretty cool concept, right?"

Wowza. This coach had a way with people. Hopefully Speech and Debate wasn't a cult, because she was sure he'd sweet-talk her into drinking the Kool-Aid.

"It is."

"And honestly?" Beezy lowered his voice. "If you want to excel at Prose and Poetry, you'll need those acting chops and you'll want your piece memorized like a Taylor Swift song. After what you did in class with *Catcher in the Rye*, you got this."

Taryn's brain told her lips to move, but her body ignored it. Beezy paused to let her reply, but, perhaps getting a hint of her brain's short-circuit connection, continued before the struggle consumed her.

"So think about it, see what you come up with. Take your time—but not too much time! The first tournament is in three weeks. Neither prose nor poetry can take up less than one-quarter of your whole piece, and you should aim for eight to ten minutes. Do you want guidance on where to start with stories and poetry?"

"I think I'm okay with the story part. It doesn't have to be a short story, right? Like, I can use a scene from a book?"

"Absolutely."

"All right. Actually…do you have any poetry books in your office?"

"I do. If you want to walk over together, I can point you in the right direction."

Elation threatened to seep from her pores. "That would be great."

Chapter Ten

Riker

It was a good thing Riker's legs weren't an inch longer, or else he would've crossed into the discomfort zone long ago. As it was, his legs were just about the maximum length possible to chill in an auditorium seat for thirty minutes.

By his feet were half a dozen scripts marked up with pencil and sticky notes. Evidence of his failing attempt to find the perfect script for this year's Speech season.

He sighed. The second Speech and Debate meeting of the season had ended half an hour ago. A few students remained in the auditorium, also reading. Like the meeting last week, other team members had scattered to different rooms to practice, find material or talk things out with Beezy or Zeb.

Riker didn't need to talk it out. He just needed the right script to smack him in the face.

He reached into his backpack and pulled out *Robin Hood*. It was the first script he'd read last week, the first one that had caught his eye. Although the pages of the thin booklet had curved, the spine was stiff in his hands, as though it had hardly been opened by anyone before him. He opened it for the second time.

As he read, he visualized the characters popping off the page. He imagined the voices he'd use for each one during competition, the gestures he'd overplay. The last time he'd read it, he'd marked a couple superfluous sections to cut out, and he'd added at least two artificial scene breaks. Now he added more notes as the scene developed clearly in his mind. He felt the pauses before each punchline, heard the chuckles from an unsuspecting judge.

Yes, this was the script. To hell with all the unworthies at his feet. *Robin Hood* would be the gem to get him to the state tournament again. Maybe this time he'd even get above tenth place.

Should've stuck with my instincts the first time around.

After a third read-through, he'd marked it up enough to make it a script he could work with. Hopefully Beezy wouldn't mind the pencil marks. He'd try to erase them at the end of the season if he remembered.

He closed the booklet around his finger and leaned back in the auditorium seat, eyes closed. In his mind, he spoke a few lines and envisioned how he'd play each one. He opened the script in front of his face with his head still tilted back, then closed his eyes and recited the next few lines. He'd have them memorized in no time. Like always.

Another ten minutes passed before he tossed the script onto the floor with the others. When he opened his eyes for good, he saw that no one else remained in the auditorium. Still, his teammates' chatter emanated from the hall. Beezy and Zeb's time on campus was far from over, if his experience on the Speech and Debate team had told him anything about their commitment to late evenings with practicing students. He almost felt sorry for them, but hey, at least they were spending time with each other, even if that meant a bunch of high school students joined them.

There were worse jobs to have.

Hell, maybe he'd end up working with his spouse someday. Doing his dream job—voice acting for video games. And his wife could be a...well, she could be something associated with all that. The director or producer or something. Then he'd never have to feel alone in the crowd, always having someone by his side when things got tough.

But all that hinged on actually getting his shit together when it came to girls.

When it came to Taryn.

He'd tried to catch her eye during today's meeting, just as he'd tried the previous week. Just as he'd tried every Drama class.

But even when he succeeded, something stopped him from taking the next step of actually talking to her.

Why couldn't life be as straightforward as *Timescale*?

State your goal. Prepare to achieve said goal. Advance. Succeed!

Or—

State your goal. Poorly prepare to achieve said goal. Advance before you're ready. Fail!

Yep, that was how he'd approached the Taryn situation so far. Like a video game where he hadn't taken the time to learn the worldbuilding.

Maybe it was time to change that.

He reached into his backpack and pulled out a notebook. Before he could stop to think how terrible an idea it was, he began to write.

Taryn,
Maybe I'm crazy to say this – or maybe I'm just crazy in general, haha – but lately being near you is like a drug that makes me forget anything else exists. Humility be damned, you're my addiction.

It's easier to write this kind of thing than say it. A lot easier. Seriously, though, everything seems pointless when I don't have the chance to look for you. In Drama class, Speech and Debate, the halls – if you're there, I want to see you.

That pretty much sums it up.
Riker.

P.S. If you only like girls, pretend I never said anything.

Was that too candid?
Whatever.

He folded the paper without reading it over and slipped it into his front jeans pocket. Ready for delivery.

Except now came the biggest problem of all — acquiring the bravery to give it to her. Which was ten times harder than writing the damn thing.

Life was unfair like that.

If he didn't stand right away, he'd lose his nerve. This was a task that had to be completed pronto, or else he'd never do it. He rose to his feet, grabbed his backpack and the scripts from the floor and headed toward the hall.

As long as Taryn was still in the building, it wouldn't be difficult to find her in one of the classrooms reserved for Speech practice. If he found Beezy, he'd likely find Taryn.

He peeked into the window of the first classroom he came across, careful not to linger too long like a creeper. Inside he saw Zeb and a cluster of debaters around a bin of files. Definitely no Taryn.

The next room had Gavin speaking at the front, a host of other students around the room either watching Gavin or looking through papers or books. No Beezy or Taryn.

He spotted her in room number three. Beezy was also there, chatting with two other students. Riker marched in as if his sole intention were to talk about his Speech piece with his coach and fellow competitors. The stack of scripts in his hand would help if he needed conversation starters on the spot. The desks on either side of Taryn were empty, so he took the liberty of selecting the seat closest to her backpack.

Taryn had what looked like a poetry book splayed on the desk in front of her. She leaned forward with such intent that the left side of her collarbone peeped out over the top of her shirt.

As he lowered his backpack to the ground next to hers, she raised her eyes. Their gazes locked for a fraction of a second before she returned to her pages.

Riker's heartbeat thumped.

He pulled *Robin Hood* from his stack, leaned back in his chair, and opened the script to the page he'd bookmarked with his pencil. Concentrating on this thing would be impossible while sitting next to Taryn, but it didn't matter—he was on a mission, and that mission didn't involve reading *Robin Hood* for the fourth time.

Movement out of the corner of his eye. Shuffling noises. He looked up from his book to discover that Taryn had left her seat and walked toward a now-unoccupied Beezy with her poetry book in hand.

He quickly pulled the note out of his jeans pocket and slipped it into the front pocket of Taryn's backpack.

Then it was back to rereading *Robin Hood* and memorizing lines.

Chapter Eleven

Taryn

Taryn's chemistry teacher scribbled across the whiteboard as the end-of-class bell rang. His frazzled black hair swayed atop his head while he wrapped up the formula stretched in a crooked line across the board.

"Write this down before you leave! I'm not putting it up here again."

She copied the letters and numbers into her notebook as quickly as her hand would allow. The time between classes was miniscule when it involved a trek to the other end of campus. Every spare moment counted.

She exhaled as she finished and closed her notebook around her pencil. After shoving them and her textbook into her backpack, she stood.

White-hot pain shot through her abdomen. She halted and sucked in a breath.

Jesus Christ!

The pain retreated just as quickly as it had come.

She looked down at her waistline, as if blood might have soaked through her clothes. The shock of it had sure as hell hurt that much. But no, nothing visible. Had she imagined it?

Taryn took a tentative step forward, then another, as the last of the students left the room. No pain. She exhaled.

More small steps, out of the classroom and down the hall. God, how she hoped no one in the sea of swarming students was watching her. When the pain still hadn't returned, Taryn began her powerwalk to the theater for Drama class. Her note-taking and temporary turtle pace might have been enough to make her late for class, but she had no time to dwell on that as she zipped past classroom doors and dawdling high schoolers.

When she reached the sectioned-off auditorium, several students lingered outside the door. She slowed. *Damn, I'm getting better at this.*

She squeezed past the group and made a beeline for her usual seat. Only when she stood in front of it did she look up at the clock—a whole thirty seconds to spare.

With a sigh of relief, she dropped her backpack to the floor and flopped onto the auditorium seat.

Holy shit!

As soon as her butt touched the cushion, she was met with another jolt of pain, this time starting in her butt and jerking up to her stomach. She gasped, then quickly looked around to see if anyone had heard. No one in the immediate vicinity was looking at her. *Thank God.*

Except—

Except Riker, at the other end of her row. He was too far away to hear her over the babble in the room. But she could have sworn he'd looked at her before glancing away. *Great.*

She faced forward and squirmed in her seat, trying to get comfortable. Crossing one leg over the other was met with more pain. She shifted onto her right butt cheek, leaning her weight against the armrest, but another stab emanated from her buttocks into the rest of her abdomen.

Might as well try to find the most comfortable knife to sit on.

Her heart pounded. This did not seem normal.

Maybe if I...

She gritted her teeth and planted both feet on the floor, butt cheeks putting equal pressure on the seat. She froze in that position, holding her breath.

One second passed, then two. After five seconds in the same position, the pain finally seemed to have disappeared again. Apparently, this was her new sitting position for the rest of eternity.

She risked a slow exhale.

Yes, this position would be fine. She preferred to cross her legs or lean into the armrest, but she'd have to make do with this. No way did she want that pain again. Especially not with Riker watching.

Turning her head slightly, she dared to look at him. He sat with one ankle crossed over his knee, his focus on the front of the classroom. Not paying her any mind. Maybe he never had been.

Still. Random pain was the last thing she needed. Not only did it suck, it was yet another thing to make her stand out at her new school.

Though, come to think of it, this school was getting a little more familiar every day.

Beezy entered then, his shoulders squared, his chin tucked down as if the relaxed half of him were missing. Without Zeb at his side, perhaps it was, a connection she never would've made without seeing them together at the Speech and Debate meetings.

Before Beezy could set his laptop bag next to the podium, Gavin jumped out of his seat and walked up to him, one hand gesticulating wildly and the words escaping faster than Taryn could decipher from her distance. Maybe — probably — they were talking about Speech. Not like it was any of her business.

What *was* her business was the array of stories and poetry in her backpack. The compilation she hadn't put together yet. She only had five days before the next check-in with Beezy, and she wanted nothing more than to delight him with an amazing, never-before-attempted Prose and Poetry piece to blow the judges away. Easier said than done.

Her mind bounced back to the idea Gavin gave her, of transforming *Catcher in the Rye* into a competition piece with Holden Caulfield as a present-day female. The idea was daunting — really freaking daunting — but it would certainly check the box for ambition if she could pull it off. And after her round of applause in Drama class, maybe she could. Hell, she even had two minutes of it memorized already.

As Gavin took his seat, Beezy cleared his throat. With everyone else now facing the front of the sectioned-off auditorium, she took the opportunity to glance at Riker again.

His eyes were already on her.

A millisecond passed before he flicked his gaze to Beezy. Taryn followed suit.

One corner of her mouth quirked up against her will. Maybe not everything was in her head.

She picked up one leg and crossed it over the other —

— and winced.

Shit.

The pain definitely wasn't in her head. She froze with her legs crossed, willing it to dissipate.

At the front of the auditorium, Beezy spoke. His words drifted above Taryn's head, a massive jumble of syllables that made no sense amid such discomfort. Should she say something? And, if so, what? "Hi, I have to go to the nurse's office, but it's going to take a while because I can't move"?

No. Better to wait it out. It couldn't possibly stay like this forever.

Unless it did. Then she'd be screwed beyond belief.

She focused on her teacher, trying to make sense of his words. She caught something about "movie" and "write down" and "discuss." The pain, though, continued to call her back, to remind her that it wanted attention.

Then suddenly everyone was shuffling around, standing up, talking. Her eyes widened. What the heck had she missed?

"Can I?"

And now someone was talking to her? Holy cow, she really was out of it. She turned her head to the right and saw two pale arms on either side of a shirt-clad stomach. She knew precisely who she'd find as her gaze drifted upward.

"Yeah," she croaked at Riker. No clue what she was agreeing to, but clearly Riker was in the know. As long as it didn't involve moving, she'd agree to anything with him.

He pulled down the auditorium seat next to her and lowered himself into it, resting a notebook and pencil on his lap. "I have a pretty good idea where this is going. Bernardo is probably the protagonist, and Riff seems like the antagonist but that's only true sometimes. I guess it depends which clip Beezy shows us. Oh, and the setting is obviously Manhattan."

She blinked twice. Bernardo? Riff? Was Riker talking about *West Side Story*?

Beezy rolled a TV on a stand toward the front-center of the auditorium. *Apparently so.*

"Good call." She smiled. To hell with any pain that remained. This was apparently a partnered class assignment, and Riker had *picked her. And* he knew *West Side Story* characters off the top of his head.

Someone pinch me.

"Everyone have their partners?" Beezy asked. The class replied with murmurs. "Good, good, good. So like I said, first is a *West Side Story* clip. You should pick up on the names of the characters pretty easily, but something like 'the guy with the red shirt' is fine, too. Remember, pay attention to the clip, and then write down the protagonist, the antagonist, the conflict, the setting and at least two themes."

Okay, this didn't sound so bad. Watch a movie clip and discuss it with Riker. No biggie, as long as the pain in her side didn't resurface. Which was apparently not a guarantee.

Riker sat with both feet flat on the floor, notebook resting on the thigh farthest from her. His closest hand rested palm down on his other thigh.

In the perfect position for grabbing.

Not that she would.

But.

She could.

Beezy flipped off the auditorium lights. Even in the darkness, Taryn saw the outline of Riker's hand. Mere inches from her own. As if it weren't a big deal, as if attractive people got this close to her every day.

His thigh bumped against her knee then, almost as quickly, bounced away. Stayed away.

She held her breath as the movie clip began.

A group of men stood in a circle, one half opposing the others. Bernardo, in the middle of the circle, stood poised to fight his Jet opponent. At Riff's go-ahead, a choreographed scuffle began.

Jesus, it was a good thing she'd already seen *West Side Story*. No way could she concentrate on an assignment when Riker was so close she could practically feel a draft from his breath. She had Bernardo and Riff pretty much memorized. She did *not* have Riker's leg memorized, nor the way his hand arced while resting on top of his thigh.

God, how she wished she did.

A few glances down and to the right helped her take him in. Discreetly, she hoped. Talk about a distraction from the pain. Hell, the jolts in her pelvic area seemed to have totally disappeared for the time being.

The lights came on and she blinked hard.

"Okay!" Beezy chirped. "You got your list of questions. Now discuss and write down the answers."

At the front of the room, the whiteboard listed the five items they were supposed to deduce from the scene. Beezy must have jotted them up there while the movie clip played.

"Let's do this," Riker said beside her.

She turned and caught his gaze—bright blue and striking—for a fraction of a second before looking elsewhere. Watching his chin would do.

"First up—protagonist," he continued. "Easy. It's obviously Tony. Unless you want to argue it's Bernardo or Riff, but you'd need to know more of the movie to debate that one."

Whoa, this guy. A dramatist at heart. And after her own heart if he kept saying things like that.

"No debate necessary. Go with Tony." She paused and smiled. "But great point."

He returned the smile before jotting down the answer into the notebook on his right thigh.

"How about Bernardo and Riff as the antagonists in this scene, even though we know they're both good by the end of the movie?" Taryn asked. She was about ninety percent sure of the answer to her own question, but after a bout of ridiculous pain followed by a thigh that was still close enough to graze, she'd estimate that ten percent of her brain had gone on hiatus.

"Got it," he replied, jotting down her answer without looking up. "And the conflict is clear. Riff and Bernardo want to beat the crap out of each other, and Tony just wants everyone to get along." He raised his eyes as he finished his sentence, one blond eyebrow quirked up higher than the other.

She swallowed hard. God, those eyes were fierce. Like watching the sun reflect off rough ocean waves— she had to pull her gaze away before they caused permanent damage.

"Right." She cleared her throat. Beezy stood a few feet away, hands clasped behind his back. Studying the class, perhaps. Maybe studying *them*. "The next answer's Manhattan, like you said before."

"Yep," he replied. Out of the corner of her eye she saw his hand move across the paper once more. "Which just leaves us with two themes. Revenge and race sound good?"

"Sure."

Riker let his writing hand collapse onto his notebook. "Simple enough. We're totally getting an A."

She chuckled. "As long as the next clip's just as easy."

Beezy, now several rows away near the shoulders of another pair of students, spoke up. "Two more minutes to wrap it up, everyone."

A couple of grumbles came from around the room. Taryn leaned back in her seat and sighed. The downside to finishing early was that she had nothing to fill the silence with. She was destined to ruin any chance of getting to know Riker better.

She shifted in her seat. Another jolt of pain shot through her side.

With a deep breath, Taryn closed her eyes. She willed away the pain, as far as that was possible. As long as she didn't move, all was okay.

She allowed herself the indulgence of closed eyes for just long enough to not be weird. Or so she hoped.

Think of something to talk about. Anything. Anything but this pain. Or the weather.

"Did you…" Taryn paused, gathering her thoughts. "I mean, are you ready for the first Speech and Debate tournament?"

"Yes!" It came out of his mouth like a burst of energy. "I…yes."

"What did you end up picking?"

"*Robin Hood*. Beezy seems to think it's a good choice. I have this weird voice for the Sheriff that really makes him stand out. But maybe everyone'll fall asleep from how boring it is. Who knows?"

She smiled at the self-deprecation. Her kind of guy.

"What about you?"

"I think I have something figured out." She hesitated, not eager to share that she had adapted her piece from something she'd already done in Drama class. Even if he'd complimented her on it that one day in Beezy's office. "I don't want to say just yet. It's not, um…it's not ready."

"Fair enough." His eyes glinted, as if he understood so much more about her own soul than she could ever understand.

Another cough, this time from the front of the room. Beezy held up a remote to signal that everyone needed to get ready for the next movie clip. "All set?"

A chorus of "yeahs" and "yeps" followed.

"Okay. *Guys and Dolls* this time, people." He turned off the lights and pointed his remote at the television.

In slow motion, Taryn settled into her seat, hoping against all hope that if she moved slowly enough then the pain wouldn't come back to bite her. The method worked for now, but there was no way to tell if it was a surefire tactic.

With the lights out and the pain staying away, she could focus her attention on more enticing things.

Like how Riker's knee had somehow gotten even closer.

Good thing I have this movie memorized, too.

She set her hand on her thigh, palm down. Maybe she'd go radical and grab his hand. Maybe she wouldn't. All she knew was that the stabby pain had better not come back, or she might accidentally rip his hand off.

So yeah, maybe best not to touch him.
She moved her hand an inch closer anyway.

Chapter Twelve

Riker

On the screen, Nathan Detroit, with his jaunty hat and smooth chin, complained to Adelaide. After a fourteen-year engagement, he'd just learned Adelaide had told her mom they were married with five children.

The conflict here was pretty clear, and he didn't just mean Adelaide's terrible fake sneezes. The protagonist and antagonist in *Guys and Dolls* might be up for debate, though. Beezy probably planned it that way.

Regardless, Riker knew *Guys and Dolls* about as well as *West Side Story*, which was really freaking well. No one went through years of Drama class without learning a thing or two about musicals. And they rarely stuck around if they didn't enjoy them.

Which was precisely why he didn't need to watch this scene. Just listening gave him the refresher he needed.

It was also why his eyes were focused solely on Taryn's right hand. Her pinky finger had twitched twice in the last ten seconds. Before that, she'd moved her hand an inch closer to his.

He held in a breath, then, very carefully, he watched his own hand as he moved it an inch to the left on top of his thigh.

And exhale.

Two days had passed since he'd slipped that note into her backpack. Two days of wondering whether she'd found it. Of not knowing what she thought about it. God, why hadn't he just handed it to her? At least that way he'd know for sure she had received it.

Or, the more important question—why had he written it at all?

If she read it, then she knew his intentions right this second.

Which would mean she could be purposely holding back. Or expecting him to make the first hand-holding move. Or thinking he was a blunt asshat.

If she hadn't read it…

Well, then he might scare her away if he so much as breathed too hard.

Maybe it wasn't too late to snatch the note out of the front pocket of her backpack. If someone else distracted her for thirty seconds, he could save himself from a world of humiliation. Then he could forget he'd ever attempted to give her that far-too-honest note in the first place.

Sigh. Not likely.

He'd only had the nerve to partner up with her on this assignment because she'd so clearly been in pain and unable to move. Beezy's requirement of partners was just the excuse he needed to make sure she was okay...even if he hadn't come up with the guts to ask. It had taken everything in him to move his feet in her direction and ask to sit down, the whole time hoping the mortification seeping into his soul didn't show on his face.

This was the second time he'd seen her like this. Something was going on. She might not be willing to talk about it, but maybe a distraction would help.

Now that he was here, something in Taryn had relaxed. Some nerve ending somewhere had let go enough so her face didn't look like she'd sat on a box of needles.

With any luck, he hadn't embarrassed her in the process.

Yeah, looking back, he doubtless had...

And to top it off, he'd fallen right into the damsel-in-distress trope, as if she needed a savior or some other ridiculous thing. As if she couldn't fend for herself like the awesome freaking person she was.

Pathetic.

The overhead lights illuminated with a smack to the corneas. Reflex told him to pull his hand back, to not appear as bold in the light as he was in the dark. Instead, he forced his hand to stay on his thigh. Forced himself to not move a muscle.

To let her know he wanted his hand close to hers. Even if he didn't have the courage to make contact.

At the front of the room, Beezy pointed to the whiteboard, mock underlining the list of requirements with one hand.

"So that's our cue," Taryn said. "The protagonist is probably Nathan, but I can see how Beezy might argue for Adelaide. Couldn't both characters be good and bad?"

He turned slightly to face her. With a silent exhalation, he pulled his hand from her vicinity and used it to hold his notebook in place.

"Definitely. Let's write down both characters for protagonist and antagonist. He'll either scratch it out or give us bonus points."

Taryn giggled, the noise radiating like wind chimes. *God, that sound.*

"And the conflict," she continued. "Totally straightforward. The characters are having relationship problems, basically whether they're going to get married."

Riker nodded as he wrote. This class was beyond easy, but he'd take any excuse he could get to spend an effortless class with Taryn.

"And this scene is set in New York City." Had they mentioned that in the clip or had he pulled that one from memory? He wrote it down.

"Wow, I was just going to go with 'dressing room,' but that works. And the themes would be…" She paused and pinched the tips of her hair between two fingers. "Love and trustworthiness."

"Nice," he replied as he jotted it onto the paper. "I added 'dressing room' too. We'll make sure Beezy's happy, whatever answer he's looking for. Not like he'd fail us for trying."

"Seems like you've got Beezy memorized." Her palm lingered over her lower abdomen, so lightly she might not have noticed she did it.

"Oh, it's not hard. Beezy's predictable. You just show him you care, and you're golden."

"That simple, huh?"

A slanted smile appeared on her face. Goosebumps ran up his arms at the sight, and it took everything in him to not stare open-mouthed. Instead he looked to the front of the room where Beezy was preparing the next movie clip. This girl was going to be the death of him, one intense glance at a time.

Somehow, that was both the best and worst thing.

"Everyone ready?" Beezy called to the room.

If it means more time with Taryn, I'm ready for anything. Lights on or off.

He set his notebook on the leg farthest from Taryn, putting his left hand palm down on his thigh. An open acknowledgment that the pending darkness meant closeness. If she noticed, if she had even looked at him, he had no clue. He refused to look her way again right now, lest he falter in confidence.

God, did she read that note?

"This next clip is from *Little Shop of Horrors*, which is right up there in my top ten," Beezy went on. "Enjoy!"

"Oh!" Taryn exclaimed, then slapped a hand over her mouth. She swallowed hard. This was apparently one of her favorites, too.

Well, crap. He'd never seen *Little Shop of Horrors*, hardly knew anything about it aside from some plant that wanted an onslaught of food. So much for knowing all the musicals. He'd actually have to pay attention to this one. Especially if it interested Taryn.

He relaxed his shoulders as the lights went out and the clip began.

Chapter Thirteen

Taryn

"All right, Ms. Platt. Show me what you got." Beezy nodded at Taryn with wide eyes and a warm smile. His finger hovered over the stopwatch on his phone.

After school at Speech practice, Taryn stood at the front of a sparsely populated classroom with her legs shoulder-width apart, a stapled set of photocopied papers in her hands. Two seats to Beezy's right sat Quinn, ramrod straight in her chair. Two weeks had passed since their first Speech and Debate meeting, and now it was time to show Beezy what she'd come up with.

However terrible it might be.

She swallowed and began speaking.

"The hardy bell rang but once,
Acknowledging release.
Escape the school, winter break,
When all assignments cease."

Her Prose and Poetry piece opened with a poem she'd found about school vacation — the anticipation of joy and the hopes of all that could be accomplished. The poem, from one of the books in Beezy's office, helped set the stage for her larger theme.

From there, she transitioned right into her modern-day female Holden Caulfield on holiday break before finishing the prose and poetry sandwich with a second poem, this one about a character completely messing up their chance at a date. The poem itself hadn't provided a gender for the narrator, so she'd been happy to fill one in by continuing in her female character's voice.

When the final poem ended, she bowed her head just so, as she'd seen her fellow teammates do at practice when they finished their own pieces.

Beezy and three other people in the room clapped politely. Quinn nodded, though for some reason she didn't clap. Taryn exhaled, relieved she'd gotten through it without bolting from the classroom in fear.

"Good, Taryn. Good," Beezy said.

She moved to sit down, but he held up a hand.

"Stay there. Let's talk about this one."

"Oh. Sure." *He's going to say it sucked beyond belief.*

"First of all, that was a great start. Really! I'm impressed with how you strung *Catcher* together with those poems to make it continuous. Solid themes throughout."

She looked to her toes, unable to hold her coach's eye. She wondered if Quinn still watched her too. "Thank you."

"I have to admit — I was a little concerned when you said you were going to use *Catcher in the Rye* again. Not because it's not good, but because I'd hoped you'd broaden yourself a little and try something new. But I was just glad you'd showed up, so I wasn't going to complain."

Oh. So there was the catch.

"That being said, though…you really found a way to add color to this story and make the character pop even more than you did in class. Bravo!"

She nodded. Beezy had a weird way of dishing out compliments.

"You'll need to make some tweaks. For starters, it's too long. My stopwatch has you at twelve minutes, and the judges will dock you above ten. So cut out two-to-three minutes before you show it to me again."

"Sure, okay," she replied, though she had no clue where to cut. She'd already condensed it more than she liked, had already chosen every line with purpose, but alas…

"And I also need you to work on eye contact. If it's hard for you, I suggest looking to the back corners of the room. Find two or three focal points and just take turns with them. That'll keep you from staring at everyone's desks instead."

Guilty. She raised her gaze from her feet. That tip was easier said than done.

He smiled. "Another big thing to work on is the way you flip the pages. We'll get you an actual black book once you finalize the content, but remember to be gentle with the page flips—not angry."

Oh. Well, she hadn't noticed that. *Oops.* "Okay."

"Good. So focus on those tips. If you want to try it again today after a few more people go, I'll be happy to watch. If you're sticking around, you'll have about thirty minutes to find spots to cut. And I recommend using pencil. It's a process."

Taryn took this as her cue to finally move. She settled into her seat next to Quinn, hoping for some expression of encouragement, but Quinn stood and headed to the front of the room to practice her own speech. So much for that.

Taryn hadn't planned to stay at practice for thirty-plus more minutes, but getting everything out of the way now would be more efficient than coming back later in the week. It was just that...well...the season premiere of *Timbre!* was airing in two hours, and she needed prep time.

Her followers would expect some chitchat leading up to the episode, then of course she'd post her reactions live during the show—one of the most popular activities she did for the fandom. Since Grandma's computer room didn't have a TV, she'd have to post from her phone. An annoyance, but oh well. Plus, she'd have to finish her homework first, because no way could she concentrate on it after the show aired. No, she'd be too busy hashing out all the details with her followers and fangirling over...well, the fangirling fuel was yet to be determined.

And to top it off, the new trailer to the upcoming *Timbre!* movie was expected to drop during the commercials—a trailer she looked forward to as much as the episode itself.

She tapped her fingers on her leg. Time to focus on chopping up her Prose and Poetry compilation. And for that, she needed a pencil. She reached her hand into her backpack and pulled one out.

Nope. Pen. After that came a highlighter. Then another pen.

There had to be a pencil in there somewhere — her math teacher would've murdered her by now if she didn't carry one.

She sighed. Her blind hands were useless. She leaned over and pulled her backpack flaps aside with her hands, then dug more thoroughly through the bag. She pulled some books out. Still nothing.

With a huff, she unzipped one of the front pockets and shoved her hand inside. Then she unzipped the next. Her fingers brushed against two objects — one hard, one soft.

She pulled them out of the pouch together.

A pencil and a folded piece of paper.

A folded piece of paper with "Taryn" scrawled across it, the edges tucked into each other like a neat little package. An honest-to-God old-school form of communication.

Her heart rose so high it threatened to explode out of her throat. Someone had *written her a note.*

But she hardly knew anyone here. She definitely didn't know anyone well enough for a secret note. She searched Quinn for any sign of recognition or expectation on her face, but Quinn was about to begin her speech, not paying Taryn any mind.

Unless…

With shaky hands, she untucked the edges and unfolded it, flattening the kinked page on the desk. Her eyes darted to the bottom of the page.

It was from Riker.

Riker!

Taryn,
Maybe I'm crazy to say this — or maybe I'm just crazy in general, haha — but lately my mind makes every moment about you…

Holy shit on a cracker.
Holy mother of all things good in this world.
Riker!

Her heart had definitely exploded out of her ribcage. Could everyone in the room see the gory mess it made?

Somewhere in the distance was the sound of Quinn's voice. No way could Taryn focus on the girl's speech right now, but she at least owed a return of the favor. She stared past Quinn's head, her mind wandering as she didn't take in a single word.

When did Riker write this? Today after the Speech and Debate meeting? He hadn't come close to her, though…

After they'd almost held hands in Drama class? Good God, that would mean the closeness between them wasn't in her head.

What if he'd written it before that day? Would that mean he'd thought she'd read it already?

Does it matter?

Yes. It matters because I want to know!

If only he'd picked a better section of her backpack, she would've found it sooner. She hardly ever checked that front pocket. Thank God for Beezy.

"Humility be damned, you're my addiction."

Yep. Her heart had perished.

Was Riker still in the building? Could she chase him down to tell him she got his letter? Not that she…well, dream as she would, she'd never have the nerve to talk to him about it. Maybe writing a letter back was the best approach. Then what? Slip it into his hand wordlessly?

Every idea seemed worse than the last.

Light applause scattered around the room. Only then did Taryn realize Quinn had finished speaking. She clapped along, the polite thing to do.

Time to file away this Riker thing. For now, she had to focus on the task at hand. The task using her godsent pencil.

Whatever feedback Beezy gave to Quinn was lost on Taryn as she read through her piece. Or tried to read. Her eyes crossed the first poem for the third time. Pretty hard to cut lines when she couldn't focus on the words.

Quinn, now sitting, was occupied with the papers in front of her, scratching a bright pink highlighter across two rows of text, using Beezy's feedback.

Quinn turned to her, a smile across her face, highlighter poised. Her eyelashes framed her brown eyes like an ornate picture frame. "You sticking around?"

"Yeah, I think so. I have to get home fast, though."

"Cool. I'll go again after you, then. Hey, did you bring your ad money?"

Taryn restrained a gulp. Ad money? She remembered Beezy talking about that at the first Speech and Debate meeting, but she'd thought there was plenty of time.

"Um. No?"

"My mom wrote the check but totally forgot to put it with my stuff."

"Oh. When is it due?"

Quinn narrowed her eyes. "You can look it up in the packet. I always get mine in right away, though."

Wait, had she said her mom wrote the check? "Does your mom own a business?"

"What? No." Quinn paused, then shook her head. "You don't have to own a business to write a check for an ad. My mom just fills out the paperwork and writes a big 'Good luck' ad for the showcase program."

"Gotcha."

Quinn made it sound so simple. Taryn's mom would never write such a frivolous check, especially if Taryn were supposed to sell ads to raise the money instead. But good lord, how would she convince a business to buy ads? Taryn had about as much skill talking to strangers as she had singing opera.

Then there was the whole thing about needing a family member to volunteer for a tournament...

Maybe this Speech thing was a terrible idea. The chances of her mom judging an event or volunteering her time at a concession stand were...not likely.

Her best hope was Grandma. Add it to her list of requests for the woman who'd already opened up her home.

She returned to her Prose and Poetry piece. At the front of the classroom, someone else had begun performing for Beezy. Which meant she had to cut out more words pronto so she could practice again and get home before the start of *Timbre!*

* * * *

"What about this one?"

Taryn's mom held up a black blazer with shoulder pads — shoulder pads!

"Mom, no."

Her mom shrugged and put it back on the rack. She'd insisted on taking Taryn shopping the moment she'd picked her up from Speech practice. When Taryn asked why, her mom said she'd read in the packet that Taryn needed professional dress clothes for the first tournament. Never mind how unusual it was that her mom had taken an interest in reading it.

The timing was…odd. But it wasn't the first time her mom had insisted on a spontaneous trip to a discount department store.

Taryn rifled through the clothes on the rack. She stopped on a blue blazer with small flowers stitched onto the front pocket. Not bad. She checked the price tag — reasonable — and picked it up.

"You like brown?" her mom asked from the other side of the rack. "There's a brown skirt over here."

"Nah. Blues and blacks. And when's the last time you saw me wear a skirt?"

"Well, I figured you might if you were dressing up."

Taryn didn't bother answering that one. She probably hadn't worn a skirt or dress since she was five.

Her mom pulled another blazer from the rack and held it up, eyebrow raised in question. This one was oddly long in the back, like a tux with tails. But all things considered, not terrible.

"Sure, I'll try it."

"Good." She handed it to Taryn. "I'll go check out the purses while you try these on."

Taryn clutched the hangers of three blazers and pressed three folded pairs of pants to her chest. She had no idea what Mom's budget was, but she made sure that each of her choices ranked low on the price scale. She rushed toward the dressing room as she checked the time on her phone. She'd be lucky to make it home with ten minutes to prep before the show — it would definitely be a late night of half-assed post-fangirling homework. At this rate, she'd hardly even get a chance to mull over Riker's letter.

Her arms flew through the air as she pulled on pants and shrugged on blazers. Only one of each fit, the navy-blue pants and the blazer with the flowers on the pocket — easy decision.

Time to go go go!

She rushed out, tossed the non-fitting merchandise onto the dressing-room rack and hurried to the accessories section, where she found her mom opening and closing the clasp of a purse to give it a test drive. Her face twisted in anguish as if examining purses gave her immeasurable anxiety. Maybe it did — financial anxiety.

"Hey, Mom." Taryn held up her selections. "I picked some."

Her mom returned the purse to the shelf before turning to face Taryn. "Great. Let's get out of here. You can show your grandma your new outfit before that show of yours starts."

"Sounds good."

"And make sure you let her know I paid for it."

Whatever spat her mom and grandma were having, she wanted no part of it. Taryn was grateful for her mom's effort — a huge "thank you" was definitely in order after they checked out — but the mention of Grandma left a sour gurgle in the pit of her stomach.

Mom was trying to prove she could provide for Taryn all by herself. The sentiment reeked of petty competition.

Three months ago, her mom had been too proud to admit to Grandma when the house was being foreclosed on. She'd been too stubborn to let Grandma help.

Until there'd been no other choice.

If Taryn had asked Grandma to take her shopping, they probably would've gone to a nicer place, maybe a department store instead of a discount store. But then the battle between Mom and Grandma might've been even worse. Too much pride in every direction.

Either way, Taryn knew one thing for sure — there was no way in hell she could ask her mom about buying ads or volunteering for a Speech and Debate tournament. This spontaneous shopping trip was already too much.

As she and her mom walked toward the register, though, it was time to put on her game face.

Step One — Get through the checkout line.

Step Two — Thank Mom and rush to the car.

Step Three — Add some pregame *Timbre!* posts from her phone, with a reminder that she'd soon begin posting live reactions to the new episode (and movie trailer!).

Step Four — Turn on the TV. Swoon. Fangirl. Post.

Step Five — Do homework. Reread Riker's letter. Go to bed.

Step Six — Wish there was a single person in real life who she could talk to about all of it.

Chapter Fourteen

Riker

Beezy winked as he handed Riker a single sheet of paper. Then he moved on to another student.

At the top of the paper was a big green "A+". Jotted at the bottom in jagged cursive were the words, "Great job! You're both masters of musicals!"

Yeah, Beezy was predictable. This was the in-class assignment Riker had completed with Taryn about protagonists and antagonists, and, as expected, Beezy didn't much care what they wrote as long as they tried. Still, the assignment was hella easy.

What wasn't hella easy was what he had to do next—show it to Taryn.

When he looked up, Taryn was already staring at him from the other end of their row, one side of her mouth scrunched up. Finding the nerve to approach her was easier said than done, but God, how he wanted nothing more.

Best to do it right away. Any hesitation would turn into a drawn-out delay, no doubt. He stood and crossed the divide between them with four long strides.

"You can keep it," he said as he handed off the paper with their grade.

She smiled. "Thanks."

Stick around, Rike. You have an easy excuse to talk to her!

He swallowed. What was there to say? *"A+ for us, fellow master of musicals. Let's go practice our musical-watching skills together."*

Hell no. His erratic heart rate was winning right now, and it told him to run back down the row before he made a fool of himself.

And so he did.

He closed his eyes before his butt even hit the auditorium seat. Good God, why did he always get this way? That letter he'd written Taryn had been bold, honest, outgoing. His face-to-face personality? Not so much.

Which meant that if Taryn had read the letter—still a big if—she probably thought he was an inconsistent weirdo. She wouldn't be wrong.

"Okay!"

Riker opened his eyes. Beezy stood in front of the room with a medium-sized metal bowl under one arm.

"Great job on the class assignment, everyone. We're starting a new assignment today with partners, but this time we're going to pick the partners randomly." He pulled the bowl out from under his arm and held it in front of him like a platter. "I'll explain what we're doing after we pick. Everyone ready?"

Riker didn't bother nodding. Beezy would begin with or without his approval. Still, several other students gave their teacher the affirmative, the loudest being Gavin with an over-the-top, "Bring it, Beezy!"

"Moment of truth," Beezy said, as if randomly chosen partners for a Drama class assignment were on par with advancing to the next round of a reality show. Either way, Riker knew exactly who he wanted as his partner. The same person he'd tried to hold hands with in the dark during movie clips.

Beezy rifled his hand through the bowl and pulled out the first slip of paper. "Mason! You'll be with"—another dig through the bowl—"Elizabethany! And, Monroe, your partner will be...Taryn!"

Womp, womp. No hand-holding in his near future.

Probably for the best. That voice in his head was laying the pessimism on thick. He sighed and ducked his head until chin threatened to touch chest. There were few others in this class he could tolerate without judgment. But hey, it was just a class assignment. He'd push through and get it over with.

"Riker! Your partner is...Gavin!"

Ah. Well, that's not bad.

Gavin was about the best alternative he could've hoped for, even though he hadn't thought to hope for it—a fellow Speechie with way more energy than any human needed but actually down-to-earth. He'd probably even do a decent job with their assignment. Though it hardly mattered anymore. An A+ was grand, but he wouldn't lose sleep over a lower grade.

"Hellooooooo. I'm still standing up here." Beezy raised his hands above his head, addressing the class. "Go find your partners instead of chatting with your neighbor."

Right. Time to get Gavin.

Across the room and toward the front, Gavin had already stood. He pointed at his own chest, pointed at Riker then gave a thumbs up and a giant toothy smile. All right then, simple enough. Riker would stay put.

He caught movement out of the corner of his eye — movement from Taryn's end of the row but coming closer. Before he could turn his head to confirm, he saw a small tan hand reaching toward him. Then there was a folded piece of paper on top of his thigh.

A note.

"Excuse me," she said. Taryn pushed her butt against the back of the auditorium seat in front of Riker to slide past him. Her eyes bore into him as she passed, her feet doing the slowest sidestep in the history of sidesteps. And hallelujah for that. He'd hold his breath forever if it meant getting this close to Taryn. Being eye-level with her navel was a-okay with him.

More than a-okay.

He exhaled as she reached the end of the row. She descended the steps then cut across a row toward Monroe, which meant maybe she hadn't taken the most efficient route. Maybe she'd crossed Riker's path for the mere purpose of handing him a note.

A note!

He fumbled for the paper in his lap. He could at least read the first and last lines — hopefully the juicy parts — before Gavin arrived.

It was lighter in his hand than he'd expected — a half-sheet of paper. There was no point rushing through Taryn's letter, because he could read the whole thing with a glance.

I got your note :)

He flipped it over. Nothing on the back.

Um. What does this even mean?

Obviously it meant she'd read his note. *But what does that mean?*

She hadn't replied to anything he'd said. He'd bared his soul to her for nothing. He was no closer to knowing her, no closer to finding out how she felt. Did her smiley face mean she agreed? Or did it mean she was just being nice and was afraid to turn him down? She hadn't even clarified whether she only liked girls, or if boys were fair game too.

He looked up to catch her eye, to see if she could give him a clue from five rows away. But she sat in an auditorium seat next to Monroe, her back to Riker.

"Hey, Riker!" Gavin dropped into the seat next to him. "You ready? I'm so ready."

"Sure, I guess."

"You going to Speech practice tonight? I already went yesterday but I really want to get this one right. I'm telling you, I'm going to blow those judges away."

Riker laughed. He had no doubt this was true. Gavin had a knack for blowing everyone away—his passion was infectious. "I bet. But no, not today. I already went once this week."

"Bare minimum, eh? And somehow you still always pull it off." Gavin winked. Infectious passion and one of the few people born in the aughts who could wink unironically.

Beezy cleared his throat at the front of the room. Next to him on the whiteboard was a single word—Sound.

"Everyone with their partners? Good. Okay, we're focusing on sound today. More specifically, how can you use sound to set a scene?"

Hm. Could be interesting.

"Acting isn't always looking pretty and speaking lines. It's also about making the audience believe you. It's about transporting them to a new time or place so flawlessly that they don't question the reality of it."

Riker sat up straight. Beezy was on to something here. In his attempts at voice acting, he'd always tried to focus on the characters themselves, not just the words. Sometimes, a groan or a cleared throat could make a character's lines pop. When audio was the only medium, details like that could make all the difference.

Beezy continued. "So we're going to dive right into an assignment about sound, then afterward we'll discuss it and figure out what worked and how we can get better. I have pictures for you all..." He trailed off as he reached for a stack of prints on the podium. Then, without another word, he walked around the room to give one print to each group.

The picture that ended up in Riker's hand was a black-and-white photocopy of a busy street, full of cars, buses and pedestrians. In the background loomed tall office buildings that continued past the frame. He passed the photo to Gavin, who nodded as he examined it.

"Okay. So," Beezy continued, now back at the front of the room. "Each of you has a picture of a scene. You have ten minutes to figure out how to perform just the sound from this scene. You can use your mouths, your bodies and anything else you happened to bring with you to class. Then each group will come up and sound out their scene, and the rest of us will try to guess where you are. The only catch is that you can't use words. Got it?"

Definitely. Riker could already hear the honks of the oversized buses, the ding of the street-crossing signs, the flap of litter flying up from passing cars. He and Gavin would have this assignment in the bag.

* * * *

Riker pulled his backpack onto his shoulders as he descended the auditorium steps toward the exit, his chin high and his chest puffed out. He and Gavin had smashed the living daylights out of their sound project, being the only group who'd sounded out their scene well enough for the entire class to yell out their location. Maybe it was the years of Drama class, or maybe it was all the work they'd put into Speech, but Riker just knew this had been the perfect assignment for him and Gavin. Beezy had even used their minute-long performance as an example afterward when lecturing about sound techniques on the stage.

This was his niche. He was born to perform with his voice.

Nothing could knock him down at this point. Not even Mr. Robin's boring calculus class, his next destination.

Daring a glance to the left — because what good was confidence if he didn't use it when he had it? — he caught sight of Taryn as she pulled her long brown hair out from under her backpack straps. He gave her a closed-lipped smile, one side quirked up higher than the other.

Taryn bit her bottom lip before ducking her head.

This was it. He had to say something.

He exited the auditorium and turned right, the direction he knew Taryn would take. Half a dozen steps later, he turned around and leaned one shoulder against the wall, waiting for her to emerge from the room.

No need for deep breaths. He'd ride this high until he crashed back down—an inevitable occurrence, but something for future Riker to worry about. Present Riker was on a mission to talk to a beautiful girl.

Taryn exited the classroom with a giant stride, as if already rushing to her next class. His heart fluttered at the sight of her, a butterfly flapping feverishly against a cage.

She stopped.

But not in front of him.

In front of Quinn, the blonde girl from the Speech and Debate team who always wore those funny sideways knit hats. She was showing off a gray and navy-blue one right now.

And her hand was on Taryn's wrist, lingering there. Taryn giggled at something Quinn said, the hallway too noisy for the sound to travel to Riker. Quinn reached up to Taryn's face and tucked a stray strand of hair behind her ear.

Shit. I can't be here.

He turned and powerwalked in the direction of Mr. Robin's class. No way in hell could he bare his soul to Taryn right now—not when she might be falling for someone else. Quinn could be insensitive at times, but she'd be a good catch. Not that Riker had personal knowledge, since Quinn only liked girls.

How had he not seen Taryn and Quinn talking at Speech practice? Had he missed a major red flag somewhere down the line? Either way, Quinn had taken the plunge before Riker.

Shit, shit, shit.

With each expletive, he felt his shoulders tense higher and higher.

There was nothing to do now but go to Mr. Robin's predictable calculus class.

Great.

Riker's legs carried him on autopilot to his next classroom, where he dropped his backpack to the floor and slumped into his chair. He bent over to pull his phone out of his backpack. Hopefully he could distract himself from Taryn for the next two minutes before the bell rang.

There were two texts waiting for him, each from a different sister.

Keira: Hey little bro, what's up? How's school?

Erin: Dad said you haven't been getting out much. All good?

He rolled his eyes. These texts were *not* helping. He closed the messaging app, not bothering to send replies.

He pulled up his email and froze.

At the top of his inbox was the subject line, "Invitation to Submit Sample."

He tapped it, his fingers tightening around his phone as the app opened the message.

Dear Mr. Lucas,
Thank you for providing your name for consideration for our upcoming online video about bridge engineering. We have reviewed the samples you provided on Voice Venture *and would like to invite you to submit a more thorough sample for consideration. Please find the script and submission instructions below.*

We look forward to receiving your sample!
Sincerely,
Holly Jolly Productions

Whoa.
Yes!

Holy crap, this was awesome. He'd thought the chances of their email had been zero, but now...

Now he had another chance to show someone what he was made of.

Maybe he could even get that microphone he'd had his eye on. Which might then lead to more gigs. God, if only he had the microphone for this sample, it might give him an extra edge.

He sighed. No way could he ask his mom to buy it. He'd like to do one damn thing for himself. The regular old microphone would have to do.

The new problem was tolerating Mr. Robin's class for the next hour and a half. With any luck, it would go by more quickly if he spent the period running through the new script in his head and tying down the voice. He jotted the short script down into his notebook so he could return his phone to his backpack before Mr. Robin took it by force.

He began reading the lines as Mr. Robin signaled the start of class. Riker had a long night of work ahead. The earlier he started, the better.

Chapter Fifteen

Taryn

Taryn gulped the moment she walked through the front doors for her first Speech and Debate tournament.

Had she stepped into a high school or a crowded airport? Hell if she could tell the difference. The ceiling must have been three stories high, and the room was filled with light from the far-and-wide windows.

If she'd thought her own team was big, then she'd been far from prepared for the number of people here. It was impossible to tell who belonged to which school, and, with the professional attire, there was a thin line differentiating students, coaches and judges.

Taryn tensed as something touched her lower back. Beside her, Quinn had reached a hand out to give her a nudge forward. Taking the cue, Taryn moved with the rest of her teammates, plowing through the crowd as a group the best they could.

Beezy hadn't been joking when he'd said they should dress up. She'd felt confident as hell this morning in her new outfit, but now that she was in a sea of crisp suit jackets, pencil skirts and reach-for-the-sky heels, she couldn't have felt more out of place.

Great. Yet another strike against me.

Quinn, her own outfit ten levels above Taryn's, slid their hands together, palm-to-palm. Taryn glanced at their hands, unable to resist the visual.

Holy effing shit. Quinn is holding my hand. In public.

She squeezed her eyes shut for a fraction of a second. If Quinn was chill about this, then Taryn would be chill about this.

Quinn sped up until she was a couple of steps ahead of Taryn, her blonde hair appearing strangely manicured without her typical knit hat. Their arms stretched between them, hands still clasped, as Quinn pulled her forward. Two guys in suits—as if all the guys weren't wearing suits—brushed past them, too close for comfort but without much choice. Behind Taryn, Gavin's voice rose above the crowd, noticeable but barely. If Quinn had said anything out loud, Taryn had no clue.

Soon they reached the auditorium, where Beezy and Zeb ushered them to two rows of plush red seats. Quinn pulled Taryn down one row, only releasing her hand after they plopped into two seats toward the middle. Gavin sat beside Taryn, though he immediately turned away from her to talk to the person on his other side.

Four seats past Gavin, Riker's pale hand stuck out from a too-short sleeve. If he'd noticed her since they'd entered the school, he hadn't shown it.

Her heart sped up at the possibility of him noticing—he'd already claimed he always did. If he'd been watching her, then he'd seen her hand clasped in Quinn's.

"Everything good?" Quinn asked.

Taryn looked back to Quinn and nodded. Was she referring to the tournament or the hand-holding? Maybe it didn't matter.

"What comes next?" Taryn asked.

Quinn shrugged. "We sit around. We practice a bit."

"Oh. But when does everything start?"

Quinn pulled her cell phone out of the pocket of her blazer and tapped the side to read the time. "The opening ceremony is in like an hour. Round one starts after that."

Damn. She hadn't expected so much downtime. There were only so many more times she could practice inside her head before it exploded. Over in the aisle, Beezy and Zeb departed the team, apparently leaving them to their own devices.

"So, do we sit first or practice first?"

Quinn shrugged again. "Whatever."

Taryn took a deep breath. She'd thought Quinn was guiding her, but all of a sudden she was sure she'd become an imposition.

Lay off on the questions. Just chill.

She leaned back in her seat and took in the auditorium. Other teams were bundled together in groups of varying size. The ceiling stretched far above them, complete with rows of stage lights. On the stage ahead was a podium with a microphone, flanked by half a dozen chairs. The shared gymnasium-auditorium at her old school paled in comparison to this. Even Fir Grove's largest auditorium could've fit inside it. Maybe this school's auditorium was so big because it only had one.

Right, "only" one.

Her teammates, for the most part, were quiet. Not a single one had stood up to practice. Maybe that meant they were practicing in their heads? Where the heck else would they do it?

Taryn pulled out her Prose and Poetry competition book and opened it to the first page. She ran through the piece in her head, staring straight ahead as she went, only glancing down when she forgot the words. By page three, her mind had wandered from the story, her thoughts unable to grasp the piece she was supposed to practice.

She turned back to Quinn, who sat back in the seat with her eyes closed. It was impossible to say whether she was practicing in her head or trying to sneak in a pretournament nap. On Taryn's other side, Gavin quietly flipped through a notebook—a rare event indeed.

Someone cleared their throat at the end of the row. Zeb, flanked by Beezy, with a stack of papers in hand. He passed individual sheets down the rows of students, announcing names as he parted with each sheet. Soon a piece of paper was in Taryn's hands with her name and competitor number typed across the top, her personal schedule and room numbers below them.

If it hadn't been official before, it sure as hell felt official now—she was a Speech competitor.

Breathe.

Once the papers were all distributed, her teammates began talking and standing.

"You ready to practice?" Quinn asked beside her.

Oh. So that really is a thing happening somewhere else.

"Sure." Book in hand, she filed out of the seats with some of the other students from her school, following their lead to leave their backpacks on the seats or floor. A thing she never would have done at her old school — but apparently this was a whole new world where people trusted each other.

Quinn fell in step beside her, and thank God because Taryn had no clue where they were headed. The group of them — moving en masse though not necessarily together — walked toward the hallway then turned in a different direction from where they'd entered the building.

Then she saw it — students from other schools, scattered throughout the halls a mere foot apart. Each one was facing a wall and talking to it. Each person was impossible to hear over the others, their voices blending together in an amalgamation of speeches and arguments and stories.

Practicing meant talking to the wall.

Her teammates broke off one by one as they squeezed into spots along the wall. Quinn, apparently expecting Taryn to get the gist, didn't bother explaining what to do. The two girls broke from each other, and Taryn found herself staring at a beige locker.

The book in her hands was clammy under the tips of her fingers. She glanced to the right and left, ensuring that talking to the wall really was a thing everyone else was doing — it was. With a deep breath, she spread her feet shoulder-width apart, lifted her chin, and spoke her introduction out loud.

Okay, this isn't so bad.

As each minute of her piece passed, her voice became louder and more confident. Not a single person was paying attention, as far as she could tell. There was nothing in front of her face to distract her in this moment—not a mirror, not a coach, not a person nodding off. A beige locker five inches away was about as non-distracting as it could get.

By the end of the nine minutes, Taryn's voice felt firmer than it had all morning.

I totally got this.

She closed her book and gave a little nod to the locker. Then she shook out her arms, repositioned her feet and started over.

* * * *

Taryn wound her way through the halls in search of Room 227. She held her competition book with an iron grip. Come hell or high water, she refused to lose track of it. The black plastic was the only lifeline she had to make it through her first tournament.

The opening ceremony had been brief yet formal, one introduction after another as the crowd clapped politely. On any other Saturday, she'd still be in bed, listening to the indistinct buzzes of her grandma's lawncare team outside the window. But today she'd already been awake for almost four hours, and she was as energetic as she could expect for nine-thirty in the morning.

The door to Room 227 was open when she reached it. Inside was a girl with straight black hair in the first row and a tall, lanky boy with porthole glasses in the third row. Taryn slid into a seat in the second row to split the difference. She set her book on her desk and pulled out the schedule. Yep, she'd made it to the right place at the right time. And she'd be the third of six competitors in this room.

Round one of tournament one, here we go.

Within a minute, the remaining three competitors took seats in the room. A minute after that, a young woman in khaki pants and a clipboard presented herself in the doorway. She whisper-counted the number of people, checked something — the time? — on her phone and closed the door to the classroom with a soft click.

The judge took a seat in the middle back of the room, as if the students had left that chair vacant for her. Maybe they had. She sifted through a stack of papers, tapped them into a neat pile and placed her phone screen up on the desk.

"Good morning, everyone. Looks like all six of you are here. Can we start with number forty-nine, please?"

The boy diagonally behind Taryn stood without a word, holding a black book identical to Taryn's. He positioned himself at the front of the room, book at his side, feet shoulder-width apart, chin up. Confident as hell.

His words came out as self-assuredly as his appearance, voice booming across the room before turning soft at just the right moments. His gaze fell just above everyone's eyes, focusing on each forehead in turn. Behind Taryn, the judge's chair creaked ever so slightly.

This guy was good. Like, good enough to win. Or at least it seemed that way, in her limited experience. The other Prose and Poetry competitors from her school that she'd watched during practices had come nowhere close to this guy.

Gulp.

He finished with a flourish and a slight bow of the head. Taryn raised her hands to clap, but, hearing no other clappers in the room, scratched her nose before setting both hands on the desk.

The girl following wore a crisp black pantsuit that might've been tailored judging by how well it fit. She opened her black book with a mastered poise, like a hand model displaying jewelry. Her shoulders were squared back, her chin lifted high. The epitome of grace and professionalism.

About twenty paces more advanced than Taryn could dream of being.

The girl began speaking, a low-pitched rumble with carefully chosen articulation. Her eyes barely glanced at the book, as if she'd scripted when to do so. She turned each page without looking down, like a pianist whizzing through a set.

Taryn swallowed. She'd thought the first competitor was good. The second was even better.

A lump in her throat had enlarged to the size of Cleveland by the time the second competitor finished. Maybe she'd get lucky and pass out from asphyxiation before it was her turn.

"Third up, please."

Damn. No ambulance rides today.

Taryn blinked hard. She pushed her chair back from the desk, grabbed her performance book in a show of confidence and powerwalked to the front of the room. She set her feet firmly in position, shoulder-width apart, and raised her chin.

You can do this. You can do this. You can, you can, you can.

After a mental countdown from three, she began.

* * * *

In the airport-esque cafeteria, Taryn was hard-pressed to identify a table that wasn't already covered in backpacks and food trays. She scanned the room for a familiar face. Anyone would do, be it in the cafeteria line or seated at a table.

She noticed Riker first, followed by Quinn. They sat diagonally across from each other at the same table. She let out a sigh of relief at the sight. She might be nervous to talk to either of them, but at least she knew them.

Upon closer inspection, she realized the table was occupied by several other people from her school. And bonus points, there were still empty seats. As she approached, Quinn gave a finger-wave with a smile spread across her face.

"Come sit with me," Quinn said, patting the empty stool next to her.

This girl made it seem so breezy. Like it was a piece of cake to just find the right table in a crowded lunchroom and invite a cute girl to sit next to her, all while displaying the confidence of a Persian cat.

Taryn lowered her backpack to the floor and slid into the seat. Quinn patted her leg twice, then picked up her fork and stabbed it into her salad. Taryn didn't dare glance at Riker, not when Quinn was paying her so much attention. Not when she hadn't given Riker's letter a proper reply.

The completely amazing letter that had said so much.

"So how'd it go?" Quinn asked.

"Me?" Taryn asked. Maybe she should've gotten in line before sitting. Quinn's salad didn't look particularly tasty, but the smell of the macaroni and cheese on someone else's plate two seats down was giving her a Pavlovian response. Not to mention the French fries.

"Of course you, silly. How did you do?"

"I did okay, I think. I mean, everyone paid attention and no one booed, so that has to be a good sign."

"Eh." Quinn shrugged one shoulder. "Everyone's just polite. You get points knocked off if you're mean to the other competitors, remember?"

"Oh." She hadn't thought of it that way. "I guess I'm not sure how I did, then."

Quinn waved her hand in Taryn's direction. "I'm sure you were fine."

Taryn thought she'd done okay in her first round, then about the same during rounds two and three. But it was so hard to tell when everyone in the room — including the judge — had a static expression. A "polite" smile, as Quinn pretty much said. They even reacted that way for the really bad competitors, at least one in each round.

Whatever. This was her first Speech tournament. There was no way she'd place. Most of the other people in her rounds were way too good in comparison.

"Can you save my seat? I'm going to get some food." And with that, Taryn stood to join the fray.

Chapter Sixteen

Riker

Three feet from Riker, Quinn's palm was on top of Taryn's.

He looked down at his slice of pepperoni pizza. If the food had eyes, it would be the only thing paying attention to him right now. He was pretty sure he could gawk openly at Quinn's and Taryn's hands without anyone noticing.

Not that he would do that. Not intentionally.

It was just that…well, maybe he'd hoped…

He picked up his pizza and took a bite. As far as tournament food went, this ranked somewhere toward the top. More like takeout than cafeteria food. The only plus side to this moment.

He sighed into the bite and glanced back at their hands.

Damn, Quinn had definitely taken the first—and second and third—step, far ahead of any boldness

Riker would've been able to muster. Unless he counted the pathetic attempt at writing a letter, something Taryn had brushed aside, as evidenced by her non-committal reply. Pouring his heart out in a hastily written note had gotten him nowhere, had probably even set him back a few steps. If he could kick himself under the table without drawing attention, he would.

Under normal circumstances, he'd back off from anyone the infallible Ms. Quinn had hit on. The girl must've had some strange sixth sense for knowing when hitting on another girl was allowed, and typically Riker would be happy to accept her judgment call for who was off the table for guys.

Yet he'd seen the way Taryn blinked rapidly at him, could still feel how his heart had pounded when she'd crept her hand toward his during Drama class—he'd been pretty sure she'd done it intentionally. She'd never stated she was bisexual or pan, but surely that must be the case.

He swallowed.

I'm not imagining it, right? I'm not one of those guys who thinks every girl is into him?

No. Hell no. He'd passed many a day noticing how often girls were strictly *not* into him. That wasn't how Taryn acted.

So hey, silver lining—he and Taryn had something in common. They were both attracted to girls. And that seemed like a pretty kick-ass thing to have in common. They could compare their celebrity crushes, could debate the merits of being a boob person versus a butt person. Hell, maybe she was even a leg person.

Riker bit down on the inside of his check. He'd never say any of this to her—it would be a surefire way to scare her off for good. Not to mention it would brand him as Fir Grove High School's resident creep.

Get it together, Rike.

Quinn removed her hand from on top of Taryn's. The latter's eyes followed the hand for a beat, as if longing for it to come back.

Yeah, Riker stood no chance in hell.

Quinn stood and sauntered back to the lunch line, seeking dessert, perhaps. Taryn followed the girl with her gaze, then circled her eyes back to the half-eaten lunch in front of her, French fries with macaroni and cheese. Her hand hovered over her fork, as if debating whether to pick it up. She set her palm, Quinnless, back on the table.

Then her gaze pierced Riker's.

Riker's neck spasmed. Was she looking at him intentionally, or had her view just happened to land on him?

He held her stare. His hand itched to rise to his arm and scratch, to do something other than stay stock still. He forced it to heel.

Taryn blinked once, twice, her eyelashes fluttering across the bright green of her eyes. One side of her mouth quirked upward before she lowered her eyes to her lunch once more.

Riker was in trouble.

Taryn picked up her fork and stabbed it into a French fry on her plate. She gingerly dipped the fry into a puddle of ketchup before biting into it, then repeated the action. After a couple more fries, she set down her fork again and rummaged through her backpack, pulling out a notebook.

When Quinn came back, Taryn glanced at the girl's dessert, a single brownie. If Riker were the one holding hands with Taryn, there was no way he would've left that line without two brownies.

Quinn peeled the plastic wrap off her brownie and tore it into four pieces, then she popped them one at a time into her mouth. Meanwhile, Taryn examined the notebook in front of her, eating an occasional forkful of lunch. Riker wondered if she'd mentally checked out, the way he sometimes did when he couldn't escape a large group of people.

The way he'd love to do right now. But instead, he was staring at Taryn like some kind of pervert.

"So tell me," Quinn said, turning to face Taryn. "What are you bingeing these days?"

Taryn coughed as if choking back a knee-jerk response. "Um. Well. I really like *Realms at Dawn*. And, um, *Timbre!*"

"Oh God," Quinn moaned. "Talk about the suffocation from the patriarchy. As if all those students need so much help from their male teacher. I stopped watching *Timbre!* a year ago."

Taryn swallowed. Visibly. "I mean—doesn't everyone need help from their teacher?" The low volume of her words lanced Riker. He recognized this stance—defensiveness.

Quinn rolled her eyes. "Not really. I mean, come on, we're not all helpless little students. They'd never put a female in that teacher role. They think we're too feeble and dependent."

"I—"

Taryn cut herself off. Riker wondered if she'd been ready to voice the obvious fact that there were several teachers on the show who helped their students, and they weren't all male.

I mean, I get the whole teachers-know-nothing thing, but some of them aren't that bad. Like Beezy...

But if he jumped in to announce this, Quinn would accuse him of being part of the...well, the patriarchy. A mansplainer at a minimum.

He had to say something, though. Taryn looked as uncomfortable as a sinner in church.

"I've seen a couple episodes of that show," he said. "I thought the singing was pretty awesome."

Quinn looked at Riker with startled eyes, as if she hadn't noticed he was there to begin with. Taryn bit her bottom lip and raised a hand to her cheek.

"Yeah?" Quinn asked. "That singing is way too autotuned. I really can't stand it."

Riker caught Taryn's eye and held it for a beat—for as long as he could stand—before looking away. "Well, I still like it. And those song selections are fantastic, with or without the autotune."

Quinn shrugged one shoulder, a silent termination to the conversation. Taryn had removed her hand from her cheek, which only emphasized the lift at the corners of her mouth. He couldn't be sure, but it felt like he'd said the right thing.

Chapter Seventeen

Taryn

The bus rumbled as it sped down the highway. Taryn's shoulder pressed against the window, jostling each time the bus hit a bump.

On her other side sat Quinn, their thighs forced to touch in the limited space of the seat, Quinn's wool against Taryn's polyester.

"I can't believe I didn't place," Quinn said. "God, I bet I was close."

"Yeah? I'm sure I got dead last." Taryn chuckled, unsure how else to react to her own self-deprecation.

Quinn apparently wasn't amused. She tilted her head at Taryn and narrowed her eyes. "You're lucky you're cute."

And if I weren't? Taryn bit back the thought before it tumbled out of her mouth. Probably best to not be snarky with someone who had actually showed interest in her.

"Seriously, though," Quinn continued. "I'm sure I was close to placing. Beezy's probably going to give us our scores any minute so we can read them before we get back to Fir Grove."

Taryn had no hope of good scores. She was already well aware that she — and Quinn — weren't in the top six. First through sixth places in each competition category had been called to the stage during the closing ceremony after lunch. Several people from Fir Grove had placed, including three first-place winners in Debate and one in Speech.

But there had been only one placer she hadn't been able to keep her eyes off. Riker had looked so damn confident as he walked up to the stage, shoulders squared and cheekbones high, to accept sixth place in Humorous Interpretation — to the standing applause of the entire Fir Grove team and the dozens of other competitors in his event.

Even after Taryn had sat back down and Quinn had grabbed her hand, Taryn's focus had remained on the sixth placer. He'd stood at the edge of the stage with a small medal in his hand as places five through one were called up to stand beside him, the others in their event standing and clapping from the audience to show their appreciation for each winner. So what if she was moony-eyed? Aside from performances in Drama class, when else did she get to stare at Riker without it being weird?

Taryn felt pressure on her thigh and looked down. Quinn's hand had somehow made it onto her leg, as if it were the most nonchalant thing in the world. Who knew? Perhaps it was.

And perhaps all that buildup about maybe-almost holding Riker's hand in Drama class had been hyped up in her head far more than it should have been.

Maybe.

At the front of the bus, Beezy stood, a stack of papers in hand. With any luck, it would be *the* stack of papers, the ones containing their individual scores.

Without speaking—surely the chatter on the bus was too loud anyway—he stopped at the first row of occupied bus seats, flipped through his pile and handed papers to each competitor. The process repeated at the next row.

Four rows to go. Then scores!

She sat up straighter, her shoulder squeaking against the windowpane. Beside her, Quinn used her left hand to scroll through social media on her phone.

Two more rows before scores... She looked out the window to take her focus off Beezy. The woods off the highway were a green and brown blur as the bus whizzed by.

"Quinn and Taryn."

Taryn turned to face her coach, hoping her sudden attention would make it seem like she hadn't anticipated him. Like Quinn, who didn't look up from her phone even now.

Beezy rifled through, pulling out sheets of paper from different spots in the stack. "I have your judges' scores and comments here. Great job, ladies."

Oh God oh God oh God. "Thanks, Beezy."

His eyes flitted to Quinn's hand on Taryn's thigh before retreating to Taryn's face. He smiled as her thigh twitched. "You had a fantastic start for your first tournament. Keep it up."

Heat rose to her cheeks at the compliment. A reply wouldn't come.

Beezy moved onward. Quinn slid her papers behind her phone and continued scrolling.

Taryn took a deep breath, then held the papers to her face with both hands. Three stapled sheets, one for each round. She quickly found the number she'd been looking for in the bottom-right corner — three.

Which meant she'd gotten third place out of the six competitors in her first round. Right in the middle. Not enough to place above the dozens of competitors in her category, but not at the bottom.

She flipped the corners to find the scores from the other two rounds. Three, followed by three.

She would've needed ones and twos to place, but threes were pretty damn good. Especially for her first time competing.

Maybe I really am meant for this!

She chuckled at the thought. Her followers, if they'd been there, would've rooted her on, told her to rock her acting skills like the actors on *Timbre!*

She glanced at Quinn, who still hadn't checked her scores. Quinn had been so harsh about Taryn's favorite show during lunch, saying things that just didn't add up. It took all her willpower to not stand up and exclaim, "How dare you!" Except of course she'd never have the nerve to do that. And she definitely wouldn't have the nerve to ask Quinn to see the upcoming movie with her in two weeks — Quinn would shoot down that idea in a flash. Time to steel herself to go to a movie solo, even if it took every dime she had.

Riker, though...he'd stood up for the show. As if maybe he liked it, too. Or maybe he'd noticed Taryn's face had been about to explode.

Wishful thinking.

She turned back to the first page to read the first judge's comments. Her eyes darted over the page, unable to concentrate on reading complete sentences, then she did the same with the second and third pages. Phrases popped out at her as she tried to take it all in.

"Creative and entertaining!"

"Work on eye contact and focal points."

"Great job on voice projection."

"Inflection needs work."

"Be careful with your feet fidgeting. You were close to stepping outside the performance area."

Deep breaths. It's not that terrible. Some of it's good! Even though some of it's bad.

Beside her, Quinn was finally looking at her own papers.

"How'd you do?" Taryn asked.

Quinn shrugged. "Just okay. A one, a two and a three. Really close to placing, probably. You?"

"Three threes."

Quinn nodded. "It's your first time. Don't beat yourself up over it."

Taryn hadn't planned on beating herself up over it. She'd done better than three people in every round. Which was better than she'd hoped. "Okay," she said, unsure how else to reply.

"At least you're not as intense as those Drama kids," Quinn continued. "They win those acting events all the time and think they're better than everyone else. I swear Beezy just teaches that class so he can recruit them."

"Oh...I—" Taryn stopped. Had she really never mentioned she was in Drama? Had Quinn not noticed she'd come from the auditorium when they'd talked in the hall the other day?

So what if she was in Drama? She'd been hitting her stride in class, and there was no doubt it had helped with her Prose and Poetry performance on the Speech team. And wasn't Quinn just as intense and arrogant about her own event as the Drama kids were about theirs?

Taryn clenched her teeth. "I'm, uh, I'm in Drama too."

Quinn turned to face her. "Ah. Well, no one's perfect. I'm surprised Beezy even let you do Prose and Poetry, then."

"He said I could pick whatever event I wanted." And that was true. Beezy had never once tried to steer her in a direction she didn't want. That was part of what she liked about him—he always seemed to encourage everyone's interests.

"Sure, okay," Quinn replied before going back to her phone.

Taryn looked down at Quinn's hand on her thigh. It hadn't moved for several minutes, not in a good way or a bad way. The pressure of Quinn's palm was firm, like a lion staking its claim on prey. About as far from warm as frozen yogurt.

Quinn was perfect on paper—smart, organized, fearless, beautiful and not afraid of PDA.

But.

But Taryn couldn't help comparing Quinn's unyielding grip on her thigh with the way Riker had gradually inched his hand toward hers without ever taking the plunge.

There was no denying the thrill in Riker's method. Even if it seemed like both Taryn and Riker had the kind of personality that prevented them from going all in.

Was it good or bad that she and Quinn had opposite personalities? Maybe Quinn's sociability was exactly what Taryn needed.

Maybe.

The bus hit a bump that sent Taryn a couple inches out of her seat. When her butt landed, she yelped in pain. A sharp stab jolted through her pelvic area, from her butt up through her lower abdomen.

She froze.

This was just like the pain she'd experienced in class. Once again, she couldn't move. Her pelvis tensed, leaving no doubt that a single change in position would bring a new wave of pain.

Quinn's hand remained on Taryn's leg as she scrolled through her phone. If she'd noticed the yelp or the now-rigidness of Taryn's thigh, she gave no indication. Taryn took deep breaths, willing the pain to subside before the bus dropped her off at the high school.

* * * *

The next day, Taryn sat in her grandma's computer chair, bent over at the waist and facing the floor. She'd been in the position for at least three minutes—long enough to know that this pain was worse than what she normally felt on the first day of her period. It always hurt, but…

Since starting her period this morning, her pain had run the gamut from light cramping to full-out Charlie horse. It was only three o'clock in the afternoon and she was already close to maxing out the daily allowable amount of ibuprofen.

Thank God it wasn't a school day.

She took another deep breath before sitting up straight, the pain finally dissipating enough for her to feel sane again. On the computer screen, several messages flashed, vying for her attention. All were from fellow *Timbre!* fans, likely discussing the upcoming movie or last week's episode. She clicked through each of the message threads in turn, adding her take, inserting way more exclamation marks and capital letters than necessary.

She leaned back in her chair as she hit "send" on the final message. It had been a solid two hours since she'd sat down in this chair—time to do something else before a new message sucked her back in.

At her feet was her still-zipped backpack. She'd brought it into Grandma's computer room with the intention of starting homework. Intention fail.

But what if…

What if there was another letter from Riker inside? What if he'd found an opportunity during yesterday's Speech and Debate tournament?

Why didn't I think of that sooner?

She bent down and unzipped the smallest front pocket. Nothing. The two small pockets behind it contained the usual, spare pens and a flash drive. No note.

As a last-ditch effort, she opened the main section. But even after pulling out each book, there was no sign of a note from anyone.

Blah.

She pushed her backpack against the wall and wandered into the hallway. Maybe her mom or grandma could distract her. Unlikely, but she'd try anything if it meant boredom wouldn't swallow her whole.

Both women were in the living room, Grandma in a recliner with a tray pulled up to it. She wrote by hand on a bifold card, as if working her way through a stack of thank-you cards. Perhaps she was — grandmas were weird like that.

On the couch sat Taryn's mom, flipping through a magazine and leaning so far back that her rear threatened to slide off the front of the couch. The television was off and they weren't speaking, the space as quiet as two exhausted women in a nineteenth-century parlor room.

They looked up as she entered. Taryn lowered herself onto the other end of the couch, leaning against the cushion of the armrest. It was unlikely she'd find entertainment here, unless her mom and grandma were okay with her turning on the TV.

"Taryn, honey?" Grandma said, setting down her pen. "Your mom said you liked watching something on one of those online services."

Taryn sat up. Now they were getting somewhere. She looked at her mom, whose face remained buried in her magazine, then back to Grandma. "Yeah."

"Well, maybe you could show me how to set it up for you."

She nodded vigorously. "Yes. When do you want to do it?"

"Oh, when I'm done writing these cards."

"Sounds good, Grandma."

"And, honey, your mom showed me that information packet for your Speech and Debate team. There were things in there that needed to be filled out.

I'm surprised you hadn't asked me or your mom about them."

"Oh. Sorry. I wasn't sure." What was Grandma talking about? The permission form for the weekend tournament?

"I filled them out and put them on your bed. There's your permission slip and a check for the ads, and I found a date that works for me to volunteer. Although, from what I understand, I won't be allowed to judge anyone from your school, which defeats the purpose."

"Wow. Thanks, Grandma. That's...that's really nice, thanks."

"You are very welcome."

Her mom's jaw tensed, fingers curling around the cover of the magazine. It was hard to say whether Grandma had done all this behind Mom's back or had talked to her about it.

So this solved the problem of begging for a volunteer judge or wandering the streets to find a business that would buy her ads. Still, it felt too simple, like she hadn't earned any of it.

Perhaps the price was all this tension in the house. Tension that didn't seem likely to disappear any time soon.

A dull ache emerged in her abdomen—again. She lay on her side and rested her head on a couch pillow. Like before, pressing a palm into her abdomen did nothing to quell the pain. At least it had subsided to a dull throb, instead of the sharp shooting she'd felt before.

Worthless freaking periods.

Taryn adjusted her hips and felt a tight ache in her pelvic area. She sighed.

"Mom?"

Her mom's eyes dragged to the bottom of the page before she faced her daughter. "Yes?"

"Um. I just… My period really hurts lately?"

Her mom raised her eyebrows. "Is that a question or a statement?"

"A statement, I guess. I started this morning and it just really freaking hurts, since yesterday."

"Well, periods can do that to you. They're just cramps. Everyone gets them. Did you take ibuprofen?"

"Yeah, a few times today." Taryn looked back to her stomach. This didn't seem like normal pain. "I don't know, Mom. I don't remember it hurting like this before."

Her mom shrugged and returned to her magazine. "I don't know what to tell you, Taryn. Periods are awful. Welcome to womanhood."

Chapter Eighteen

Riker

Riker lowered his chin to his chest and held the pose for three seconds — the classic end to a humorous interpretation performance.

"Thank you," the judge said from a small desk in the back of the room. She continued writing without looking up.

Riker nodded and worked his way down the aisle to the desk he'd chosen at the beginning of this round. The five other competitors were silent, unmoving — another of the strange traditions at these Speech and Debate tournaments. The silence unnerved him every time. In Drama class, clapping was customary, an indicator of how well he'd performed, but for Speech tournaments, clapping only happened during opening and closing ceremonies.

Silence engulfed the room as they waited for the judge to call up the next competitor. Riker was glad to be done with his turn. This might have only been the third tournament of the season, but it was the ninth time he'd performed in front of a judge in the course of fifteen days. If he'd bothered to multiply how many times he'd done this in the past two years…

Not worth counting — the number would be too disheartening.

Sure, he did okay at these things. Sometimes more than okay. At one point in history he had even loved the tournaments, looked forward to them. But lately he just wondered what the hell he was still doing there. The monotony, the repetitiveness, the strange traditions.

At least he had better success here than he did for voice acting gigs. He'd thought the Speech performances would make him a better voice actor, but if so, he hadn't seen the results of that yet.

He snapped back to reality and realized the next competitor was already performing at the front of the room. He'd seen this girl before — an average speaker who'd placed a couple times since he'd first seen her two years ago. Now here she was performing a piece from *Mean Girls*, still trucking along two years later. Why?

Great, now I'm projecting my problems onto her.

This competitor plus two more meant about thirty minutes before they broke for lunch. It took everything in him to not slam his forehead on the desk.

He'd rather be home, alone with these dismal thoughts. Far from the conventions that told him to pay attention, to be polite, to enjoy himself.

He lifted his chin in a mock show of confidence. *I am not miserable. I love being here. I'm great at what I do. I want this.*

But thinking the words did nothing to make them feel true.

* * * *

Maybe it was in Riker's head, but Taryn and Quinn didn't seem nearly as close this weekend.

Another Saturday of competition in the morning and lunch at a random high school while waiting for the tournament results — such was the cycle on the Fir Grove Speech and Debate team. And just like the previous two Saturdays, Taryn and Quinn sat diagonally across from him.

Except this time, he had yet to see hand-holding. Which was fine by him.

"Taryn! There you are."

The voice came from Taryn's side of the lunch table — a woman with spiky white hair walking toward them.

Taryn's eyes widened, and she sunk into her shoulders. "Hi, Grandma."

Her grandma stepped over a backpack on the floor to get closer. She put a hand on Taryn's shoulder. "I wasn't sure I'd find you. Listen, I'm all done, so we can head home."

"Oh." Taryn blinked twice. She replied so quietly Riker barely heard her over the lunchroom crowd. "I have to stay here for the closing ceremony, to see how I did. Then we all ride back to the school on the bus."

Her grandma pulled her hand from Taryn's shoulder and touched it to her chest. "Well then, what on earth am I doing here, Taryn? If we weren't driving together this morning, I at least thought we'd drive home together."

Taryn sputtered. "It's just...I needed someone to volunteer so I could be on the team."

Her grandma sighed. "They're expecting too much. I drove all the way out here to judge some kids from *other* schools, and I didn't get to see you all day. Then they didn't even let me pick what I judged. One of the events had me almost falling asleep! I'm going to call that coach of yours later and tell him how terrible this system is."

"Okay, Grandma."

If Taryn were in an acting event for "seeing ghosts," her wide eyes and blanched cheeks would have won her the top prize.

"I'll see you at home, Taryn." Her grandma turned and scuffed her feet against the backpack on the floor. She brushed her hands down her hips before stepping over it and winding her way out of the table rows.

Quinn finally turned to Taryn. "Wow."

"Yeah," Taryn said, her eyes cast down to the table. "Sorry about that. My grandma, she's...she's really intense."

"Understatement." Quinn laughed. She turned her shoulder back to Taryn and pulled out her phone.

Riker couldn't help it. He leaned forward, his elbows on the table and his hands stretched toward the only girl he had eyes for. "Taryn?"

She looked up at him, eyelids fluttering. "Yeah?"

"Are you okay?"

Taryn's shoulders slumped as she exhaled. "I...I am. I think. Thank you."

Riker shifted in his seat. Now that he'd started a conversation, he'd have to continue it or risk sitting in awkward silence in a loud room. "So your grandma lives with you?"

Taryn chuckled, a touch of bitterness attached to it. "Not quite. More like I live with Grandma."

Well shit, now he'd stepped in it. Alluding to her apparent lack of parents only made this conversation harder to push forward. "Oh. I'm sorry, I didn't realize..."

She shook her head. "No, no, I didn't mean... My mom's not dead or anything. She lives there, too. I mean, I haven't seen my dad in like ten years, but he's still alive. Not that you, um, care about all that..." Taryn trailed off.

"I do!" *Oh God, way too enthusiastic.*

Taryn hesitated, scratching her jaw. "Me and Mom, we moved in with Grandma a few months ago. That's why I'm new here."

"Where did you go before?"

"Trippe. Don't make fun."

Riker mock-gasped. "I would never." He'd certainly heard of Trippe—only twenty minutes away, with a reputation for being underfunded. But that wasn't Taryn's fault.

"Good." Her hand hovered over her fork, though she didn't pick it up.

"Do you miss it?"

Taryn set her hand down. "Eh. I didn't really have friends, so..."

"So no?"

She shrugged. "I guess not. It's not like I really have friends here either, but...I like Drama class and the Speech team."

His face brightened. Just having Taryn here made this tournament seem tolerable. Even if the rest of it bored him to tears these days, the reminder that Taryn would always be there might be the motivation he needed. Not that he would ever admit that to her.

"Well, I hope you make some friends here. We're not that bad, all things considered."

Of their own volition, his eyes drifted past Taryn and landed on Quinn. The girl swung her legs up and over the table bench, then left without a word. Taryn hadn't said whether Quinn was her girlfriend. Maybe that meant he still had a chance…

Taryn leaned forward on her elbows and lowered her voice. "I liked what you said about *Timbre!* That's my favorite show."

"Oh! Well, I've only seen a couple episodes. But yeah, I think it's really good."

"Ah." She sat back up.

Pulling away, it seemed. *No, no. Not now.*

"What's, um…what's that one guy's name, with the blue hair?" he asked.

"Oscar," she said quickly.

"Right. Oscar. I saw that episode where he sang *Maria* from *West Side Story.*"

Her eyes widened and she nodded. He pushed on.

"And it really stuck with me, you know? He belted out those notes like he was Tony pining his way through Manhattan. I always meant to watch more episodes, but…I haven't seen that many."

"You should!" Taryn leaned forward on her elbows again. "There are so many great episodes. The one where Oscar sings *West Side* and kisses Maria is good, but some are way better."

"Yeah? Got any suggestions?"

"Mmhm. There's a set of three episodes in Season Three that's perfect. Seriously. There's this part where

Valerie—she's the one who always wears the straw hats—finally admits she's in love with—"

Taryn stopped abruptly. Riker vaguely remembered Valerie. Besides the straw hats, the only thing popping into his head was her bisexuality.

"With who?" he prompted.

"Well, I shouldn't say. It would ruin it for you."

"Ohhh, I see. We definitely can't have that," he replied. "But maybe…do you have something else to go on? How will I know which episodes they are?"

Her words came out before he'd hardly finished his question. "The first episode in the set is called *Excepting Fishes*."

Riker chuckled at the *King and I* reference. "Nice."

Her eyes brightened as she continued. "There are so many ups and downs in it, and I have lots of favorite parts, but Valerie sings *Something Wonderful*, and it is so freaking mind-blowing, you wouldn't even believe it. It's different, though, because Valerie, um, she changes the pronouns in the song since she's singing to a girl. Anyway, it's one of my favorite songs, and I swear, I've listened to it…well, a lot."

Her shoulders slumped, her body deflating at the end of her sentence. It was the most he'd ever heard her say at once, except for when she'd been on stage during Drama class. Even so, he hadn't one-hundred-percent understood what she was talking about. Her excitement oozed out of her like sweat from pores.

"I'll have to watch it. Definitely." He nodded once in confirmation. Because after this conversation, how could he not watch? "I love musical theater, so there's no reason I shouldn't."

She placed one of her hands on top of the other. The fingers on the bottom clenched against the table. "Yeah?"

"Yes! Sounds like I'll have to start from the beginning, though, so I don't miss anything."

"You can stream it, and, um, you could let me know what you think?"

You mean take advantage of another reason to talk to you? Hell yes. "I'll do that. Might be a while till I get to the *Fishes* episode, if it's in Season Three. Is it worth the wait?"

"I think it is." She switched her hands so the other was on top.

Riker nodded as further conversation prods escaped him.

"Hey."

Riker looked up to find that Quinn had come back to the table, her timing perfectly imperfect. She slid onto the bench next to Taryn.

"Hey again," Taryn said.

Quinn put her hand on top of Taryn's hands on the table. Though Taryn's shoulders tensed, a giant grin crossed Quinn's face. "I was over there talking to some people from William Hopkins. Remember they won a ton last week?"

Taryn nodded. Riker resisted nodding as well. Despite his proximity, he wasn't part of this conversation.

"So there are these two girls in Original Oratory, and *they* said that one of the best people—he's from Dogwood—they said he's out with pneumonia. Seriously, who still gets pneumonia? Anyway, he wins all the time, so this is good. Better chances for me to place today!"

"Oh, cool," Taryn said.

"Mmhm. So I told them, I wish I would've known sooner, because…"

Riker turned away. He couldn't bear to hear more of this. Nothing against Quinn, but he just didn't care.

He picked up his food tray and stood. As he crossed the lunchroom toward the trash can, he couldn't help but wonder if Taryn would be at the upcoming overnight tournament. They'd always been a bore for him in the past—long trips were boring when he was mostly alone with his thoughts, and messing around on his phone just didn't cut it—but just the thought of Taryn near him on a four-hour bus ride was enough to send goosebumps up the length of his arms. Not to mention the hotel. Even if all they did was talk about *Timbre!*, he would be the happiest miserable person alive.

He gulped. This was ridiculous. Clearly, Taryn was interested in Quinn instead. He could write her ten letters—could slip one into her backpack by the end of today's closing ceremony—but none would make a difference. He'd never get close enough—always just out of arm's reach.

Chapter Nineteen

Taryn

Taryn ascended the steps of the school bus that would take the Speech and Debate team back to Fir Grove High School.

She adjusted the backpack straps on her shoulders. There were fellow competitors in front of and behind her, but, unfortunately, neither were people she knew well. Quinn had sat with her during the closing ceremony but had bolted ahead as the crowd let out. To be with other friends, Taryn assumed. Not seeming to notice that Taryn didn't really know anyone else on the team.

The hot and cold of it grated.

Taryn reached the top step and looked quickly down the bus aisle for a seat, hoping to delay the embarrassment of lingering too long with nowhere to sit. In the back, Quinn sat up on her knees on a seat she shared with one of the Domestic Extemp speakers, speaking rapid-fire to the pair in the seat behind her. No room for Taryn.

Her eyes raked up the aisle as she took baby steps forward. Most seats had at least one person in them.

Including, halfway back, Riker's seat. Only one person.

With room for one more.

She squared her shoulders. *No time like the present.*

He stared out the window as she approached, though there was nothing to watch but the parking lot beyond the glass. She stopped at the edge of his seat and tapped her fingers on the vinyl seat in front of him.

He turned to face her, and his eyes widened.

"Can I sit here?"

He pulled his backpack off the empty seat and slid it to the floor. "Yep."

She lowered herself into the seat and shoved her own backpack between her feet. "Great job today," she said. He'd gotten fourth place in Humorous Interpretation this time, one step up from the previous week. At this rate, he'd be riding the first-place train in no time.

"Thanks. How do you think you did? I should've asked you that at lunch..." His statement left out the obvious — she didn't place in her event.

Taryn put her hands in her lap and clenched both fists. For some reason, talking about herself was more difficult than talking about other people. "I think I did better than last week. It's so hard to read the room, though, when everyone just stares at you with those blank faces. Unless —" *Shit. I'm not the only one who gets those blank faces from the room, right?* "Is every event like that, where the people in the room don't clap or anything?"

"Yep. It drives me nuts. Like, it's so hard to push through sometimes when no one in the 'audience' clues me in on how I'm doing."

"Exactly! I'm so glad it's not just me."

At the front of the bus, Beezy stood, taking a silent headcount. Apparently satisfied with his number, he turned to say something to the bus driver before sitting back down. Taryn racked her brain for how long the initial ride had been to this tournament. Forty-five minutes, maybe? Enough time to make her happy next to Riker. Hell, any time next to Riker would make her happy.

She lifted her left hand from her lap and placed it on its side in the small space between them. If her hand twitched, her knuckles would brush his dress pants.

She peered down just long enough to see Riker's right hand move from his knee to the edge of his thigh.

We're on the same page.

Oh God oh God oh God.

She resisted the urge to check the time on her phone as the bus pulled out of the parking lot. She wanted to know exactly what time it was, and exactly how much time they had left. But it would ruin the moment, take them out of sync.

Because right now, "in sync" seemed to be the perfect phrase. And not in a bad-nineties-band type of way.

Why had it never felt this way with Quinn?

Stop. You know why.

Because.

Because because because she's beautiful but a terrible personality match.

So what was Riker? A great personality match? She had no idea.

"Hey, Taryn?" he asked. He was hard to hear over the rumble of the bus engine and the chatter across the rows.

"Yeah?" She tilted her head closer to hear better, though her eyes remained on the seat in front of her.

"Are you...I just need to ask..."

Her heart fluttered. She dared a glance at him and nodded to prod him along.

"Are you dating Quinn?"

Oh.

She shook her head slowly. "No."

"Okay. Because I wondered if maybe...you were. Dating her."

"For a little while I thought maybe I would, but...no."

The words settled around them, as much a realization to herself as she assumed it was to Riker. The bus pulled onto the highway, roaring as it accelerated to merge. Apparently, Riker really had been watching her all along, like his note claimed.

"Did you want to be with her?"

"Well." Taryn turned to face him. Was there a correct answer to this? Would her response make it back to Quinn's ears? Had Riker asked as a friend, or...? "I guess I used to. But not anymore."

"I see."

His eyes flicked down to their hands, still not touching. But so close. She cocked her wrist until the back of her hand broached the fabric on his thigh.

Riker's chest heaved at the contact. He let out a shaky breath.

He slid his right hand down along his thigh, then interlocked his fingers with Taryn's, their hands mashed sideways into the space between them on the seat.

If her heart weren't attached to her body, it would have flown right out of its cavity and shot up to the moon above their school bus.

This. This felt so right.

Even if she had trouble looking at him. Even if she was lost for words. Even if it'd taken her far too long to figure out his name.

"I did an online search after lunch," he said.

Random, but sure, I'll go with it. "Oh? About what?"

He cleared his throat. "*Timbre!* You didn't tell me a movie came out yesterday."

She sputtered. Hell yes, the movie had just come out. Was he hinting at…?

"Did you see it yet?"

She shook her head.

His hand shifted within hers but didn't release its grip. "So I thought maybe…I could watch some episodes and then we could go see the movie. You could fill me in on everything I'm behind on, so I'm not lost."

"Really?" She met his eyes. "You'd do that?"

He nodded.

"Yeah, okay."

Oh my God. She was about to share a part of her world with someone who had no idea how much of a fanatic she really was.

And he might hate it.

Riker shifted in the bus seat. He leaned his back into the corner between the seat and the window, then rested his head on the window. He pulled her hand with him.

Taryn hesitated. Then she slipped her hand from his and turned her back to him, sliding against his chest until her head rested under his chin. Riker exhaled as she settled in. He rested his left hand on her stomach, the right hand trapped beneath her.

"Beezy'll pass out our scores soon," he said, his voice so close to her ear it sent shivers down her neck, unrousing words somehow turning sultry.

Will I have to sit up when he comes? Please say no.

"I bet you were right about doing better this time. Sometimes you just feel it," he continued.

"Thanks. I hope you're right."

His fingers twitched against her stomach. She held her breath, waiting for God knew what.

"Do you want to eat before the movie? Your choice."

Okay, this was happening. Really, really, really happening. A whole damn date. They'd gone from an elbow-ram almost two months ago and hardly talking to this. It was as if he'd acquired a burst of confidence, the final push he needed to take the plunge.

She nodded "yes" against his chest. "I have a place in mind…" And hopefully he wouldn't hate it.

"The overnight tournament is next weekend. So maybe we could go Thursday night?"

"Thursday," she confirmed.

"It's a date, then."

Taryn relaxed into Riker. With nothing else to talk about, she let her eyes drift closed. She'd have to open them again when Beezy came around, but for now she wanted to savor this moment. Her back cramped slightly on top of Riker's bunched-up right hand, but it didn't matter. Even if the bus ride took three days with no interruptions, she'd stay there, content with Riker's rising chest against her back and his palm against her navel.

Chapter Twenty

Riker

Riker looked up at the wide double doors of the restaurant Taryn had chosen. Above was a gold-lettered sign with the name of the business — Violette's. To the right, a rainbow flag flapped in the wind.

To his left, Taryn shifted her feet, hesitant.

He pulled open one of the doors and stepped back to let her walk in first. She stopped in front of a "Please wait to be seated" sign.

The host appeared, a person with short hair and four earrings up the cartilage of one ear.

"Two?" they asked.

"Yep," Taryn squeaked.

The host grabbed two menus from the podium. "This way."

Riker held back to let Taryn walk ahead of him through the tables of the half-empty restaurant. The host stopped at a booth by the window, placing the menus on it before Riker and Taryn slid into opposite sides.

"I can take your drink orders if you want," they said.

"Um," Taryn began. "Water, please."

"Me, too," Riker said.

Riker adjusted against the vinyl of the seat, not much different than the texture of the bus seat they'd shared last weekend. Roomier, though. Across from him, Taryn examined the single-sheet menu, hands clasped in her lap.

"Have you been here before?" he asked.

"No. I've always wanted to try it."

"Ah. So you can't tell me what's good. I guess we'll have to find out."

Her eyes glanced up at him, twinkled and returned to the menu. He took in her rounded cheekbones, examined the same dark-blue sweater she'd worn to school earlier in the day. A Thursday evening date was unusual, he knew, but they'd be busy the next two days with the overnight Speech and Debate tournament. And no way was he willing to wait an extra week when Thursdays worked just as well as weekends.

Tomorrow they'd leave right from school on a four-plus-hour bus ride for the weekend tournament. Four-plus hours of sitting next to Taryn. Four-plus hours of hand-holding, more skin against skin.

More cuddling in the bus seat, if he was lucky.

If he was even luckier, a glimpse of Taryn in pajamas back at the hotel. Not that it would get any further than that with Beezy and Zeb laying down the iron first of keeping students to their assigned hotel rooms.

He swallowed.

"Not going to lie," he said. "I had to look this place up. I didn't even know it was here." Part of his search was for directions, the other part for the menu. In the meantime, he'd discovered that Violette's was an LGBTQ-owned-and-operated restaurant, one of the few places advertised as such in town.

She folded her hands on the menu. "I never had the chance to come, and you said I could choose. Is it…is it okay?"

"Yes!" he said too quickly. "Yes. I want to try anything you want to try."

"Good. I thought, maybe…maybe you'd run away as soon as you saw it." She chuckled, a nervous laugh.

"Never. Consider me an ally. Glad we could get you here."

"I just…I never had anyone to come with. And it seemed like you'd be open to it."

He nodded. The implication that Quinn hadn't taken her here didn't escape him. "Are you bisexual? Am I allowed to ask that? I want to make sure I get it right."

"You can ask. Yes, bi." Her nervous laugh came again. She picked at the corner of her menu. "Sorry. It's like…a way I've always thought of myself, but not something I say out loud very often."

And here she was, saying it to him. Like she trusted him—like he was worth telling.

He hoped he was.

"Don't be sorry. At all. If that's who you are, embrace it." Riker cleared his throat. *Just tell her. It's honest—tell her!* "In fact, I…I think it's really cool we have something in common. Liking girls, I mean. God, that probably didn't come out right. It's just that…it's something we can both talk about. It almost makes it less scary that way," he ended, deflated.

Oh God, you said it. She's going to tuck and roll out of this booth.

Or maybe I'll do a tuck and roll from embarrassment.

A wide smile crossed Taryn's face as she stopped picking the corner of the menu. "That's a really good way of seeing it."

Maybe it hadn't come out as asinine as he'd thought!

The server, a lanky man with a small black apron around his waist, arrived at their table then with two glasses of ice water. "Hi, my name's Branson, and I'll be taking care of you. Are you ready to order?"

Nope. Haven't even looked at the menu.

Riker raised his eyebrows at Taryn, who nodded that she was ready. "You go first," he said, then scanned the menu quickly for anything that sounded appetizing on short notice. By the time Taryn ordered macaroni and cheese with French fries, Riker had sufficiently narrowed in on a steak and cheese sandwich.

The server wrote down their orders with a flourish of his pen before saying, "I'll get that right out for you."

Riker put his elbows on the table. "So fill me in on this *Timbre!* movie. What do I need to know?"

"Well, were you able to watch any episodes?"

"Yes! I made it through Season One. Finished up the finale last night, actually." Yeah, it had been a ton of bingeing, and it had really cut into *Voice Venture* hunting and *Timescale*, but it was all worth it to get closer to Taryn. Bonus points for enjoying it — once the pilot had hooked him, he'd had no desire to stop.

"So...what did you think?"

The question was simple, though based on her expectant look, he knew a lot hinged on his response. "It was great. That episode with the *White Christmas* music was brilliant. I know it's the wrong month to listen, but I had to pull up the music online because I just couldn't get it out of my head."

Taryn nodded vigorously. Sensing she wanted to hear everything possible about the show, he continued.

"And I can totally get behind that Valerie character. Remember that episode where she was swooning over Oscar? I laughed so hard, plus she's such a good singer! I think she's my favorite character."

"She's my favorite, too." Taryn's smile could have stretched from sea to shining sea. "Okay, so you know the essentials about Valerie and Oscar, and you caught the big pregnancy scare at the end of the season, so obviously you know Tessa was cheating on Julián. You won't have to know everything about the show to understand the movie, but you'll need the basics. Which means I have to spoil a couple things…"

"That's fine. I figured."

"So what you don't know — and I won't give you too many details so it'll still be exciting when you watch Season Three, because it's seriously the best part — is that Valerie is now with Molly, finally, but Valerie is hiding a huge secret about Julián being Molly's brother."

"What!"

"I know, right? From the trailer, it looks like the movie's going to focus a lot on that. Also, Oscar is with Ariel now — that's the girl with the purple tips in her hair, so yeah, now the two people with colorful hair are together, which of course the writers just couldn't resist. The fans were waiting a long time for them to get together, so I'm not surprised it happened."

"Fans?" he asked with a smile. "Like you?"

She bit her bottom lip. "Yeah, I guess so."

"Do you..." He trailed off, unsure whether to ask the question directly in case it embarrassed her. "Do you write fanfiction?"

She shook her head. "No, I just... I'm really active online."

Riker cocked his head at that, eyebrows raised in question. She shrugged, pointedly not clarifying.

"So now you need to tell me something you're really into," she said. "Because I've been talking a lot, and it's only fair."

"Crap! I was hoping I wouldn't have to say anything about myself," he said with a smile. "There's really not much to know."

"Sure there is. I need some sort of nugget to take away about you. I know you have sharp elbows, and I know you're really good at Speech."

"There's not much else. I lead a boring life."

"False." She sat up straighter. "You're interested in something. What do you want to be when you grow up?"

He laughed at her choice of phrase, as if they were elementary school kids with futures in the distance instead of around the corner. "When I grow up? Well, okay, that one's easy." *Easier to think about than say, anyway.*

She nodded in encouragement.

He licked his lips. "I want to do voice acting. Like for commercials or video games. Especially video games. I know that doesn't sound exciting, but..."

"It *does* sound exciting. I've never heard anyone say they wanted to do that."

"A lot of people do it, but it's pretty hard to break into. I've been trying to get small gigs, but I haven't gotten many bites. I'm starting to think I'm terrible at it, actually."

"Oh, there's no way you're terrible — I've heard you in class. Remember that monologue you did where you spoke in that weird old-timey voice? That was really good."

"Walter Matthau," he said. "I love trying to do voices like his. Not that there's a huge market these days for 'People Who Can Impersonate Walter Matthau.'"

"So what do you have to do to get gigs? Are there auditions?"

He took a deep breath. He hadn't talked about this before, hadn't opened up to anyone about the process or how much he wanted to make it work. What if his response sounded ridiculous?

"Kind of," he said. "There's this website that hosts all these jobs, and basically I comb through it and try to find stuff. Sometimes they post casting calls or invitations for private samples. But there's like a million people on the site doing the same thing, so it's a big shitshow of voice actors clawing their way to the surface. Or trying to, anyway."

"Wow. That's super intense."

"Yeah. That's a good word for it." It felt strange, unloading on Taryn like this. But she acted like she gave a damn. Maybe she did.

"Did you ever get close to the big stuff?"

Riker scratched his chin. "I've gotten invited to submit some samples for big projects, but nothing ever came out of them. I still have one invited sample out there that hasn't been rejected, but I don't think it's going anywhere."

"Ah. Well, here's to hoping." Taryn raised her glass of water and held it toward him. "And if not this time, then maybe next time."

He lifted his glass and clinked it against hers. They locked eyes for a flash of a second, just long enough for Riker to see the flicker of her eyelids over the green sea of her irises. "Thanks, Taryn. And thanks for, you know, listening to me babble."

She took a sip of her water, taking her time to swallow before replying. "I like hearing you babble. You can babble to me any time you want."

Riker's cheeks warmed. This girl was perfect. Beyond perfect. She was beautiful, passionate, sympathetic. And though he liked the nervous side of her he saw at school and Speech tournaments, he also enjoyed this opened-up side, as if he'd earned the right to dig deeper into Taryn's personality.

Their server returned, pulling Riker from his trance. He straightened up in his seat as the man set a plate in front of each of them.

"Is there anything else I can get for you?" the server asked.

"No, thank you," Taryn replied.

Riker shook his head, suddenly at a loss for words after opening up to Taryn. He watched as the server retreated, then reached for his napkin. For being the go-to local LGBTQ restaurant, this place had about zero differences from other restaurants. Well, one difference if he counted the rainbow flag out front. Still, it was an honor that Taryn had chosen to bring him here—an honor that she trusted him enough to share this part of herself.

Taryn squirted ketchup into a puddle on her plate, then stabbed a fork into a French fry. Her other hand rested palm down on the table, fingers fidgeting against the wood. His eyes raked over her as she dipped one French fry after another with her fork, an entire process she seemed to savor. How had he gotten so lucky to be sitting at a restaurant across from this beautiful, perfect girl? What favor had he unwittingly given to fate?

* * * *

On the movie screen, Valerie sang the opening notes of *Take Me or Leave Me* — which Riker recognized as a *Rent* classic, though he'd never seen the musical on stage or screen. Molly returned some of the lyrics, and the two girls took turns singing, fighting out their problems in style. Taryn had prepared him well for their relationship in this movie. He hadn't missed a beat, so to speak.

What she hadn't prepared him for was her awe-filled expression as her eyes locked on the screen.

From the moment the lights dimmed, joy radiated off Taryn as if it had invaded her very essence. It only increased the more Valerie was on screen, even more so as her relationship with Molly bloomed and deepened.

He'd watch a thousand movies with Taryn if they all brought this elation.

Taryn's hand fidgeted next to her thigh. He wanted to squeeze it and never let go, to signal that a love of love was one of the greatest possible things Taryn could possess.

Instead he set his hand on the armrest between them. His heart hammered in his chest.

The next time there's a big moment, I'll grab her hand. Next time.

On screen, Valerie belted out a final note to the song, her arms spread wide and her chin high. With a heavy beat, the song ended. Valerie froze where she stood, her dress still swaying around her thighs. Next to Riker, Taryn's chest rose high then fell, a happy sigh as far as Riker could make out. Based on how she tilted her head downward but kept her eyes on the screen, he suspected he'd detect blushing if the theater weren't so dark.

This was what made Taryn happy, what caused her face to light up in a way he'd never seen. Her celebrity crush on a giant screen, singing her heart out for all to hear.

Was it really that easy? Jesus, he'd buy her every digital copy of Valerie and Molly's version of the song, every poster of Valerie ever printed, the special edition copies of every season, all with the money he'd been saving for a new microphone, if that's what it took to make Taryn so ecstatic.

Was this what "being an ally" felt like? Damn, why weren't more people doing it?

Taryn slid her hand an inch away from her thigh. Closer to the armrest.

Closer to Riker.

He gulped.

On the screen, the camera switched away from Valerie, focusing now on a group of teenagers in a classroom. The intensity of the musical number was over, but Riker was no less at attention. He tilted his wrist until his pinky finger dangled off the armrest.

There. He'd leave his hand in that spot and try to get closer in a few minutes. Whenever another song came on and Taryn's face lit up again.

Why is it even harder now?

Every time they were in close proximity, Riker felt the process start all over again, as if any previous attempts at contact didn't count. Inching toward each other's hands in Drama class. Holding hands then cuddling on the bus ride home from last weekend's Speech tournament.

And now here, in the dark, with the plastic armrest acting as a barrier.

It was almost as if the absence of touching since the beginning of their date made this moment so much more difficult to initiate.

Why did my confidence fly out the window?

Taryn reached up her pinky finger and curled it around Riker's, locking their tiniest extremities instead of their whole hands.

He sucked in a breath. All the oxygen in the theater had disappeared into a vacuum.

Leaving just him and her. Just his pinky hanging off an armrest, and hers reaching up to meet him.

Chapter Twenty-One

Taryn

"Are you still watching?"

Taryn looked at the message on the television. She had taken one bathroom break during the credits, and all of a sudden the streaming service wanted to know if she was still around.

Wanted to know if it should keep auto-playing *Timbre!* episodes.

Yes, yes, the answer's always yes. Because now, two hours after her date with Riker, the show would forever be associated with him.

She used the remote to click "Yes, keep watching" — to hell if it was midnight — and the intro graphics she knew so well appeared on the screen.

Ahh, this is the life. How had she survived so many months without such easy access to the episodes?

From the moment she'd pressed "play" on the first episode of Season Three, peace of mind had oozed through her bloodstream. Now she could happily watch her favorite series and engage more fully with the fans on her account and soak in the show's connection to Riker. A win all around.

She adjusted her head on the armrest and stretched out her legs across the couch cushions. On screen, Valerie watched Molly from across a choir classroom, in the first episode of the arc she'd gushed about to Riker. She couldn't rewatch the movie yet, but at least she could swoon over the romance on the show, could savor every little drop of love blooming between Valerie and Molly.

She could only dream of having Riker feel that way about her.

Because in all honesty, he probably wouldn't watch *Timbre!* again. Taryn had surely scared him off with all her chatter at Violette's, her moon eyes during the movie. She'd taken him to an LGBTQ-owned-and-operated restaurant, for Christ's sake.

But he'd stayed with her. He hadn't backed out.

He'd held her pinky finger through the end of the movie, sending jolts of electricity across every nerve in her body.

Maybe she should have grabbed his whole hand instead of just a finger. Except the intensity of outright hand-holding might have sent her into cardiac arrest.

There was no way he felt such intensity for her in return. Even though his letter a while back had indicated…

She sat bolt upright. It'd been a while since she'd checked for a new letter. She rushed to her bedroom and kneeled on the floor in front of her backpack, where she unzipped all the front pockets and shoved her hand into them one at a time. But her fingers didn't graze paper.

She opened the large section and pulled out every schoolbook and notebook, then flipped through them to see if anything fell out of the pages. Nothing.

Ah, well. The thought was nice.

Her phone buzzed. She lunged.

Please be Riker, please be Riker, please be Riker. She closed her eyes, tried to count to three and looked at her phone on "two."

Quinn: Hey hot stuff. What you up to?

Taryn's shoulders fell. Quinn could give her all the compliments in the world, but none of them would provide the elation she felt with Riker. If Riker had sent her this exact text, she would've been over the moon.

But he hadn't.

Taryn: Hey, not much. Bored.

She winced. *Not much except that I just went on a date with Riker. And now I'm watching* Timbre! *Again.*

Taryn: You?

She walked back to the living room, where the first episode in the three-part arc was still playing. She plopped onto the couch, one thigh propped onto the armrest with her foot hanging off the other side, and rewound through the parts she'd missed. Grandma would scold her if she walked in and saw her posture — or lack thereof. The phone buzzed again.

Quinn: Just got done hanging out with Alyssa. She said you got better scores last weekend. That true??

Taryn paused the show and racked her brain for the name "Alyssa," but nothing came. Someone must've mentioned Taryn's scores at the meeting earlier this week. Odd that Quinn had waited so many days to mention it, though.

Yes, Taryn had done better at her third tournament than she had for the first or second. Then she'd made extra effort this week to practice, to refine, taking in Beezy's praise before implementing his suggestions. They'd get her piece polished, he'd assured.

And good thing, because tomorrow's tournament was the overnighter, with the team leaving together on a bus in just fourteen hours.

An hours-long bus ride with the team. With Riker.

The amount of cuddling they could do in a few hours...

Taryn: Yeah, a little better. I didn't see you after the meeting on Monday. Did you stick around to practice?

Quinn: Nah, I promised Alyssa I'd take her to dinner. I practiced Tuesday.

Dinner? Quinn had never taken Taryn out for food in any form — dinner, ice cream, whatever. Never even alluded to it. But what would Taryn have gotten out of a dinner date with Quinn, anyway? More frustration at their clashing personalities?

She laughed at the thought. That ship had sailed. She'd love to find a girl to fall in love with, a girl who showed an interest when Taryn bared her soul. But Quinn was not that girl.

Besides, Riker was checking all the right boxes.

Taryn: Cool

She placed her phone face-down on the couch and pressed "play."

Someone entered the room, and Taryn jerked as if they'd caught her using the couch as a hammock—which she kind of was. But it was only her mom, phone held to her face and thumbs typing. No need to sit up straight when it wasn't Grandma.

"Hey, your grandma's making homemade gnocchi tomorrow." Mom spoke and typed as she walked to a striped accent chair and sat down.

Taryn glanced at the TV, catching Oscar dancing across the screen, his blue hair moving with him as if glued into place. Nah, Mom's comment wasn't worth pausing the show.

"Nice. Try to save some for me?"

"Sure," her mom replied.

Taryn's phone buzzed. She glanced at it but couldn't find the effort to read. Quinn could wait. She plopped her head onto the couch cushion, leg still dangling in the air. Oscar had stopped dancing and now was talking to Molly, who was about six episodes away from a faint-inducing kiss with Valerie. For now, Molly was more worried about perfecting a performance of *Getting to Know You* for the musical theater club, and Oscar was more than happy to assist.

"Taryn," her mom began.

Taryn looked up at her mom to find that her eyes were no longer glued to her phone. "Yeah?"

"What would you think about moving?"

Taryn blinked. "Moving where?"

"I'm not sure yet. Close to our old place, maybe."

So outside of Fir Grove's district, even though Taryn had finally started to feel settled. "Umm. I think I don't want to go back to my old school if I don't have to."

"Oh." Her mom's face fell. "I thought you'd be happy to get out of Grandma's house. This place is so…" She waved her hand through the air. "Suffocating."

Partially true. But it wasn't the worst situation in the world — suffocating it might be, but it had its perks.

Taryn shrugged. "I like Fir Grove. It has a Drama class and the Speech team, you know?"

Her mom nodded, as if actually considering Taryn's opinion. Doubtful, but hey, it wouldn't be the first time her mom had surprised her.

Taryn looked back to the TV. Molly sat on a stool next to Oliver, getting ready to spill her feelings about Valerie. A scene Taryn had seen a thousand times — she'd never tire of it.

But now the scene had a new connotation for her. It made her think of Riker, how he'd completely supported her love of the Valerie/Molly relationship tonight. How he'd eaten it up, gotten into the movie just as much as she'd hoped.

Suddenly, a dull ache emerged in her abdomen.

Shit, not again.

She moved a hand to her left side on reflex, as if touching her palm to her shirt would make it at all better. She adjusted herself on the couch, finding a more comfortable position. When was her next period supposed to start? Not for another couple weeks, she'd thought.

A sharp pain shot through her side before running down her pelvic area. She groaned and rolled onto her side, pulling her knees to her chest.

"Shouldn't you be in bed?" her mom asked, apparently oblivious to the five hundred tiny knives stabbing her daughter.

Taryn looked to the clock below the TV. Yeah, it was late. And if she kept watching *Timbre!*, she was liable to get sucked into the entire three-episode arc.

"I guess so."

She stopped the show and held her position for a few seconds longer, taking one deep breath after another. The pain was mostly at bay for the moment, but, in her limited experience, she suspected there'd be another pang the instant she moved.

Closing her eyes, she moved her legs slowly away from her chest and to the floor.

Ow, ow, ow.

She planted her feet on the ground and used her hand to hoist herself from the couch.

Ow, ow, ow.

Finally standing, she hunched her shoulders to make the position an ounce less painful. Yeah, going to bed sounded perfect right about now — no movement meant less pain.

She looked to her mom, who was once again engulfed in her phone.

Taryn made her way to the bathroom, where she hunched over the sink as she brushed her teeth. Then she shuffled to the bedroom, pulled on her pajamas with the speed of a sloth, and gingerly climbed into bed with the intention of absolute immobility.

* * * *

Ughhhhhhhhhhh.
Shit shit shit, fuck.
Ugh.

Taryn had no idea what time it was, but light filtered through her bedroom window.

She froze in her position, hip digging into the mattress and body bent in a chair formation. She'd thought she had pain before, but holy shit on a stick, she couldn't move.

She lifted an arm, then set it back down on her hip. Okay, that much didn't hurt. She wiggled her toes — no additional pain from that, either. She extended the knee of one leg —

— and yelped in pain.

This was not how today was supposed to go. She was supposed to leave school early for a teamwide bus trip to their overnight tournament. Hopefully sharing a seat with Riker.

She lay motionless for another two minutes, each inhalation deep to ward off the pain. Though none of it helped. With a final deep breath, Taryn stretched out her leg again. She gritted her teeth at the pain that shot through her abdomen. It was infinitesimally less terrible than before.

She pressed her palm into the bed and used the leverage to roll onto her back. A loud groan escaped her lips once again at the agony of the movement.

"Taryn?"

The voice came from down the hall. Her grandmother.

"Yeah?"

"Is that you?"

Taryn closed her eyes and exhaled. Did she really want to have this conversation right now?

"Yeah."

Her grandma appeared in her doorway. "What's with all the groaning? Are you okay?"

"I—I'm not sure. Something really hurts. Kind of like cramps, but way worse."

Her grandma nodded. "You had all that pain a couple weeks ago. When you were on your period."

"Yeah, but...I'm not on my period now. It just feels like I am. I seriously can't even move, Grandma." She adjusted her butt against the bed in an effort to get more comfortable. More pain, more discomfort. Wetness formed at the corners of her eyes, threatening to spill tears if this kept up.

Her mom appeared, sharing the doorway space with Grandma. "Hey, time to get up," Mom said. "You're going to be late. Is your suitcase packed?"

Taryn groaned again, but not from pain this time. In all the excitement of her date, she'd forgotten to pack for the trip. She'd have to get up soon to have any chance of making it to school on time.

Except...the idea of getting out of bed sounded impossible.

"No, I didn't pack. I think...I think I need to stay home."

Her mom crossed her arms over her chest. "What?"

"I'm really in pain. Like, I don't think I can get up."

"If you don't go to school, you'll miss the tournament."

Crap, true. But how could I possibly...?

Grandma piped in. "She's in a lot of pain from cramps. I think we should just let her stay home."

Taryn's mom rolled her eyes. "This is ridiculous. You don't miss school for cramps. You take ibuprofen and suck it up."

"I mean, I usually do," Taryn replied. "But...this is really bad, Mom. I think I need to see a doctor or something."

Her mom dropped her arms to her sides. "Fine, whatever. Mom, you can call the school for her if you're that insistent." She turned on her heel and walked away, down the hall.

Grandma sighed. "Taryn, I'll let them know you're not coming. I'll give them a message for Mr. Banley-Zimmerman, too."

"Thanks, Grandma." The words came out as a moan. "Do you think you could get me some ibuprofen?"

"Sure, sweetie. And what's the name of your gynecologist? I'll try to set up an appointment."

"Um. I'm not sure. You'd have to ask Mom. I only went once, like a year ago."

"You're due for a visit, then. You just get some rest. I'll be back with the medicine and a heating pad. Try not to move too much."

She laughed, low and dry. "Trust me, I won't move too much."

Taryn closed her eyes. Riker — she hoped — would be so disappointed, but she couldn't bear the thought of texting him about this. And Beezy…Beezy had said she needed to give an eight-day notice for a missed tournament. Did that include sick days? She couldn't possibly have known she'd have this problem ahead of time.

Ugh.

Chapter Twenty-Two

Riker

"Great, great, great job, everyone!"

Beezy stood at the front of the sectioned-off auditorium with his arms spread wide, as if welcoming his Speech and Debate team to a cult.

A really bizarre cult where well-performing Speech and Debate kids were forever expected to perform the same scripts and debate the same hot-button issues over and over again.

"Everyone did amazing this weekend!" Beezy continued. "We had thirteen people place, and almost everyone else improved their scores from the week before. Really awesome job, folks."

A few feet away from Beezy, sitting instead of standing, Zeb beamed at the competitors in the room. His giant hand slapped his knee twice in affirmation.

This husband–husband duo got their kicks out of the weirdest things.

Riker had been one of the thirteen placers at the overnight tournament. After two days of competing with a lonely hotel stay sandwiched in between, he sure as hell had deserved to place.

Repeating his lines for the hundredth time had been his only purpose there. So he'd gone in, performed his humorous interpretation piece, sat in silence for the other performers and exited. A machine on autopilot. And it had gotten him all the way to third place.

But the single thing he'd looked forward to hadn't materialized — Taryn.

Taryn, who he'd gone on a date with the night before the tournament.

Taryn, who'd held his finger like she was afraid to lose him in a crowd.

Taryn, who'd said she'd be there…

She'd sent Riker a single text after the team bus was almost at its destination.

Couldn't come this weekend, sorry.

Alone in his bus seat with his temple against the window, he'd stared at his phone, wondering why on earth it didn't contain more info. She'd been so open with him at dinner — why hold back in a text?

He'd replied with a *"Hope everything's okay!"* but had never heard back.

Now he looked down his row of auditorium seats. There she was, sitting in the same seat she always occupied during Drama class, hands folded in her lap. Except today wasn't a Drama day, and here they were at a Speech and Debate meeting, listening to Beezy bask in the team's awesomeness. Had she been sick over the weekend? She certainly didn't look it now, and she hadn't on their date.

She turned her head toward Riker as Beezy talked. He lifted a hand at waist-level and waved so that only she could see it down their row.

She scratched her shoulder before turning back to their coach. As if their date had meant nothing.

Taryn hadn't acknowledged Riker once since entering this room for the afterschool meeting. Because once again, Riker was the guy who failed at everything. He'd never escape this curse.

"So!" Beezy continued as Riker clenched his failed wave into a fist. "If you're sticking around to practice today, you'll know where to find me and Mr. Z.-B. I know a lot of you have been coming in on other days, and that's okay, too. Don't forget you need to practice at least once a week to compete! Any day, Monday through Thursday!"

Riker nodded as if this were news. He wasn't sure why Beezy said it so often. There were likely only one or two people in the whole bunch who thought they could escape Beezy's and Zeb's hawk eyes.

"So break away, my faithful competitors. Come down the hall to practice when you're ready. If you're not ready, this room and the office are open for you, and you can always talk to the wall in the hallway." He clapped twice to dismiss them. Then he made a beeline to Taryn's auditorium seat.

Her eyes widened as he approached. She clearly hadn't been expecting the visit. Was it about missing the tournament? God, he hoped she wasn't in trouble.

Beezy sat in the auditorium seat in front of her, then put his arm on the back of his seat and turned to face her. He spoke low enough that Riker couldn't hear him from the other end of his row. Not that it was his business, anyway. If Taryn actually liked him and wanted to talk about why she ditched, she would have done so.

But she hadn't.

And yeah, he could've been the one to approach *her*, could have been the one to ask direct questions. But she was the one who had left him to bide his time for two days of competition. For four hours there and four hours back, the other half of his bus seat had been cold with her absence.

Whatever. He didn't need this.

He scooped his backpack off the floor and flung it over his shoulder. His long legs carried him down the stairs to the bottom of the room. Exit stage left.

He powerwalked down the hall toward Beezy's office, where he could kick back before it was his turn to practice. Voices drifted down the hall, becoming louder as he approached. He wouldn't have the space to himself. When he got to the cramped office, he found Gavin and Quinn already chatting away, Gavin with one hand on his popped hip, Quinn sitting on Beezy's desk like it was a barstool. Riker helped himself to the chair behind the desk.

"Riker, you were so good this weekend!" Gavin said.

"It wasn't that impressive." The words came out before he could analyze how rude they'd be. *Why do I sound like such a dick?*

"It totally was. You're two inches away from first place."

"I guess so." He tried to remember whether Gavin had placed over the weekend, but he'd been too deep inside his own head at the time to commit most of it to memory. Even Beezy's recap during today's meeting had gone in one ear and out the other. Best to not say anything about it, then.

Quinn leaned back against her palms and looked at Riker over her shoulder. "I can't believe the scores I got. Only sixth place!"

He chuckled, unsure how else to reply. There were probably sixty people in her event that would've far preferred sixth place over their own rankings. But Quinn never seemed satisfied with anything. She might as well have transformed into Angelica and belted out *Satisfied* from *Hamilton*.

Something moved out of the corner of his eye. He turned to look at the doorway and found Taryn, knuckles clutching the straps of her backpack. She was blinking three times more than normal.

"Taryn-Like-Karen! Hi!" Gavin said with a rapid wave. Riker wished the kid could speak a single sentence that didn't sound like it was punctuated with seven exclamation marks. But hey, if that were the only negative thing about him, Riker could deal with it in small doses.

Taryn smiled and pointed at the bookshelf. "Beezy sent me to grab..." She trailed off, pointed hand flailing in the air before she lowered it to her side. Quinn, her back to Taryn, swung her legs until her heels banged against the desk.

Riker clenched a fist. If Taryn would just turn in his direction, she'd see the questioning look in his eyes. *Are we okay? Did I do something wrong?*

"So," Gavin began again. "It's too bad you missed the overnighter. We had such a blast."

Quinn looked over her shoulder at Taryn. "Mmhm. We were up pretty much all night in the hotel room, after Beezy and Zeb locked us in. Alyssa snuck in a bottle of gin."

"Oh. Right. I couldn't go." She shifted her feet, lingering in the doorway. Then she raised her eyes to

Riker's, locking them in silent communication. Now if only Riker could figure out the code. "Something came up."

He squinched his mouth to one side. So many questions, none he dared ask in front of Quinn or Gavin.

He wasn't sure Taryn would answer them anyway.

"Taryn, are you practicing today?" Quinn asked.

Taryn broke the eye contact with Riker. The moment—and it must've been only a second or two—was gone.

"Yeah, I need to since I missed that tournament. You?"

"I am, and I have to get down there." Quinn hopped down from the desk and brushed invisible dirt down the leggings on her thighs. She waggled her fingers and said, "See ya," as she squeezed past her ex—or whatever she was to Taryn.

Gavin looked to Taryn, then to Riker, the sudden silence in the room stretching between them like a cheesy pizza. Riker leaned back in Beezy's not-so-comfortable office chair. It creaked.

"Welp, I'm getting the hell out of here," Gavin said. "I have to work in an hour. You two try not to have too much fun without me." At this, he winked at Taryn and sauntered out of the room after Quinn.

Riker squeezed his eyes shut at Gavin's insinuation. He took a deep breath. When he opened his eyes again, Taryn was still there, watching him.

"I just need to…" She waved her hand toward the bookshelf. "Beezy asked me to find something."

"Ah. Right." He stood and pushed the chair in to make room for her behind the desk. "What's the name of it?"

She stepped behind the desk and browsed the shelf. "*Cat on a Hot Tin Roof.* I'm not sure what it is, but..."

"Oh, I know that one. Tennessee Williams. I saw it around here once, but it's been a long time." He faced the bookshelf with her, scanning the spines. Knowing the color would make this search a heck of a lot easier.

Though why he was helping her, he wasn't sure. He wished he didn't want to.

Would she help me in the same situation?

Would she have come if she'd known I'd be in here?

She inched closer to him as she continued looking, then took another tiny sidestep his way. At this proximity, she smelled faintly of flowers.

He slow-blinked, taking it in. Even on their date they hadn't been this close.

"Riker..." she said. It came out like pleading, a soft whine with the "i".

He swallowed. His eyes froze on the scripts, unable to concentrate on the words. He couldn't dare look at her right now — his heart would explode.

"Yeah?"

"I meant to go on the overnighter. I just...couldn't."

"Oh."

He wanted to ask why, wanted to know every detail. But the words caught in his throat. Instead, the staccato title stood out to him on a spine.

"I found it," he said, pulling it from the shelf and finally turning to her with the book in hand.

She turned to face him. She reached for the script, both of them watching the book as it exchanged hands, a replay in slow motion.

They looked up at each other.

Noses inches apart.

She blinked twice. Then she crossed the space between them and pressed her lips to his. A million tiny grenades detonated behind his eyelids as he closed them.

Her lips trembled against his, just slightly.

And he kissed back, lips linking into place with hers, tongue sliding through.

Her hand found its way to his lower back, where she dug her fingernails in as if squeezing a stress ball. A soft whimper from her throat put every one of his hairs on end. He lost track of who held the book smashed between their stomachs.

She groaned, sharply, and pulled away as though he'd bitten her. She slapped a hand over her mouth and groaned again.

Not a good groan. An I'm-in-pain groan.

"Are you okay?" he asked. The book was still between them, both of their hands on it. He reached out to touch her arm with his free hand, but then thought better of it.

Taryn nodded fiercely, as if trying to convince herself of its truth. "I'm fine. Fine. I think I just need to…" She swayed on her feet, shoulders stiff.

His hand shot out, landing on her waist. Balancing her. "Do you need to sit down? Let me get the chair."

"No, no. I don't…"

He added pressure to his grasp. She lowered her gaze to the floor, inhaled, exhaled. "I need to get this script to Beezy. He's probably wondering where I went."

"He can wait a minute."

"No, I'm good."

"Right. Okay."

He let his hand drop to his side. Should he say something else? About her apparent pain, about their out-of-the-blue kiss? Did this thing — whatever it was —

have anything to do with Taryn missing the overnight tournament?

Don't be ridiculous. She doesn't want you prying.

He gave up the book when she tugged on it. Then she turned, her shoulders hunched and her hips looking more like creaky hinges than functioning body parts, and walked out of the room with slow steps. Something was up—something wasn't right. But she hadn't said a word about it.

Probably because she didn't trust him. Probably because she hadn't meant to kiss him.

Probably because…everything.

Because he was worthless, and he'd never in a million years impress a girl he liked, never be able to talk to Taryn like a normal human. Never be able to help her like he wanted.

And the little voice screaming inside his head would never let him forget it.

Chapter Twenty-Three

Taryn

A bell jangled as Taryn opened the wooden door. She'd been in this gynecologist's waiting room once before, a year ago. This time, she had pain to talk about on top of her annual exam. Two birds, one stone.

Taryn's mom placed a hand on her daughter's back as if to nudge her forward. Behind a window at the far end of the otherwise-empty waiting room sat a young woman with jet-black hair. The woman slid open the window with a clang before tapping a long orange fingernail against a clipboard on the counter. "Sign in here, please."

Taryn scratched her name onto the paper and turned to pick a seat. The moment her butt hit the cushion, the woman behind the counter spoke again.

"Ma'am?"

Taryn looked up, then around. The only other person in the room was her mother, and she wasn't a patient today. "Me?"

"Yes. Can I have your ID and insurance card, please?"

"Oh. Um. Yes."

Taryn fumbled to open the latch on her purse and pulled out her wallet. She wriggled her identity card out of its slot with a shaky finger. When she looked up, she found her mom in the seat next to her, holding out what could only be an insurance card. Taryn nodded and took it, then handed the information to the receptionist, who traded it for a clipboard of paperwork. Taryn took a seat again.

The first page was easy — basic info, date of last period, medications — but her eyes widened as she reached Page Two.

"Mom?" she whispered.

"Hm?"

"Can you help me with this section? It's something about family medical history."

Her mom nodded. "Let me see."

Taryn held the clipboard in front of her mom and watched as she scanned the page. Her mom sighed. "I already filled this out for you last year. Not sure why they make you do it again every year. You can mark 'no' for most of these. But two of your great-grandmothers had breast cancer, and your grandpa had a heart disease. Can't remember what it was called. Oh, and diabetes — two of your grandparents had that. Mark yes for those."

Taryn nodded, jotting down the information. Did all that mean she was destined to get breast cancer and heart disease? And diabetes, too?

Great, another thing to worry about today.

After finishing up the paperwork, Taryn pulled a book for English class out of her purse. She could definitely use a distraction from whatever the hell was about to go down in the doctor's exam room—from whatever the future held, truth be told.

Five minutes later, the door to the back rooms opened and a nurse called her name. She took a deep breath and stood. Then, frozen, she realized she had no idea if her mom was supposed to come too.

"Do you want me back there?" Mom asked.

"I—I don't know?" She paused. Her mom had gone into the exam room with her at this same time last year. But she was seventeen now, so that no longer seemed necessary. "I think I'll be fine alone."

Her mom nodded and lifted a magazine from a side table. "I'm out here if you need me."

The nurse welcomed Taryn into the hallway and directed her toward a scale. After taking her weight, the nurse pointed her to a room down the hall and asked her to take a seat at the open chair.

"Okay," the nurse said, her voice chipper and direct as she examined the tablet in front of her. "Last period started three weeks ago. No regular medications. No drug allergies. Are you allergic to latex?"

"No."

Tap, tap on the tablet. "Are you sexually active?" The nurse looked up.

A lump tightened in her chest. "No."

"All right. Do you give yourself breast exams?"

"Um." Taryn squirmed against the stiff-backed chair. "No. I'm not quite sure what that means."

The nurse nodded. "That's fine. I'll make a note for the doctor to walk you through it." She tapped her fingers on the tablet. "For your periods, would you say you have three heavy days followed by three lighter days?"

Taryn nodded. "That sounds about right."

"Good. And have you had any problems you'd like to discuss?"

More squirming. "Yes. Um. I've been having a lot of pain, like around the time my period starts, but other times too."

"All right. Can you describe what it feels like?"

"Kind of...shooting? Like, when I sit down it feels like someone's stabbing me."

The nurse tapped away on the tablet, her face expressionless. "Where do you get this pain? In your abdomen, your vagina, your anus?"

Taryn cleared her throat at the sound of the technical terms, which, now that she thought about it, were more appropriate than the non-technical terms — but perhaps more embarrassing.

"All of those places. It starts low and then shoots up when I sit down."

"And how bad is it? Where one means you barely notice it, five means it's noticeable and uncomfortable, and ten means you can't move and can't think about anything else?"

Taryn tilted her head to think. "I guess it depends? Sometimes it's at level ten for maybe five seconds, then slowly goes down to level five. And then there are other times during the day where it's a one."

More tapping on the tablet. The nurse gave no indication what she thought — she might've been typing "patient is a persistent liar" for all Taryn knew. "Okay. I've made some notes for the doctor. She'll talk to you about it. Do you have any other questions, or anything else to add?"

Taryn shook her head. Her heart beat rapidly.

The nurse stood and pulled open a drawer, selecting two pieces of linen. "Go ahead and get undressed. The green one" — she placed a finger on it — "goes over your shoulders, like a shirt. The yellow one goes on your lap after you sit on the table. The doctor will be in soon."

"Thanks," Taryn replied, almost in a whisper. After the nurse closed the door behind her, Taryn took off everything but her socks. She folded her bra and underwear inside her jeans and put the bundle on the chair before hopping onto the patient table, covering herself with the sheets and lying back with her eyes closed.

Breathe.

The hum of the fluorescent lights took over the otherwise-silent room. She placed her hands on her stomach and inhaled slowly, counting to five before exhaling. No pain right now. No drama. No worries.

There was a knock at the door, followed by a soft, "Taryn, are you ready for me?"

Welcome back, worries.

"Yes," she called.

The doctor came in and closed the door, then held out a hand. Taryn wiggled to sit up and keep the sheets on, then shook the doctor's dry, firm hand.

"Let's cut to the chase. I hear you're having pain."

Taryn nodded. "Yes."

"Tell me about it."

She swallowed. She'd already told the nurse—wasn't that enough? "Um. Well, my periods hurt really bad, especially the day before it starts, and the first couple days. Sometimes it hurts to, like, sit down."

"Mmhm. When you sit down, where does it hurt?"

"Well…it, um, it starts in my butt and then kind of shoots up to my stomach."

"So the pain moves quickly?"

"Yeah, that's it."

"Any other pain?"

"Well, my sides hurt really bad sometimes too. Usually the left side more than the right. Like someone's pushing a blunt stick through my skin. It's not just when I'm on my period, either."

The doctor nodded as she made notes on the tablet. "Tell me about your periods. Are they heavy?"

"I'm not sure. I mean, there's a lot of blood, but that's normal, right?"

The doc laughed. "Yes, a lot of blood is normal. But 'how much' is a different question. Okay, let's pretend it's day one of your period. What size tampon or pad are you using? Or do you use a cup?"

"Day one would be…" She tilted her head to the side to think about it. The exposed skin on her upper arms prickled. "The biggest tampon. Those 'ultra' ones."

"And how often do you have to change it?"

"It starts leaking after maybe two hours, so that's when I change it."

"And how many days does it last like that?"

"Maybe two, then it starts to calm down."

"Okay, so we'd call that heavy. Would you consider your bleeding and your pain debilitating? Does it keep you from doing what you need to do?"

Depends what you mean by "need." Did I need to go to the overnight Speech tournament? Did I need to keep kissing Riker in Beezy's office?

Is Beezy still annoyed with me for missing the tournament? Did I one-hundred-percent mess up every chance I had with Riker?

Maybe, maybe not.

Taryn flattened the linen sheet over her lap. "Sometimes it hurts too much to move at all, like I can't even roll over in bed. Or if I'm already at school, it hurts so much I'll be stuck in my seat and I can't concentrate."

The doctor entered some final taps. "That's exactly what I needed to know. Okay, Taryn. Do you have any more questions or concerns before we get started?"

"No, nothing."

"Great. Lie back for me then, and I'll do your breast exam."

Taryn did as instructed, lifting one arm above her head, then the other, while the doctor's dry hands touched her breasts. The doc talked her through it, explaining how to do it at home too. It lasted for a mere eight seconds, faster than it took Taryn to wrap her mind around the oddity of it.

"Okay! Everything up here looks good." The doctor reached for a box of latex gloves and pulled one glove over each hand. "I need you to scoot your butt down to the far edge of the table and put your feet in the stirrups."

Taryn did. Under the sheet, she bared her nether regions to the cool-as-a-cucumber doctor, who'd moved her rolling chair between the stirrups.

"A little farther down, if you will."

Taryn adjusted. Surely if she moved another millimeter she'd fall right off the table.

"Perfect. Okay, just lie back and relax. I'm going to start with the speculum and take a sample."

Despite the doc's calm, there was nothing soothing about lying on a table with her lady parts catching a breeze. Especially with big words like "speculum" that might or might not have been some sort of tongs. Taryn took a deep breath, pressing her palms into her stomach on the drawn-out exhale. She felt tightening in her vagina, then a click as something snapped into place.

Her body cramped up, starting somewhere in the mess of her pelvis and pushing its way out to the rest of her. Her abdomen stiffened, as if rejecting whatever foreign entity had found its way into her body. She felt a scrape against something inside her, and the doctor's hand emerged with a large cotton swab that she dropped into a vial.

Breathe. Breathe. Breathe.

"Just breathe," the doctor said.

Okay, mind reader.

She closed her eyes and swallowed hard.

Moments later, the tongs-of-crampy-death slid out of her, and the pressure on her abdomen slithered away with them.

"You okay?"

Taryn nodded and opened her mouth to say, "yes," but nothing emerged.

"Good. Keep lying there. I'm going to do a manual check of your ovaries and uterus."

The doctor hadn't even finished her sentence before she'd inserted two fingers inside Taryn. She placed the palm of her other hand to the left of Taryn's belly button and pressed down.

"Holy—" Taryn's knee jerked on reflex at the doctor's touch. The cramping of ten seconds ago was nothing compared to this sorcery. She clamped her teeth together and clawed the vinyl bed.

"That hurts?"

What do you fucking think? "Mmhm," she managed.

The doctor nodded then did the same motion to Taryn's right side, then the center. Taryn jerked again at the pain, but slightly less so. Maybe because she'd been mentally prepared, even if only at a split second's notice.

The doctor stepped away as she tugged off her latex gloves.

"Taryn, I'm concerned about this pain you're having."

Taryn gulped. "Okay."

"I think something's going on down there. It could be one of a few things, so I'm not going to make a conjecture right now. But I want to see you back here for an ultrasound so we can get this straightened out."

"Straightened out? Like, there's something you can do to fix it?"

"Well, it depends what the problem is. I can't make any promises, but I don't want to assume the worst either. I can tell you that most people don't have pain when I feel their ovaries, especially not at your age. And the way you described your pain further tells me this isn't just regular period cramps."

"Oh." She nodded, unsure what else to say. Did this mean none of it had been in her head? All that pain she'd been having might have actually been something wrong with her?

"Now don't go thinking something's wrong with you. We're going to take this one step at a time."

Holy shit, am I talking out loud?

"Okay. One step at a time."

"Exactly. Go ahead and get dressed, and I'll go talk to your mom about setting up an appointment."

Taryn nodded again. Words drifted from her mind like dust motes, impossible to catch as they floated out of reach.

Chapter Twenty-Four

Riker

Riker stared at his laptop.

It was giving him bad news. Again.

He'd forever be resigned to getting the short straw. With school, with voice acting, with family, with girls.

With mental health. Because yeah, it was really starting to feel like he was going crazy here.

The email glared at him.

Dear Mr. Lucas,

Thank you for submitting your voiceover for our bridge engineering video. We have listened to it with interest, but, unfortunately, we've determined it's not a good fit for us at this time.

Please consider submitting to us again for future projects.

Wishing you the best in your future endeavors,

Holly Jolly Productions

Future endeavors, my ass. These voice acting attempts are a waste of time.

He slammed his laptop closed.

It had been three weeks since he'd gotten anything to do through *Voice Venture*. It had been one week since Taryn had kissed him in Beezy's office then made a dash for it. It had been two days since he'd last seen Beezy frown at his tournament scores—which had taken a sharp decline from the previous weekend.

Which was apparently what happened when Riker went through the motions too much.

And now...

Now he was home alone once more, skipping the Monday Speech and Debate meeting that all competitors were supposed to attend. But if anyone noticed, they hadn't checked in with him.

And why would they? Even people who noticed him didn't actually care about him.

Like Taryn, who'd never followed up after their kiss, who couldn't stand to be around the pathetic waste of space known as Riker Lucas. What he needed to do was write her another letter—to end it once and for all, burn the bridge down, so he could wipe her from his thoughts. Something she'd likely already done in return.

She doesn't need to get mixed up with my worthless ass anyway.

His gaze landed on his backpack, where he could easily grab the pen and paper that would push her away and free him from worrying about it.

But then he tapped his fingers on the top of his closed laptop. He slid his thumbs under the lid, rubbing them back and forth along the crack.

Don't open Voice Venture. *There's nothing there for you.*

Don't open Timescale. *It'll suck away the rest of your night.*

"So what if it does?" he said out loud.

There was nothing better to do, nothing better to think about. He couldn't stop Taryn from floating away. He was a failure at voice acting, miserable on the Speech team. Not to mention he hadn't seen his mom — hadn't seen a single family member — in twenty-four hours.

I could watch Timbre!

He shoved the suggestion from his mind. It would be impossible to focus on the show when every single song, every single kiss, screamed, "This is what Taryn loves!"

He opened his laptop in one swift movement and clicked through to his game.

* * * *

Riker snorted awake.

Something was out of place. The atmosphere, maybe.

A loud clank came from the kitchen down the hall. He looked around, gathering his bearings. He sat hunched over on his bed, laptop still open to *Timescale*. The overhead light was on, but the hallway was pitch dark.

He clenched his jaw, then pulled out his phone to check the time. Almost one a.m.

Jesus.

He shoved his laptop off his lap and climbed out of bed. If his shoulder could speak, it would've groaned at the movement. A large knot had formed where his shoulder met his neck.

Another clang came from the kitchen, followed by a thump. The latter at least sounded like a closing cupboard, something he recognized.

The kitchen light was already on as he eased toward it. Someone was banging around in there—hopefully his mom instead of a late-night kitchen robber.

He recognized her bunched-up blonde hair from behind. The color could've easily belonged to any one of his sisters, but the style—and messiness—was undoubtedly Mom's. He tapped his knuckles on the wall.

She gasped and turned, pressing a palm to the top of her chest. "Riker, honey. You scared me."

Riker rubbed his eyes with the back of one hand. The light in the kitchen seemed to have multiplied in brightness.

"Mom, what are you doing?"

"Just...making dinner. I wanted chicken fingers, but I couldn't find a pan." Her words were slightly slurred and she wobbled on her feet. It was then that he noticed the stench of alcohol, evident from a few feet away. "Are you hungry?"

Was he? He thought back to what he'd been doing at dinnertime. Playing *Timescale*? Wallowing about Taryn?

His stomach ached, a sharp and sudden message from his body at the mere thought of the meal he'd skipped.

Well, shit.

"Yeah, I guess. Here, let me—"

He stepped further into the kitchen and pulled out a medium-sized baking pan. Then he opened the under-sink cupboard for aluminum foil.

"Thank you, honey. For some reason I just couldn't figure it out. I kept looking…"

"It's fine, Mom."

She opened the box of frozen chicken fingers on the counter. Riker preheated the oven before reaching into the box and grabbing a few tenders to put on the foil-covered pan.

"Thank you, honey," she said again. She swayed. "Can you let me know when they're done? I need to change my shoes…"

She trailed off as she exited the kitchen, leaving Riker alone with the preheating oven. He opened the oven door and shoved the pan inside, to hell if the preheat hadn't finished. The universe was playing a cruel trick—he'd wanted his mom home, but not like this. Not when she was so distant her presence hardly mattered.

* * * *

The next evening, Riker's second-oldest sister, Jaclyn, sat upright on the couch as he leaned back in the reclining armchair and clasped his fingers together. Jaclyn's shoes were flat on the carpet, like a guest biding her time. As if she hadn't grown up in this house, just like him.

"So are you going to tell me what you're doing here?" he asked, twiddling his thumbs. If she was going to show up then act like she wanted nothing to do with the place, she might as well leave. At twenty-four, she wasn't that far from the nest.

Jaclyn sipped a can of pop, then set it on top of her leg with her hand still clutching it. "I'm just checking on you. Dad said you might be bored."

Understatement.

"I'm fine. And I actually have homework to do, so…" What he failed to mention was that he hadn't even gone to school today. Hadn't had enough energy to get out of bed and missed his chance for a ride from Mom once he'd finally pulled off the covers. She'd left the house without even making sure he'd woken up.

Jaclyn waved her can-free hand in the air. "Whatever. No one looks at your grades after high school."

"I'm pretty sure that's not true."

Jaclyn rolled her pale blue eyes so far back he was sure he'd glimpsed their backsides. "No one looked at mine, anyway. You know what I mean."

Did he, though? God, why was talking to his sister as tough as pulling teeth? Hadn't they played video games and read books together once upon a time?

"Okay fine, so you're not bored. Are you hungry?"

"Not really."

"Hm. Well, what do you need?"

He laughed, two hairs shy of a snort. What did he need? Well, for one thing, he needed Taryn back. For another, he needed his mind to stop spitting out self-derogatory words.

"I literally need nothing. I have a bed to sleep in, and Mom keeps the pantry stocked. So, yeah, I'm over here living the life, all alone in a five-bedroom house."

"Come on, there has to be something Mom can't give you. Like, something you can't ask her for."

Other than a constant presence in this house? Or enough sobriety to stay awake for chicken fingers?

"Okay. You know how I'm on the Speech and Debate team?"

She shook her head. "Nope, I had no idea. So you just debate people all the time?"

It was his turn to roll his eyes. Whatever this was, it wasn't brother–sister bonding. It was more like a brother–sister torture room. "No, I'm on the Speech side. I act stuff out."

"Okay, so?"

"*So*, to stay on the team I have to find an adult to volunteer for me at one of the Saturday tournaments. And I can't really ask Mom, even though she did it for me last year." He crossed his arms over his chest. Yesterday he'd wanted nothing to do with the Speech team when he skipped the meeting. Today he…well, he wasn't so sure what he wanted today. But if he decided to keep competing, he'd need the volunteer part out of the way.

She nodded. "So you want me to do it. When?"

"I don't remember exactly. All the tournaments are on Saturdays. There's one coming up at Fir Grove next month, so you wouldn't have to drive far…"

"What do I have to do?"

"You can either be a judge or work the concession stand."

"Whoa, Rike. You want me to judge this shit? I couldn't debate a preschooler."

"The concession stand, then?" he asked hopefully.

Jaclyn sipped her drink again, then again. "Fine, I can do that. I work Friday nights, though, so send me the date as soon as you know it. The date for the one at Fir Grove."

"Okay. Thanks." He twiddled his thumbs again, unsure where to lead the rest of the conversation.

Jaclyn tipped her pop back and finished it. Then she smacked her knees with her hands and stood. "All right, I'm out of here. Nice seeing you, kid."

"Sure, you too."

"Tell Mom I said hi. I'll be back next week or something."

Right. Or something. All five of his sisters claimed they'd check up on him "next week or something." Like it was the most common generic phrase to say to family burdens.

Jaclyn showed herself out as he ambled to his bedroom. A flash of dinner crossed his mind, but it disappeared quickly. He didn't feel like bothering with it.

He collapsed onto his bed and opened his laptop. He'd just check *Voice Venture* real quick, then move on to *Timescale*. No, check email first (likely empty), then *Voice Venture*, then *Timescale*. A surefire way to be a vegetable for the rest of the night—to forget about everything else going on around him.

He clicked over to his email, then, knowing there'd be nothing there before he even looked, moved his mouse to the *Voice Venture* bookmark.

But—

His finger halted. There was a new email. And it looked like...

He clicked it open. His eyes bulged as he read it quickly, then he reread to make sure he understood.

Another company had invited him to submit a voiceover sample.

Holy shit.

When did I even apply to them? He must've added his name to a list at some point...

This one required reading a five-minute script with three different voices. A month ago, he would've jumped on it, confident as hell. Today, though, he was about ninety-five-percent sure this task was futile.

Because he was never going to be a video game voice actor. Ever.

Gamer, yes. Voicer, no.

His head fell back onto his pillow. This whole thing was so fucking senseless. Like everything he did.

Like school. Like Drama class and the Speech team. Like trying to get anywhere close to Taryn. Pathetic, pathetic, pathetic. Ad infinitum.

None of these things was fun anymore. None gave him joy. He might as well yeet his entire life out the window.

He kicked his heels at his mattress, like a child throwing a tantrum. *I don't want to!*

Except he couldn't turn this down. Because there was still that five-percent chance his sample would wow the recruiter.

Fine.

This was pointless, but he had to do it. He moved himself and his laptop to the kitchen table. More professionally situated, he was ready to buckle down and begin. Ready to go through the motions and get this task over with.

Chapter Twenty-Five

Taryn

Gavin waved to Taryn the moment she walked through the rear auditorium door for Monday's Speech and Debate meeting. Before she could set down her backpack, he hustled up the stairs toward her with a giant grin.

"Taryn-Like-Karen! Hi. I'm so freaking excited for the tournament this weekend. I kid you not, my mom started crying when I practiced for her yesterday at home. I mean, it's just my mom, and she cries a lot, but still. Now I'm hoping for a mom judge!"

Taryn chuckled. "Nice. I'm not sure if all moms are like that, but good luck."

"I'm going to make Beezy cry, too. I just know it. He claims he's seen it all, but...life goal."

"All I want is to get better scores. I don't think *Catcher in the Rye*'s going to make anybody cry."

"Ah, Taryn-Like-Karen. They might not cry, but they'll sure as hell laugh at the way you do it. I hope you get a judge drinking water, 'cause they'll spit it out all over the table."

The corners of her mouth rose. God, this kid could make a cynic blush with the compliments he dished. She reached her hand around her backpack until she grabbed a zipper, anxious to fiddle with anything at all before she said something ridiculously hokey.

Her fingertips landed on something poking out of the smallest pocket. The corner of a folded note? Her heart stuttered.

She nodded and smiled, hopefully a reasonable response for whatever Gavin had just added. God, how many more hours were in the day? If this were a note — if it were from Riker, which it must've been — she had to open it pronto.

Did Riker think everything was okay between them? Would his letter acknowledge that he hadn't messaged her once after they'd kissed?

But God, I'm such a hypocrite.

She hadn't messaged him or been able to hold eye contact longer than two heartbeats.

She hadn't explained what had made her run away.

Come on, come on, come on... The clock past Gavin's shoulder said 3:55. Five more minutes until the Speech and Debate meeting and still no sign of Riker, note notwithstanding. Jesus H., she had to read it before he showed up. Had to know whether to be happy or pissed.

"...So then I told him, 'No freaking way! That's not how it works!'" Gavin said.

Taryn laughed. She made an exaggerated effort to look at the clock so Gavin would notice. "Crap, I have to go to the bathroom before Beezy and Zeb get here."

"Knock yourself out."

She slipped out of the room and powerwalked down the hall. She hurried into a bathroom stall, dropped her backpack to the floor and pulled the folded piece of paper from the outer pouch. The jagged font across the top read "Taryn."

With a deep breath, she lowered herself to the toilet seat, pants still on. Then she unfolded the letter, one flap at a time, careful to not rip it from the precise folds.

Taryn,
I guess I should start by saying sorry.
Sorry.
Life has been…messy. Maybe you could say the same?
I know I missed my chance. I've been MIA. I'll continue to be MIA. Because so much shit is happening inside my head, I'm lucky if I can get out of bed on time to catch the bus these days — and when I miss it, I'm too late to catch a ride to school from anyone else.
But I haven't stopped thinking about you. Not once. And since I'm laying it all out there, I guess I can also say I really wanted things to go differently. It's too late, though. We missed our chance, because I fucked everything up. I'm still fucking those things up. No going back at this point. I'm too far removed.
Holy hell, what are we doing? All you bring me is temporary happiness and indefinite suffering. Because don't think for a second I don't suffer every day without you.
Sometimes I have to wonder. Am I only chasing you in a desperate attempt to feel happy for once in my life?
That doesn't sound fair to either of us.
Thinking of you from afar,
Riker

Taryn's fingers clawed around the letter.

I will not *barely hold on to him. Not having him at all would hurt so much less than this dance.*

He should've either told her he was all in, or else told her he'd moved on. It had to be one way or the other, nothing in between, or Taryn risked officially breaking down.

Her throat tightened.

She'd shared so much of herself for nothing.

Including a completely amazing and unforgettable kiss that had lit up the dark like a lantern festival. A kiss she wasn't even sure he'd wanted, one that had been completely ruined when her damn cramps had showed up for a surprise visit. Those cramps had shattered her chances with Riker more than once *and* kept her from a Speech tournament. What would happen when they started seeping into other aspects of her life? That ultrasound could not come soon enough.

It was too late to talk to Riker about it. She'd missed her chance when she'd been too embarrassed to put the problem into words. No explanation about it now would make him change his mind — his letter made it damn clear he didn't think they were a good match.

Riker was right. Nothing could happen between them. There was no use — for either of them — putting up with the frustration just to feel beautiful and wanted and ecstatic for five minutes before the weight of crushing rejection took over. She'd be better off screaming into a void and waiting for an echo.

She'd just have to be better at avoiding him.

Better at putting distance between them.

Better at letting him go.

She flattened out the paper across her lap, then refolded it along the original creases. She had to get to the meeting, had to hold her head high without wavering. It was safe to assume things were over with Riker—although, now that Taryn thought about it, she wasn't sure they'd ever really begun.

She slipped the note back into her backpack, took a deep breath that rattled her chest more than it soothed her and opened the stall door.

Thank God I'm not crying. For now.

She retreated to the auditorium with purpose, chin up, imagining she was a businesswoman power-walking through New York City in four-inch heels.

When she entered the auditorium, she went straight to her seat without looking around. If she caught sight of Riker, that would be it—the floodgates would open, and the tears would force their way out.

She set her backpack down and dared a glance to the front of the room, where Beezy and Zeb were each speaking to a different student. The clock on the wall indicated that the meeting should have started a minute ago.

Thankfully, no one was talking to her. No need to put on a front. Because she sure as hell had no idea how she felt. Talking might prompt some unexpected emotions.

She had to know what Riker was up to, though. Was he watching her? Was he purposefully avoiding her? She closed her eyes with a deep breath, then opened them and looked toward Riker's usual seat.

He still wasn't there.

She flicked her gaze around the room, then turned around in her seat to look behind her. No Riker.

So he ditched me and *ditched the meeting two weeks in a row? Great.*

He said he'd be MIA, though she hadn't assumed that included today. When had he even had the chance to give her this note? Maybe it was less awkward with him missing, but what if she didn't see him again until they put on their A game (well, his A game, her B+ game) for Saturday's tournament? Ugh.

Or what if…

A heavy weight dropped inside her stomach as she realized the deeper implication of his letter.

What if he wasn't here because he hadn't woken up on time to catch the bus to school, like he'd said in his letter? What if he hadn't been able to get up?

What if there were a way she could make sure it didn't happen again…?

Stop. He doesn't want your help. He doesn't want you to think that way about him anymore.

At the front of the room, Beezy cleared his throat as Zeb took a seat. Taryn slumped in her auditorium seat. Without Riker to steal glances at, this would be the most boring Speech and Debate meeting in the history of meetings, on par with last week.

Aside from Gavin, the only other person she really knew here was…

Well, it didn't seem appropriate to even think of her after being so invested in Riker.

Taryn looked diagonally toward the front of the room, where Quinn always sat. Sure enough, there she was, a forest-green cap tilted on her head and a thick scarf hanging loosely around her shoulders. As focused as always. Beautiful as always. Exactly what Taryn needed right now, though only half-heartedly what she wanted.

But if she and Riker were never going to be on the same page, then what the hell was she waiting for? Maybe it'd do her some good to cut the cord completely, to one-hundred-percent move on.

As if on cue, Quinn looked up. She caught Taryn's eye and smiled. Taryn returned it.

Chapter Twenty-Six

Riker

The doorbell rang, but Riker didn't move.

You've gotta be kidding me.

Riker, lying on his side, stared at the blank television. He hadn't thought to grab the remote before plopping onto the couch after school. And now, of course, it was too far out of reach.

The doorbell rang again. None of it mattered. If it were one of his sisters, they'd let themselves in and bother him without invitation. If it were someone else, they'd go away eventually.

It must've been past four o'clock by now, though Riker didn't have the energy to check his phone for the time. Surely the Speech and Debate meeting was underway without him. Taryn would be there, her dark hair splayed over one shoulder and her eyelashes fluttering as she took in every word Beezy said.

But there was no point going back to Speech and Debate—even the sight of Taryn wouldn't fix any of his problems. Besides, he hadn't looked for anyone to buy his ads—all the more reason for Beezy and Zeb to not care if he gave up. If that were Jaclyn at the door, he'd have to let her know she didn't need to volunteer at the concession stand, either.

After two skipped meetings, Beezy and Zeb had probably already marked him off as hopeless, complaining on their car ride home that Riker didn't belong on the team and never had. Just like Taryn would write him off as nothing more than the lazy ex-competitor who didn't like her enough to make a move. Especially after she found the note he'd left in her backpack.

Whatever. Taryn could have Quinn in a heartbeat. They'd be better for each other anyway. It would be a total dick move to tie Taryn down with someone who was obsessed with her but not open enough to show it.

He'd always be second place. Or worse. All the more reason he couldn't go to practice today.

He just couldn't.

The doorknob rattled as Riker heard a key clicking into place.

Large families are so overrated.

The front door opened, and Riker's oldest sister, Clarice, stepped inside. Her blonde hair was pulled back in a frizzy ponytail, each strand seemingly attempting to escape.

Clarice stomped her feet on the rug inside the entryway. "Why the hell didn't you answer the door?"

"Why ring the doorbell when you have a key?"

"It's called decency, Rike. You ever hear of it?" She tugged off her jacket and tossed it on the arm of the couch by Riker's feet. "Is Mom here?"

He sniggered. "She's never here."

Clarice crossed her arms over the chest of her dark-blue hoodie. "Do you know where she is, then?"

"Jesus." Riker swung his legs forward and sat up. "I have no idea, okay? Mom shows up in the middle of the night if I'm lucky. Dad stops by for like two seconds once a week. You'd know all this if you were ever here. This is your house too, you know."

His sister sighed. "I moved out years ago."

"There's still a bedroom with your stuff in it…"

"I don't have room for all that junk at my place. It's not my fault Mom never moved any of it."

Riker lifted his butt to tug his phone out of his back pocket. What the hell was the use in listening to Clarice right now? Like she said, she hadn't lived in the house for years now. She had no idea what Riker went through every day, no clue what it was like to live in a house with one or zero parents at a time in the middle of a divorce.

He tapped the *Voice Venture* app and watched as the latest postings populated his phone. The site was easier to use on his laptop, but the damn thing seemed miles away. He doubted his legs could move even if he told them to.

Clarice walked past the couch and out of the room. Off to the kitchen, maybe, to do God knew what. Fine by him. He was used to not having her around.

He scrolled through the postings, reading quickly to ensure that he didn't miss any good ones before other people snagged them. He was vaguely aware of his oldest sister rummaging around somewhere in the house. He continued scrolling until he reached postings that sounded familiar, ones he'd already read and knew he wasn't qualified for.

I should just get my laptop and play Timescale.

Should, should, should...

He groaned. He really did not possess the motivation to get up. Maybe he could ask Clarice to grab it from his room.

He scrolled back to the top of the postings and refreshed.

Rinse and repeat.

By the time he glanced at the clock on his screen, it was past four-thirty. The Speech and Debate meeting was over, replaced with individual practice sessions with Beezy and Zeb.

"Hey, so I got a hold of Dad." Clarice sauntered back into the living room with a can of pop. He'd momentarily forgotten she was in the house. "He said to call him if you need anything."

Riker snorted, his gaze still locked on the phone. "Like what? Dinner?"

"Wait." She put a hand on her hip. "Do you need food?"

Riker looked up at his sister. "No. Mom's at least alive enough to buy mac and cheese."

"Okay. Well if you need anything else, just shoot Dad a text."

Right. Like Dad would run over at his son's beck and call. It'd never happened before, and it wouldn't happen now unless there was a legit emergency. And being bored to tears on his laptop probably didn't count as an emergency.

"Sure, I'll do that."

Clarice set her pop can on an end table and picked up her jacket, then shrugged it on. "Let me know if Mom calls, okay? I have to talk to her."

"Yeah, sure. I bet she'll be rushing right out to talk to you, just like she does for all of us."

She sighed and picked up her can. "I know, Rike. Seriously, I know. She's never been there when you needed her. But she's still our mom, and that's not changing anytime soon."

Right. At least Clarice had lived in a house with two parents throughout her whole childhood. "Sure, Clary. Hey, there's one thing I could use…"

"Yeah? What?"

"Could you go get my laptop off my bed?" There, he'd asked. A humiliating favor, but whatever.

Clarice took another drink and raised her eyebrows at him. "Are you serious right now?"

"Yeah, pretty much."

She rolled her eyes before stomping down the hallway toward his bedroom. He was sure she'd use this request against him in the future, but he didn't have the effort to care about that right now.

Clarice returned, laptop in hand. She held it out for him.

"Thanks."

"Whatever, Rike. Just let me know if Mom calls."

He opened *Timescale* as Clarice left. This was where he needed to be, even if the excitement of the game had faded long ago. He had cities to build, characters to create. If he dropped the ball on the game, he'd have to start over from scratch. And for a reason he couldn't explain, that sent tremors of dread through him — tremors that didn't dissipate as he played.

He curled up on his side and balanced his laptop on the edge of the couch cushion. The sky darkened as he continued to play, all thoughts of dinner gone.

Chapter Twenty-Seven

Taryn

If Taryn's bedroom at Grandma's house had been bland before, it must have appeared even more so with Taryn in it.

Appeared so to Quinn, that was.

Taryn sat stiffly on her bed, feet flat on the floor. It was at this moment that she wished she'd chosen her shirt more carefully, put more thought into her hair.

She could *feel* how lackluster she looked next to Quinn.

Quinn stood out in Taryn's bedroom like a pristine pearl in a dungeon. With one leg crossed over the other, her lavender leggings elongated her lower limbs like taffy. She leaned back on her palms, emphasizing the angles of her cotton-clad arms. It was Quinn's first time here, and she seemed completely at ease in this clinical excuse for a bedroom.

Taryn was not at ease.

Taryn was sitting on a bed with a beautiful girl, and she couldn't think of a single thing to talk about. And for some reason, that beautiful girl seemed completely okay with not talking, as if conversation were an unnecessary add-on to hanging out.

Taryn clasped her fingers together in her lap and squeezed. If she'd been sitting this close to Quinn on a bed two months ago, different thoughts would've run through her mind — kissing and butterflies and skin on skin. Not today. Not anymore.

"So," Quinn said, breaking the silence. "You want to watch a movie?"

Taryn shrugged. For some reason, a movie sounded worse than sitting on a bed next to each other. A movie meant even less talking. A movie meant the possibility — expectation? — of sitting closer together, maybe holding hands or more.

And, well, Taryn hadn't thought that far ahead when she'd invited Quinn over. Fantasies of doing much more than that with faceless girls were a resounding yes — but lately, her mind hadn't been able to put Quinn's face in those scenarios.

Do I want to get close? Would hand-holding even mean anything?

It would mean something to me. Maybe not to her. But if it were Riker...

No, don't bring Riker into this.

"Maybe a snack instead?" Taryn asked. "My grandma just bought this really good hummus..."

"Oh my God, I love hummus." Quinn stretched her legs out before pulling them back in, then stood. "Lead the way."

Not that that'd be difficult. Grandma's house was large, but it wasn't a sprawling mansion Quinn could get lost in.

Taryn stood as well, happy to have an excuse to do something other than sitting tensely on a bed next to Quinn. In a few minutes she'd be sitting tensely at a table next to Quinn instead, but she'd worry about that later.

Quinn followed her down the hall without a word, her socks padding softly on the hardwood floor.

Grandma's kitchen was bright and spacious, a room that made Taryn think of the phrase "entertaining guests" (not that she'd ever had the opportunity, and serving hummus hardly counted). The stainless-steel appliances against the wall glinted in the sunlight streaming through the windows, as if each one called, "Use me! Cook with me!" Which her grandma did a lot, always whipping up elaborate dinners as if they took minimal effort.

Her mom? Not so much. Before they'd moved here, Mom's diet had mostly centered around food that a microwave could zap.

"Take a seat," Taryn said, gesturing to the bar stools at the kitchen island. Quinn did so as Taryn pulled the hummus out of the refrigerator and grabbed a bag of pita chips from the pantry.

"I could seriously eat hummus all day," Quinn said.

Taryn leaned her elbows against the island, across from Quinn. "Me too. I'd never even had it until I moved here."

Quinn pulled out a pita chip and dipped it into the mashed concoction. "What, they didn't have hummus at your old school?"

Taryn laughed. Did they have hummus at any school? "No, I mean my mom never bought it. She still won't eat it, says it's just for rich people."

She bit her tongue. She'd never opened up to Quinn about where she came from and certainly not about her mom's financial situation.

"Cool," Quinn said around a bite. "You got any carrot sticks?"

Taryn swallowed at the response, which didn't quite seem to work. But whatever. "I can check…"

She wouldn't put it past Grandma to randomly have a bag of carrot sticks sitting around. She turned back to the refrigerator and opened the vegetable shelf, finding three full-size carrots, complete with knobs and peel. Five minutes ago she'd wanted a distraction, but peeling and cutting carrots wasn't exactly what she'd had in mind.

"Nope, no carrot sticks." She closed the drawer and the refrigerator and turned back around to the island, grabbing a pita chip from the bag. She racked her brain for conversation topics, even though Quinn seemed in no hurry to push the conversation along.

God, why wasn't this easier?

"So…did you always live around here?" Taryn asked.

"Yep, pretty much," Quinn said, licking crumbs off her finger.

"Okay, cool." Taryn could've followed up with another question. Could've offered a piece of her own history. But Quinn just seemed to not give a single shit.

Why was she even here?

Why had Taryn bothered inviting her?

Taryn groaned out loud before she realized what hit her. Her hand flew to her lower abdomen, clutching at it as if that would make the pain disappear.

"Shit," she said quickly. "Shit, sorry."

Quinn raised one eyebrow in question.

Taryn took a deep breath, then another. She rolled her shoulders as the pain dissipated. "Sorry, sorry. I get these weird pains out of nowhere. Like, period stuff but not always when I'm on my period."

"Oh, that sucks. Cramps are the worst."

"Right!"

She groaned again, this time the pain bending her forward. She took deep breaths as she waited for it to dispel again.

"Sorry." She moaned as she stood up straight. Her heart pounded in her chest as her body tried to recover from the flash of pain. Talking about this with Quinn was about the opposite of sexy, but, being a girl, Quinn would be able to at least sympathize. "It just...really freaking hurts. I have an ultrasound coming up soon, to see what's going on in there."

Quinn laughed. Literally laughed. Taryn gritted her back teeth.

"Sorry to break it to you," Quinn said, "but I know exactly what they'll find. A uterus and some ovaries."

Wow. Okay.

Taryn chuckled nervously. "Well yeah, but they might find something else, too. Like, something that's making it hurt so much." Like what? She wasn't sure...

Quinn shrugged one shoulder and grabbed another pita chip. "Period pains are just part of being a girl. You pop some Motrin and you deal."

But it wasn't that simple. Was it?

I'm not just worse at handling this than everyone else, right?

Taryn glanced at the clock on the microwave. She wondered how much longer she had to entertain Quinn, how much longer she had to wait before she could kick out her guest without looking like a total bitch.

This fight wasn't worth having.

Chapter Twenty-Eight

Riker

Riker sat down at the kitchen table, coffee mug in hand. He'd made it a full thirty minutes without his laptop or phone since waking up.

It took three sips of coffee before he noticed the note on the table.

Let your dad know I paid Marion's student loan this month.

Okay. Great. Tell him yourself?

What was Riker supposed to do, text his dad this sentence about his sister? Take a picture of the note and message it to him? Why the hell couldn't his mom do that herself? Marion was *their* kid.

After however-many-years of marriage (twenty-five?), he would've thought they'd be adult enough to manage a divorce without putting their kids in the middle.

Their *kid*, rather. Because Riker was the only one still living in this house. The only one passing messages back and forth like a middle schooler's wingman.

If either of them noticed him for anything other than his memo-passing capabilities, they'd notice he wasn't at today's Speech and Debate tournament at Fir Grove. If his mom had a single nugget of care inside that heart of hers, she'd notice he'd turned off his morning alarm and gone back to bed instead of asking for a ride to the school like he did every Saturday morning.

And now here he was, with no one talking to him but his mom's handwriting. The clock read one-thirty, which meant the tournament itself was over. His teammates would be huddled together in the cafeteria right now, biding their time until they could go to the auditorium for the closing ceremony and find out if they placed. Then, since it was a tournament at their own school, they wouldn't leave together on a bus. They'd wait around for their parents to pick them up.

Oh.

Shit.

Volunteering.

The doorbell rang. Riker clenched his fingers around the handle of his coffee mug.

Shit, shit, shit.

He knew exactly which sister was on the other side of the door. Jaclyn had volunteered for the Fir Grove Speech and Debate tournament.

Shit, shit, shit.

The doorknob rattled as the key went in the lock, then he heard the swoosh of the door bottom dragging against the floor.

"Riker! Are you here?"

He resisted the urge to drop his forehead to the table and bang it there a few times. That wouldn't get him out of this situation.

"Yeah, here."

"Kitchen?" she shouted.

"Yep."

Three seconds later, her flats pattered onto the kitchen tile. She stopped next to the table, looking down at him. "What the hell, Rike? Where were you?"

He shrugged. "I forgot."

Jaclyn crossed her arms over her chest. "You *forgot*? You forgot to go to the place you asked me to volunteer at? The place I went to for you?"

"I don't know. I guess so. And I guess I didn't want to go. I'm so over these Speech tournaments." He shrugged again.

Her arms flung into the air before slapping down at her thighs. "You've gotta be fucking kidding me. No wonder Mom doesn't want to volunteer for your shit— you don't fucking show up when you're supposed to, just like her. And then you don't answer your damn phone when we try to find you."

"Wow, okay. Tell me how you really feel, Jac."

Jaclyn sighed. She pulled a chair out from the table and plopped down into it. "You know what I mean. You can't just skip your tournaments like that. Your coaches looked just as surprised as I was."

"Well, they'll deal."

"I seriously cannot believe you. 'They'll deal'? Like, you completely let them down, and you don't even care?"

She smacked her palm onto the table. He jumped, coffee jolting and spilling over the edge of his cup.

"What are you even drinking?" she asked, her voice rising. "Coffee? When did you start drinking coffee?"

He shrugged.

She sighed, her shoulders slumping. "Riker. Little brother. Kiddo."

Riker blinked at her expectantly. "You still going?"

"Sweet sibling of mine who once loved his toy farm animals."

"Unnecessary. What are you getting at?"

She scratched the back of her neck, eyes on the table. "Every time I visit, you're off in your own world. You're either lost in your video game, or you're staring at nothing."

"So?"

"So, I've been talking to Dad, and I've been thinking...you might be depressed."

Riker laughed. "You're hilarious, Jac. Seriously. I already know I'm miserable."

She looked up at him and nodded several times. "Okay, okay, so you recognize you're unhappy. That's good!"

"That doesn't mean anything." He sighed and took a sip, the bitter liquid flowing down his gullet. It had already started to cool, had already lost the rich taste it carried when extra hot.

"So the next step is to get help, you know? See a doctor. I can take you, or I bet someone else would if I can't. We just want to see you get better."

Riker clutched his hands around the coffee mug. "Just because I'm miserable doesn't mean I need help. Not everyone needs to talk to a doctor just to feel better."

"Yeah, but—I think you do." She lowered her eyes to the table again.

He tipped his cup back and finished off the lukewarm liquid. "Nah, I'm good. Thanks for thinking of me though, sis."

Riker stood, put his cup in the sink and headed straight to his bedroom. There was a laptop waiting on his bed for him. Thirty-five laptop-free minutes was pretty damn impressive, if he said so himself.

I deserve to play it now.

I proved I can go without.

So now I can go with.

He opened his laptop as he heard the front door slam from his sister's departure. Leaving on bad terms, but whatever. Not his problem. She had no idea what she was talking about. And she'd talked about it with Dad? So ridiculous, so petty.

He didn't need a doctor. No therapist or psychiatrist or whatever was going to make him feel like going to Speech tournaments. They weren't going to make him better at talking to Taryn, better at getting voice acting gigs.

Nothing they could do would make him enjoy this shit anymore.

I'm sure of it.

He clicked through the opening prompts of *Timescale*. He was all in on the game today, no *Voice Venture* to bog him down anymore. The site hadn't done him any favors, and he was sure it never would.

Timescale, though — it'd done him plenty of favors.

It took his mind off everything. Off everyone. And if he played all through the night and never ate again, then so what? If it made him so tired he didn't wake up in time for school on Monday, then whatever. He wanted nothing to do with school, and no one would miss him anyway.

* * * *

Something was making noise.

Some goddamn thing was chiming, somewhere in his bedroom.

Godddddd.

Stopppppp.

He put his arm over his eyes, blocking the light from his retinas. What the hell time was it? What the hell day was it? Riker was on his bed, all the covers kicked to the floor, his jeans and button-up shirt still on — a wrinkled mess for sure.

The chime came again, somewhere near the base of his bed. He flung his arm around, patting the floor randomly until his fingers landed on something hard.

He lifted his phone to his face to find the culprit of the noise. Surely it wasn't his alarm, which he hadn't bothered setting for days. The time on the home screen read 7:44 a.m. If it was a school day, he wasn't far from cutting it close.

Is it a school day? Fuck.

There were two text messages.

Taryn: You said you had trouble getting up for school. So I thought maybe I'd wake you up.

Taryn: So…good morning! Rise and shine! I hope you catch the bus on time.

A smile crossed his face for the first time in what must have been days.

Chapter Twenty-Nine

Taryn

Taryn's grandma leaned back in a stiff chair, a paperback novel held to her face. Taryn fidgeted in her seat, her bladder full — it was impossible to get comfortable.

Ultrasound day had come.

So yeah, getting comfortable would've been impossible with or without the firm waiting room chairs and the "drink lots of water before your appointment but don't pee" instruction. Taryn was pretty sure nothing could calm her nerves right now. Not even the prospect of tonight's *Timbre!* episode and interacting with her faithful followers.

"Taryn?" her grandma asked, lowering the book. "What's wrong, love?"

She shrugged. "I don't know. I'm nervous."

Grandma closed the paperback around her finger, holding her place, and nodded. "You'll be fine, Taryn.

It's uncomfortable and strange, but I'm glad you're getting one."

"Okay, yeah," she replied, unsure what else she could possibly say in this situation. She was grateful Grandma had picked her up during the school day to bring her here, was happy to have a family member who seemed invested in the outcome. She tried to ignore the awkward nagging feeling of discussing — implicitly or otherwise — vaginas with her grandma.

Still, she could get used to chats with Grandma. In fact, she was finally starting to feel comfortable with the whole living arrangement they had.

Taryn pulled her backpack onto her lap, then winced at the discomfort on her bladder. If the nurse took any longer to call her name, she risked peeing her pants. She might have to resort to homework as a distraction.

Instead, out of habit, she unzipped the tiny front pocket of her backpack.

Surely there'd be no note in there from Riker. He'd had the nerve to not show up for yesterday's Speech and Debate meeting, again, even after missing the Fir Grove tournament. He'd missed Beezy's entire spiel about how the team's top competitors would perform at the upcoming showcase in front of their families. In fact, she hadn't seen Riker for a while — yesterday wasn't a Drama day, and today her grandma had pulled her out of school before Drama class started.

She had no idea if her morning text yesterday had helped him wake up and get to school.

More than likely, he'd ignored it.

Had she overstepped? Probably. Still, there was a chance she'd find — she shoved her hand into the front pocket of her backpack — a folded letter!

In the same place he always put them. Well, where he'd put three of them now. When on earth had he slipped it in there?

She unfolded it, feeling her grandma's eyes on her.

Taryn —
You managed to get me out of bed for once. Thank you.
RL

So her morning text had worked! Heat rose to her cheeks as she failed to suppress a smile. God, even if they couldn't be together, she could live indefinitely off the occasional handwritten message from him.

"Is that from your friend?" her grandma asked, finger once again a bookmark.

"Hm?"

"Your girlfriend that came over on Sunday. Started with a 'Q'..."

"Quinn," she filled in. Her hand went to the back of her neck. She wasn't sure if her grandma had meant "girlfriend" in the "friend that is a girl" kind of way that old ladies used sometimes, or if she meant the word "girlfriend." Not that she'd consider her grandma an "old lady."

"Quinn, right. She didn't stay long."

Taryn shook her head. "No, I guess not." *Not enough carrot sticks and excitement for her.*

Grandma cleared her throat. "Did you two break up?"

"What?" Taryn's eyes widened. Apparently, Grandma really did know how to use "girlfriend" in the twenty-first century. "No, I—we...never started going out. Not officially."

"Ah. But you wanted to?"

Taryn looked up at the ceiling, unsure how to reply. "Well...I used to. But I think maybe we're not very good for each other."

"Did she want to be your girlfriend?" Grandma prodded.

Taryn hesitated. "I think she wanted something informal, and that just...wasn't working for me. Plus I think she was annoyed with me all the time."

"I see. Well, it's better to figure that out earlier than later. Now you can focus your attention on the people who matter. I'm guessing your letter wasn't from Quinn, then?"

"No, it's from Riker."

"Is that a girl's name, or...?"

Taryn shook her head. "Boy. Very cute boy." Taryn's eyes widened again. Why was she talking about this with her grandma?

Grandma nodded, understanding. "Bisexual, then. I'd wondered."

Taryn sighed. "Sorry, we don't have to talk about this." *Here or anywhere.* At least she'd momentarily forgotten about her full bladder.

"Nonsense. I voted for Hillary, you know. What kind of monster do you think I am?"

Taryn laughed. "I don't think you're a monster, Grandma."

"Well, good. Because then we'd have a problem."

The door leading back to the exam rooms opened. A nurse with periwinkle scrubs consulted her clipboard, then asked, "Taryn?"

Taryn stood. She looked down at her grandma, who gave her a reassuring nod. Then Taryn followed the nurse to the exam room.

* * * *

Taryn sat at the edge of the patient's table, now fully clothed. The nurse had said the doctor would be in shortly, which meant it was time to wait more.

She clutched her fingers in her lap and looked down at them. Her pelvic area still reeled from the transvaginal ultrasound. The technician had told Taryn she wouldn't feel any pain, and that had been true during the initial on-the-belly ultrasound that had squished her bladder but was otherwise fine. The nurse had then released her to use the restroom, and when Taryn had come back, the transvaginal equipment was ready for her.

That was when the pain had come. The wand had gone in fine enough, but once the nurse turned it toward one ovary then the other, her body had jerked reflexively from the agony, her hands grasping at the patient bed for any sort of grip.

Was this how it would always go with something in her vagina? Was sex going to hurt like this? She shuddered to think of it.

Her experience with sex was, well, almost non-existent, be it girl or boy. Maybe everyone felt this much pain when they did it?

Maybe. Maybe not.

The door opened, and the doctor stepped in.

"Nice to see you again," the doctor said, holding out her hand to shake.

"You too."

The doctor pulled up a stool and sat down. "Okay, Taryn. I looked over the sonogram images. Combining those with the symptoms you told me about before makes me pretty confident you're experiencing endometriosis."

Taryn blinked hard. She'd heard the term but wasn't entirely sure what it meant.

The doctor continued. "In short, it means the lining of your uterus is growing on your other reproductive organs, likely the ovaries in this case. I can't be certain without getting inside there, but the signs point pretty strongly toward it. The only way to officially diagnose endometriosis is through surgery."

"Oh." She swallowed. "Does that mean I need it?"

The doctor nodded slowly. "You probably will someday, but I'm not recommending it today. For now, I'd like to start by putting you on hormonal therapy — birth control pills, really. They'll regulate your uterine lining and hopefully get some of that pain under control."

"Is it a cure?" Her voice broke over the final word.

"No, it's not. And it's not a guarantee, either." Her doctor looked directly into Taryn's eyes. "There's no cure for endometriosis, but we'll do what we can to keep it at bay. We're going to keep monitoring it, and we'll assess later if you'll need surgery and when. How old are you now?" She looked down at her clipboard.

"Seventeen."

"Okay, so it'll be a while before you have kids, if you want them. I have to let you know that endometriosis might make it difficult to get pregnant when you're ready. But I don't want you to worry about that too much — there will be options for you when the time comes."

Taryn nodded. The sting of tears formed in her eyes, her throat tightening. "Okay."

"Do you have any questions for me?"

She racked her brain. A million questions surfaced, but she couldn't form the words for them. Only one solidified into a sentence. "Will it take a while for the pain to stop?"

"Well, I'm not sure it will completely go away, to be honest. But after a couple months on the hormone treatment, the pain should be considerably less."

Taryn exhaled. She could manage that. Anything less than her current pain level would be a dream. For now, she'd focus on that—and not on all the other scary-as-hell things her doctor had just outlined.

Chapter Thirty

Riker

Taryn: Hi. Good morning. Time to wake up!

Riker blinked the sleep out of his eyes.
God, this girl.
This perfect human specimen.
He read the text again, soaking up each word. He ran a hand over his face, forcing himself to get up, up, up, out of bed.

How could he not get to school after a wake-up text from Taryn? They might have drifted too far apart to redeem what they'd once had, but he'd take any nugget of Taryn he could get — a text from her here, a Drama-class glimpse there.

He tensed. Drama. The class was already sounding as awful as the rest of them, even though it used to be his favorite. Hopefully, Beezy wouldn't make them perform anything. That kind of energy did not exist today.

Besides, you're terrible at acting.

His eyes drifted closed as he shuffled down the hall to the bathroom, the obstructive thoughts seeping into his brain.

You're never going to do voiceovers for video games.

You lost your shot with Taryn.

She'd never be with you, anyway.

He opened his eyes, catching himself swaying on his feet. He turned on the showerhead and peeled off his pajamas, letting them crumple to the floor.

Was Jaclyn right? Do I need help?

How the hell would I possibly know?

* * * *

The school day hadn't been quite as awful as he'd anticipated, all things considered.

Because on this day, Taryn had woken him up with a text. Then he'd seen her across the row in Drama class.

Just seeing her had been enough to make the light brighter.

At the end of class she pattered down the auditorium steps and out the door, which didn't make a difference to him — he didn't have the nerve to say a word to her, dream as he might.

He caught movement from Beezy out of the corner of his eye. Sure enough, his Drama teacher waved him to the front, a guilt trip he didn't need after a relatively good day. He hoisted himself from his seat and descended the steps.

"Riker," Beezy said, that cheery smile plastered to his face. "Glad you came to class today. I've been wanting to ask—will you perform at the Speech and Debate showcase? I need to finalize the programs."

Riker scratched his chin. He'd assumed Beezy wouldn't let him perform at the showcase, not with how absent he'd been from the team lately. But apparently Beezy had some sort of forgiving bone in his body, one that forced him to overlook transgressions.

Had Beezy asked a week earlier, even yesterday, Riker would've hidden from the prospect of doing the showcase. He would've reminded himself how terrible he was, how pointless the whole showcase would be. How blue it would make him.

But Taryn had woken him up again today. And that was a pretty damn good reason to put himself out there. To say "yes."

"Okay. I'll do it."

"Great! I'll mark you down. And while I have you here, can I count on you for Saturday's tournament?"

Gulp. Could he? Riker wasn't confident his own answer would be trustworthy. But still, he'd missed the deadline to cancel, so Beezy only expected one response. "Yeah, I'll come."

"Glad to hear it. And since you missed the meeting this week, just a friendly reminder about those ads. The deadline's in a week."

Alas, no conversation could be perfect.

* * * *

The bus rumbled under Riker as it drove him home, the school day now behind him.

The school bus slowed to a stop, the brakes squealing and the door opening, pulling Riker from the day's memory. He examined the surroundings outside the window to gain his bearings, taking in a red brick house with a black cut-out deer in the yard. A visual indicator that his stop was next.

With the next brake squeal, Riker grabbed his backpack and exited, then walked past three houses to get to his own, careful to avoid spots of ice on the sidewalk. He unlocked the door, pushed it open and stopped.

His mom sat on the couch, her checkered pajama pants riding up her legs, exposing her calves. A far cry from her usual going-out clothes and a good sign she'd be around all evening. For once.

"Hey…Mom?"

"Hi, honey." She lowered her phone to her lap and smiled at him.

He kicked off his shoes in the entryway and shrugged off his coat. "What are you, um, up to tonight?"

"Oh." She tucked her legs under her on the couch. "Well, I figured I should have a night in. What do you think?"

Riker scratched the back of his neck. She made it sound so simple, like it wasn't the strangest thing in the world for his mom to stay home. "Sure, good idea."

He sat in the recliner next to the couch and leaned back. It must've been months since he'd chilled with either of his parents, but hey, no time like the present.

"How was your day?" she asked.

"Fine. You?"

"Oh, fine, honey. I've been thinking I'll make shepherd's pie for dinner. Maybe see if your sisters want to come over."

Riker blinked. What the hell was happening? All those evenings away and suddenly she wanted to chat and have dinner together?

He wanted to hate it, wanted to be pissed at her change of heart, her hot and cold.

But he couldn't hate it. He couldn't hate *her*. Because what he wanted — all he wanted — was for their relationship to go back to the way it was. To stop feeling abandoned by every blood relative.

"That sounds good, Mom."

She smacked her palms on her thighs. "Great. Want to help me in the kitchen?"

"I can help, but chicken fingers and mac and cheese are pretty much my culinary limit."

She laughed. "It's not hard. Come on."

He followed her to the kitchen, still unsure how to approach this opened-up version of his mom.

"First things first — meat." She pulled a package of ground beef from the freezer and set it on a plate to defrost in the microwave. He leaned against the kitchen table, watching her move with ease in the kitchen, as if she'd actually used it recently. "Second step — text your sisters. Tell them it'll be done in forty-five minutes. Can you do that part?"

"All right." He pulled his phone out of his pocket and set up a group text to his two local sisters, Jaclyn and Clarice.

Riker: Dinner? Mom's making shepherd's pie.

Jaclyn: Sure, fine.

Clarice: OK. When?

Riker: Like forty-five minutes?

Riker pulled a chair out from the table and sat down. How strange to not have his laptop in front of him here, or a bowl of macaroni and cheese.

He watched as his mom pulled green beans from the refrigerator and washed them in a colander in the sink. He thought back to his childhood, of sitting in this very seat while his mom chopped carrots at the kitchen counter, his five older sisters flitting in and out of the kitchen, one at a time, distracting their mother but inducing a smile. Where had his dad been during all that? He couldn't remember.

"Riker, honey?" she asked, shaking the colander over the sink to let the water drip from the green beans. "Can you get the box of mashed potatoes out of the pantry? I'm taking the lazy route today."

"Sure, Mom." Boxed potatoes or not, he knew full well this meal required effort. Effort he hadn't seen his mom exude at home in ages, though who knew what she did outside of the house. "Want me to get it started?"

"Yes, please."

He read the instructions on the side of the box as she chopped the green beans into bite-size pieces. The simple thunk-thunk enveloped the room as he turned the stove on and waited for the salted water to boil.

Even though his mom was in pajamas, she looked more put together than he'd seen her in months. With slippers on instead of heels, she looked calm, clean. Sober. A quiet kind of in charge that earned respect without demanding it.

God, how he'd missed it.

"Hey, Mom?"

"Mmhm?"

"Remember last year when you and Dad went to that Speech and Debate showcase?"

"Oh yeah, that was great. You were so good, sweetie."

"Thanks. But—I was wondering…could you come to it again this year? It doesn't have to be with Dad, but I thought maybe…"

His mother turned to look at him, knife poised in the air. "Well sure. When is it?"

"Next Saturday. It's a week before the state qualifying tournament."

"Ah. So it'll be good practice for you."

"Yeah, I think so."

She turned back to her food prep. "You should ask your sisters to come, too."

His nod went unnoticed. Asking Jaclyn to come would reopen the wound of *"I can't believe I volunteered at the tournament you skipped!"* One step at a time.

He stopped, eyes fixed on the boiling water but not seeing it.

The ads.

He still had to find someone to buy his damn ads. And he knew just where to try.

"Mom, could you drive me somewhere after dinner? It'll only take like twenty minutes."

"Sure, honey."

* * * *

Riker pushed open the heavy wooden door of Violette's, stepping from dim mood lighting to even dimmer evening air. A chill wrapped around his sweatered arms, and he pulled them tightly to his chest, careful to not crumple the paperwork in his hands. Beside him, a rainbow-colored flag flapped in the breeze.

He jogged down the sidewalk to his mom's car, where she sat with the heater running. He pulled open the passenger door and sat down, reflexively grabbing his seatbelt and pulling it over his lap.

"Did they buy it?" she asked.

"Yep." He held up the paper as evidence, unable to control the grin spreading across his face.

"Great." She put the car in drive and eased forward. "So. Is there something you want to tell me?"

"Huh?"

She glanced at him as she turned on the blinker to pull out of the parking lot. "About selling ads to Violette's?"

He scratched his chin. "Well, there's this girl..."

"A girl?"

"Yeah, she...well, we went on this date once, and it's over now, I don't have a chance, but I thought maybe..."

His mom turned off the blinker and reversed back into the parking lot. She put the car in park and turned to him.

"Riker. What's going on?"

He cleared his throat. Hadn't he just said? Maybe it didn't make sense. He tried again. "I went here on a date. We're hardly talking now, but I still like her, so I wanted to put a Violette's ad in the showcase program."

"To impress a girl?"

He blinked. "Well, yeah. She probably won't care, but…"

"So you're not gay?"

He coughed. "What? Why would—" He looked back toward the restaurant, where the six-colored flag flapped in the cold evening air. "Oh."

She smiled and nodded, as if encouraging him to go on.

He chuckled. "No, not gay. Just went to a restaurant that supports it. Taryn, though—that's the girl—she's bi. That's why we went."

"Ah!" She matched his chuckle. "Now it makes sense. Though if you ever need to tell me anything—"

"Yep, okay."

"Good." She put the car back into drive and pulled forward.

Riker shook his head and rolled his eyes, though he couldn't help the smile on his face. He pulled his phone out of his pocket and hovered his thumb over the messaging app. Should he text Taryn to let her know Violette's had bought his ads—that the restaurant from their *date* had bought his ads? Maybe he'd even tell her about his mom's misunderstanding.

But.

What good would it do? She wouldn't care. She was doing him a service with the morning texts, and the communication stopped there.

His thumb bypassed the messaging app and tapped the email app instead.

He froze.

At the top of his inbox, a subject line read "Casting call invitation."

He clicked it open as quickly as his thumb would move.

Dear Mr. Lucas,

Thank you for your previously provided demo for voice acting work. Although it was not deemed a good fit for Seasons of Dust, we kept your information on file for future consideration.

We would like to invite you to attend a casting call for an as-yet-untitled video game for which we believe you're a good candidate. If cast, voice recording will occur over approximately two weeks in June at Goldblarg Entertainment's studio in Columbus, Ohio.

The casting call will require a three-to-five-minute prepared monologue and a cold reading. If interested, please RSVP by replying to this email, and we will provide you with further information.

We look forward to your response.

Sincerely,

Goldblarg Entertainment

Chapter Thirty-One

Taryn

"Yes, Taryn. Yes!"

The grin across Beezy's face was infectious. So infectious that Taryn felt her own mouth curve up at the corners.

"That was fantastic!" he continued.

She stood at the front of a classroom during Speech practice, feet shoulder-width apart, Prose and Poetry book still poised in the air where she always held it during performances. She lowered it, officially ending her presentation.

Not many people were watching. Just Beezy, really, and a couple other Speech teammates who were more focused on homework than hearing *Catcher in the Rye* for the twentieth time. Likely biding their time before they could practice in front of Beezy.

"Okay, Taryn. I love the way you've improved the narrator's voice in the Prose portion—it really has a kick now, something unique the judges are going to pick up on. And the cadence of your second poem has really improved. Stick with that."

She shifted between her feet, her smile growing. "Thank you."

"Now, there's still some room for improvement before the state qualifier. I want you to dive deeper into that first poem—really make the audience feel it. And for the whole performance, I want you to lift your chin just a little higher—yes, like that!—and make sure you don't move your feet at all—no shifting between them."

She nodded vigorously. "Got it."

"And, Taryn? Do you want to perform at the showcase? I usually have about ten performers, and we could really use a Prose and Poetry person..."

Her smile vanished. "Wait—what? Really?"

"Yes! And invite your family."

Beezy wanted her to be a part of the showcase even though she'd never placed at a tournament? She'd have been excited to be a mere spectator.

But hells yeah, she was all in.

"Wow, okay. Sure."

His smile widened, if that was possible. "Good. Are you sticking around to practice again after everyone else goes? That'll give you time to work on the points I had."

"Yeah, I will."

She returned to the seat by her backpack, making way for the next person to practice. She pulled her phone out and tapped it to life, itching to tell someone the news. But her chats were all with fellow *Timbre!* fans, and she'd never broached into the personal with them.

Maybe Riker?

No, their text exchanges didn't operate that way, and maybe they never would. She'd texted him that morning, for the third time. Another message that she hoped would brighten his day and encourage him to go to school.

But aside from the handwritten note he'd slipped her, he hadn't replied to any of them. She'd hardly even seen him except for when he flitted in and out of Speech practice and kept to the periphery in Drama class. At least that meant he'd come to school. At least it meant he hadn't officially given up on everything.

Maybe he'd slipped her another note...

She shoved her hand into the front pocket of her backpack. Nothing.

What the hell am I doing?

She pushed her phone out of sight and grabbed her Prose and Poetry book. As her teammate began their practice, she slipped out of the room. Just like in the mornings before tournaments, she'd be better off practicing in front of the wall to hone the items Beezy mentioned.

The door closed behind her with a soft click. She looked up and down the hall, ensuring no one was around. She was alone, thank God. She positioned her feet in her stance in front of the wall, book poised in the air—

Pain reverberated through her abdomen, the shock of it prompting a gasp.

With one hand pressing into her side, she closed her eyes and took a deep breath, letting the silence in the hall surround her. Not even a solitary moment of Speech practice could help her escape this haunting illness.

Endometriosis. The pain that keeps on giving.

The pain that might lessen with a few more weeks of meds. Lessen, not disappear.

Who could she even tell about what the doctor had said? Aside from her mom and grandma, she didn't know anyone well enough to vent about her medical problems. Her Speech and Debate teammates were great, but...none of them had actually gotten close to her.

Not close enough to talk about this. Certainly not Quinn.

Certainly not Riker.

Though she'd give her left ovary to be close enough to him to open up about this. And hey, maybe removing her left ovary would get rid of most of the pain to boot.

Now there's an idea.

She opened her eyes and stared lazily at the wall in front of her. A pit formed in her stomach at the reminder of what endometriosis meant — of the risk it carried for the viability of her reproductive organs.

Okay, focus. Prose and Poetry time. You're going to kick ass at this.

What was the feedback Beezy had just given her...?

She had to get this right, had to make this the best she'd ever done — for the state qualifying tournament and for the showcase.

For herself.

She lifted her chin. When she began, she spoke in a whisper — loud enough to get the words out, quiet enough to not draw attention to anyone lurking down the hall and around the corner.

As she finished, she let her shoulders slump and the book droop at her side. Beezy would probably be impressed, or at least she hoped. She'd know soon enough.

She turned away from the wall and froze.

Down at the end of the hall, the boy who caught her attention froze as well. Riker.

Riker, with one hand in his pocket. Riker, with the ridges of his pale arms visible even from this distance.

He didn't smile, didn't speak.

He raised a hand to chest-level and waved. She returned it. Then he kept walking.

The moment he was out of sight, she exhaled. She counted to five, then five more. Then she reentered the classroom to wait for her turn to practice again.

* * * *

Taryn slid into the passenger seat of her mom's car and closed the door beside her.

"Hey," her mom said.

"Hey. I have good news!"

"Oh! So do I. You first." Her mom pulled away from the curb and the car moved along through the parking lot.

"Well, um, there's this Speech and Debate showcase coming up next weekend. Like, a performance for our families. I wasn't going to bother you with it because I didn't think you'd want to go, but now..." She cleared her throat and straightened her shoulders. "Now my coach asked me to be one of the performers!" She waited, letting the good news sink in.

Her mom nodded three times as she stared out the front windshield—less enthusiastic than Taryn had hoped, but she'd take what she could get. "Sounds good. So you just get up there and do the thing you've been doing at all the Speech and Debate tournaments?"

"Yep!" Taryn said, trying to keep pep in her voice. Trying to make this opportunity sound as awesome as it felt. "I think I'm the only person performing in my category, or at least that's how Beezy made it sound. So can you come watch? It's next Saturday in the auditorium."

"Sure, probably. I don't see why not. How long is it?"

"About nine minutes. At least, that's what I've been clocking in at."

"Ah. I meant the whole thing. The, uh, the showcase."

"Oh!" she said. More false pep. "I'm not sure. An hour and a half, maybe."

"Okay. So, my news now. I got a new job."

Taryn blinked hard at the sudden change of topic. "What? Mom, that's awesome. Where?"

"Back at the middle school in Trippe School District. I'm a special education aid!" Her mom took her eyes off the road for a fraction of a second to send a beaming smile at Taryn.

"Wow. That's great, Mom. Really."

"And you know what? Now we can move out of Grandma's house. We don't have to worry about living somewhere that's not ours."

Taryn chuckled. "I've gotten kind of used to living with Grandma, to be honest."

Her mom laughed, full and hearty. "No way. I can't live there another minute."

"Do you have a place picked out? Can I help?"

"There's an apartment available right by our old house. With a washer and dryer and everything."

Taryn's heart dropped, thudding onto the floormat. By their old house meant she'd be back in her old school district. It meant no more Fir Grove, no more Speech, no more…

Her voice caught in her throat as she squeaked out the next words. "You mean back at Trippe."

"Well, yeah. Where else?"

"But, Mom, I…I like my school. I like my Drama class and the Speech team and…" *And all the opportunities Trippe can't give me.*

"Seriously, Taryn?" Taryn winced as her mom's tone turned sharp. "I can't afford to live in this school district. You know that. We were only here temporarily."

"Can't I finish out the year, at least?"

Her mom sighed, the patience wearing thin. "That's not how it works. The bus wouldn't pick you up, and they won't let you live out of the district anyway."

"Yeah, but…" Was there even a defense for this? She'd known it was temporary all along, right? What had she expected—for her mom to magically get a high-paying job that allowed them to live in the wealthy suburbs?

An impossible fantasy. Had Taryn really thought she could stay until she graduated?

Taryn swallowed down her disgust—disgust at her circumstances, disgust at her naïvety. "When do we move?"

"In a few weeks. Right after Christmas."

If the bottom of the car had dropped out, leaving her stranded in the road, Taryn was sure it wouldn't have felt different than this.

Chapter Thirty-Two

Riker

Riker stared through the windshield on the passenger side, heart palpitating erratically against his sternum. Jaclyn's car sat idling in front of the large office building containing the Goldblarg Entertainment casting office.

He'd never been this nervous about a performance. Compared to this casting call, tonight's Speech and Debate showcase would be as easy as reading a book to an attentive dog.

"Do you want me to come in?" his sister asked.

"No, I don't think so. It probably won't take long."

"Well, text me if you need me. I'll wait out here."

He turned to look at her, his throat swelling with a mix of dread and nerves. "Thanks for the ride."

"No problem. Good luck in there."

"Thanks." He squeezed his hands into fists, then released. "See you in a bit."

Riker opened and closed the car door, then headed for the wide building. He checked the office registry sign for his destination—Goldblarg Entertainment was on the fifth floor. His heart threatened to pulsate through his chest as he stepped into the elevator and pressed "Five."

As the elevator doors closed in front of him, he let his eyes drift shut.

One, two, three, he counted to himself. *Inhale, exhale, inhale, exhale...*

Go back to being the confident asshole you are. You got this.

Ever since he'd received the invitation email from Goldblarg Entertainment, Riker had been on the fence about coming to the audition at all. Part of his brain had told him the obvious, incessantly and unforgivingly—*You'll never get this part. It's a waste of time. You might as well play* Timescale *all day instead.*

But the other part of his head, a tiny part in the background that was vying for attention within the muddled mess of Riker's consciousness, said otherwise—*This is what you've always wanted. Video game voice acting! You can't miss this chance.*

Somehow, the tiny voice had won out.

The elevator dinged. Riker opened his eyes, confidence mask at the ready as he walked down the hall toward the Goldblarg Entertainment offices.

A woman with a blue blouse greeted him from behind a desk as he entered. "Can I help you?"

"Hi, I'm Riker Lucas. I'm here for a casting call."

She checked the computer and looked back at him over the top of her round glasses, the bright blue of her eyes matching the hue of her shirt. "I'll let them know you're here. You can take a seat."

"Thanks."

Only two other people sat in the waiting room, one bouncing his knee and the other listening to earpieces with his eyes closed. Riker pulled out his phone for a distraction.

Five minutes passed before a man with a clipboard came around the corner and asked for him. Riker stood and followed him down the hall, like a patient after a nurse.

The man led him to a room no bigger than Riker's bedroom. Two men and a woman sat in folding chairs, turning to look as he entered. The man with the clipboard gestured for him to take his place in front of the tiny audience.

"This is Riker Lucas," the man with the clipboard said to the room at large. Then he left the space, closing the door behind him.

One of the men in the room, this one with a button-up dress shirt with rolled-up sleeves, cleared his throat. "All right, Mr. Lucas. We'll have you perform your monologue, and then we'll do a cold reading from a script. You can begin whenever you're ready."

Riker nodded and planted his feet firmly on the ground, shoulder-width apart, just as he did for Speech tournaments. He lowered his head, staring past his feet as he took a deep breath, followed by another.

After one more breath, he lifted his head and began speaking.

* * * *

"How did it go?" Jaclyn asked before he was even sitting in the car.

He pulled the door closed beside him. "I don't know. I probably didn't get it. The chances are so low..."

She crossed her arms over her chest. "Seriously? None of that pessimistic shit. I asked how you did."

Riker sighed as he buckled his seatbelt. "Okay, I guess. They had pretty much no expressions on their faces, so it was hard to tell. But, I mean, I did what I needed to do, and I think it sounded okay."

"Good. So when will you find out if you got it?"

"Oh." He scratched his chin. He hadn't thought to ask about that, and they hadn't volunteered the information. Would they call no matter what, or just if he got the part? "No clue."

"Well, let me know. Are you just going home now?"

"Yeah, I have like three hours before I have to go to the school. You're coming to the showcase, right?"

"I'll be there. Wouldn't miss the chance to see what the hell you actually do at all those Speech and Debate tournaments. You're not just going to stand there and debate someone, are you?"

Riker rolled his eyes. He'd hashed this out with his family members before, but he'd resigned himself to accepting they'd never remember he wasn't a debater. "No, it's an acting event."

"Sure, whatever. Is Mom giving you a ride?"

He shrugged. He'd assumed so, since his mom had said she'd watch him perform. But she wasn't exactly one-hundred-percent reliable, so there was always a chance she'd back out—always a chance she'd go off somewhere without warning, even if that had happened less and less in the past couple weeks.

"I'll let you know if she can't take me."

"Sounds good," she said as she put the car into drive.

They drove in silence for a few minutes, the office buildings of downtown quickly fading into suburbs before Jaclyn merged onto the highway. As the cement wall beside the road blurred past the car, Riker thought back to the upcoming showcase, to what it would really mean to be there.

Did he want to go? No. Did he want to perform? No. But really…

"No" wasn't the right answer for any of it. "I don't feel like it" was.

"I don't feel like" going through the motions of another performance that meant nothing. "I don't feel like" trying to catch Taryn's eye in the crowd, knowing she'd moved on.

He'd come to terms with the lack of Taryn, shitty though it might be. He'd come to terms with the intrusive thoughts churning in his brain, dragging him down, making him too difficult to date.

He would just perform at the showcase and the final tournament, then move on. After next week's state qualifier, which he'd surely not place at, that bridge would burn to the ground, and he'd never have to look back and wonder what the team was up to.

Then he'd ride out the rest of the school year in Drama class and drop it before senior year.

No more.

No more of this shit that made him unhappy.

Or will I be unhappy no matter what I do?

Why was it such a thorny question?

"Jaclyn?" he asked, still watching the concrete wall out the side window.

"Mmhm?"

"You said to let you know if I need, uh, if I need help. Like, from a doctor or a therapist or whatever."

Silence came from her side of the car. He took this as a cue to continue.

"So, I think I'm ready. To talk to someone." He turned to look at her. "Ready to stop feeling like this."

She nodded.

"I'm not really sure how to find who to go to."

"I can help you figure it out." She reached over and put her hand on his leg.

He stiffened at the touch. Not because it was bad, but because it was unusual. The Lucas family wasn't touchy-feely. The Lucas family didn't show affection.

He turned back to the window, his sister's hand still on his leg as they continued the ride in silence. He could probably get used to this. Or maybe this closeness would never happen again, and his sister wouldn't mention it. Either way, he'd deal.

His pocket buzzed, and his sister pulled her hand away, placing it back on the steering wheel. Riker reached in and pulled out his phone. He didn't recognize the number, except that it was local.

"Hello?"

"Is this Riker Lucas?"

"Yes, that's me."

"Hi, Riker. This is Bethany Luck from Goldblarg. I'm calling to follow up about your audition today."

His eyes bulged as he turned to his sister. She took her eyes off the road long enough to glance at him and raise an eyebrow in question.

"I…" He laughed into the phone. "I just left ten minutes ago."

Bethany chuckled in return. "True. Listen, we were really impressed by your audition piece and the cold reading."

He squeezed his eyes shut. Was this about to be the fastest rejection of all time? Or something way better? *There's no way...*

"So we want to offer you the role for the video game. It'll be a two-week recording session in mid-June, from nine to five. You don't have an agent, right?"

"No," he croaked. "No agent."

"That's fine, I just had to ask. Okay, since you're a minor, I'll need one of your parents to sign some paperwork, and then we can get the ball rolling on the financials. I can email you the details later today, if you're interested."

"Wow. Okay. Um." As if this needed much thought. Not to mention he'd be able to finally get the microphone he'd been pining over, though he might not even need it anymore. God, he could probably buy twenty of them. "Yes. I'm interested. Definitely yes."

"Great! So I'll send you the paperwork. Read it over and give it to one of your parents, and we'll take it from there."

"I will. Thanks so much."

"Thank *you*, Riker. We're really looking forward to working with you. Bye now."

"Bye."

He opened his eyes and lowered his phone to his lap. He looked at his sister, who returned the glance.

"I got the part."

"What!" she shouted at the road.

"I got the part!"

"Holy shit!"

"I know! Holy shit!"

Chapter Thirty-Three

Taryn

Taryn stood in the wings of the stage, her hands clutching the black book that had become a formality instead of a crutch—she'd long ago memorized every word within the pages.

You got this.

You really freaking got this.

On the stage, a spotlight lit up Beezy, outfitted in a suit and tie. He stood in front of a microphone, completely at ease in addressing the audience of friends and family.

"As a reminder," he announced, "the state qualifying tournament is next weekend, beginning on Friday during the school day and concluding Saturday evening. I'm confident in all of our competitors, and I think we have a great shot at sending several of them to the state tournament next month."

God, she could only dream. She was just happy to be here, in this moment, ready to perform her Prose and Poetry piece on an actual stage, in front of an audience who, she hoped, would clap instead of staring at her blankly like the other competitors did.

Even after the dozens of performances — for judges, for Beezy, for Drama class — she'd never once stood in the wings of the stage, never had a literal spotlight on her.

A bittersweet denouement to the end of her time at Fir Grove. Before she returned to her old school, with no Drama class and no Speech team. With only her *Timbre!* episodes and fan account to remind her of how much she loved performing.

"And now, without further ado," Beezy continued, "our first performer this evening is the remarkable Ms. Taryn Platt, who competes in our Oral Interpretation category, which we like to call 'Prose and Poetry.' This is her first year on the team, and she's made incredible progress since she first dipped her toes in at a Speech and Debate meeting." He looked toward the wings, directly at her, his characteristic smile crossing his face and his arm stretched toward her. "Taryn, the stage is yours!"

She tightened her fingers around her book as she stepped from the wings and onto the stage. The audience clapped politely as she took her position and Beezy adjusted the microphone down to match her height. The spotlight seared into her eyes, blocking the audience from view. Though she couldn't see them, she knew her mom and grandma were nestled in the middle of the third row.

As Beezy retreated to the wings, Taryn planted her feet firmly, shoulder-width apart — the base position that she'd drawn comfort from since Beezy had first taught it to her at Speech practice. Looking down at her feet, she counted to three. Then she raised her head, opened her black book with the crispness she'd perfected and began.

* * * *

As Taryn held her bowed-head pose at the end of her performance, the audience's clapping was more than polite. It was enthusiastic, encouraging, excited.

It was for her.

She forced herself to smile at the audience, to keep her cool instead of withdrawing to her awkward place. She held the smile for two seconds before turning and retreating to the wings.

One of her teammates — what was his name? God, she was bad at names — raised his hand in a high-five as soon as she was in the black curtains and out of view of the audience. She returned the high-five with a smile, careful to not make a sound with her mouth or her hand. With his other hand, her teammate held a rolled-up program in front of her and mouthed, "You want this?"

She mouthed, "Sure," and took it from him, unrolling it.

When she turned back to face the stage, Beezy was already there, introducing the next performer before raising the microphone and exiting stage right. The pulse in Taryn's neck thumped like a bass drum, but it didn't matter anymore. Her leg of the show was over, and now all she had to do was enjoy the other performers.

The high-fiver crossed the stage then, leaving Taryn to herself in the stage-left wings. Beezy had told her in advance she could watch from the sidelines, or she could take the hallway around to the back of the auditorium to watch from there. For now, she waited and flipped to the second page of the program.

Her name and event were second from the top, just below "Thomas Banley-Zimmerman — Introduction." Under her own name was the name of the current performer. "Harvey Kingsley — Declamation."

Harvey. Wow. How had she missed a name like that?

She looked down the program to the next performer. "Riker Lucas — Humorous Interpretation." That was followed by "Gavin Varns — Dramatic Interpretation."

If Riker was next, that would mean...

She turned around, half expecting him to be waiting in the wings behind her. But no, the space around her was vacant. She looked across the stage, past Harvey and his choreographed gestures.

And there —

Riker stood directly across from her, his hands clasped in front of his thighs, feet shoulder-width apart as if the performer's stance came naturally to him.

Was he watching her or Harvey?

He raised one hand in a small wave. An acknowledgment that he'd seen her, acknowledgment that he knew she had seen him.

She waved back, a small flick of the wrist.

A somber smile flitted across his face before he turned and whispered something to Gavin, who Taryn now saw stood beside him. She returned to the program in her hand, scanning the list of performers and finding Quinn farther down the list. She flipped to the next page.

Instead of more performers, it contained the first set of ads — the same ones she and her teammates had been tasked with obtaining as part of their dues. Except Grandma had given her an unexpected cop-out by writing a check.

Taryn turned the page and froze.

A full-page ad stared back at her, the business's name in a familiar loopy script — Violette's.

Below that, their slogan, "Bringing people together, one French fry at a time." And finally, at the bottom, "Rated top LGBTQ-owned and -operated restaurant!"

Her stomach flipped. No, not just a flip — her stomach did a double back tuck with an imperfect landing.

Violette's. The place she'd forever associate with Riker's intense blue eyes and gleaming smile. The precursor to a night of barely touching through the *Timbre!* movie.

Anyone on the team might've procured this ad. But for some reason, her intuition said it was Riker.

Was he trying to tell her something?

She looked up to see if he was watching her, but she came face to face with Harvey, walking across the stage toward her as the audience applauded, his performance finished. He reached up a hand to wipe the sweat from his brow.

"Good job," she mouthed at him, careful to not make noise.

He mouthed "Thank you" in return before stopping beside her and turning back to the stage to watch from the wings.

Beezy was back in front of the microphone, addressing the audience. "Thank you, Harvey, that was wonderful! Our next performer has been consistently placing in the top six this season, and last year he got tenth place at the state tournament. Please welcome our master of Humorous Interpretation, Riker Lucas!"

The crowd applauded as Beezy and Riker crossed paths on the stage. Riker caught Taryn's eye, holding it for three beats as he walked toward the microphone between them. Her chest constricted as she returned the gaze, as she pondered what this meant.

When he reached the microphone, he turned to face the audience instead. His feet settled into the typical base position, and he held it, head dipped down, for two seconds before beginning.

From this vantage point, Riker was a gleaming statue of perfection. Even with the sharp elbows. Especially with the sharp elbows.

And she might as well look now, because she wouldn't have the chance later. After leaving this school, she'd probably never see him again, never watch him on a stage again. Which was unfortunate, because *God*, he was striking, and the voices he came up with sent shivers across her arms.

She'd miss him.

But.

But maybe it was for the best. Even if she stayed, she'd never get the chance she wanted with Riker. He was always off in his own world, far from her. And her disease — that godforsaken chronic illness — would just continue driving a wedge between herself and everything she wanted.

Still, it had been a great year, or part of a year. She'd joined a great team, bonded with them even if only at surface-level. She'd felt more at home with this Speech and Debate team than she'd felt with her followers — an experience she hadn't anticipated.

After this showcase, she'd have one tournament left with them — two in the unlikely event she'd make it to State. Tonight was the final hoorah before they all buckled down for the state qualifier tournament. And while she should have wanted to celebrate with all of them, to throw her metaphorical hat up in the air like they'd graduated, all she wanted to do was hide.

Hide in the darkness of the stage wings. Hide from any possibility of getting closer to these people she'd soon leave. Hide herself from getting in Mom's car and going home — then going to a new home.

But first, she'd let Riker's performance lull her into a happy calm that little else in her life could provide.

Chapter Thirty-Four

Riker

If he'd had perhaps ten times more bravery than usual, Riker would've recorded Taryn. That way, he could've watched and rewatched the look on her face when she'd studied the Violette's ad in the showcase program.

Instead, his memory would have to do. And not gonna lie, that look on her face was imprinted pretty well. He knew exactly what would be running through his head tonight.

If only he could feed himself with this type of joy all day, every day. If only this fuel could prevent him from crashing back into hopelessness and despair.

Maybe this was the sign he needed — the indicator that they were finally ready to take the plunge. Her expression had to be proof that she liked him, right? Inasmuch as someone *could* like him.

He looked up from his seat in the back of the auditorium, where he'd slipped in after his performance to watch the rest of the show. The performances now over, his teammates and their family members congregated several rows ahead of him, their conversations fluttering in and out of earshot. Jaclyn, Clarice and his mom were among them, talking to each other without the presence of the guy they'd come to see.

He'd make his way up to them — he would. He'd bask in their attendance, thank them for showing up on his behalf. But not yet. Right now, this whole atmosphere felt like another night alone, only this time he was surrounded by people.

He needed the silence he'd grown used to. Even if just for a moment. Could it be so simple? Could he really slip out with no one noticing or stopping him?

Riker stood, then exited through the back door of the auditorium. He turned a corner to get to the side hallway.

His shoes padded softly on the tile of the empty hall. If anyone else were already headed toward their cars, this wasn't likely to be part of their path. Ten steps forward would find him at Beezy's office. Twenty steps past that and he'd arrive at the classroom where Beezy made him practice his Speech piece once a week.

And in between the two locations was the side auditorium door.

The door opened at his touch without a peep. He slipped inside.

The backstage area was mere feet from where he'd just performed, and, with the stage lights now off, light of any kind hardly reached the space. The muffled voices from the auditorium drifted toward him, innumerable and indistinguishable.

That's better.

He rested his forehead against the wall and closed his eyes. He couldn't stay here forever — they'd shut the place down by the end of the night, not to mention his mom and two sisters would be waiting — but for now he was afforded this moment of solitude.

For now, the only person listening to his heavy breaths was him.

"Hey."

He startled, pulling his forehead away from the wall. Standing three feet away, in all her glory, was Taryn, her back against the wall. There was no way she'd just arrived. She must've been there the whole time, on the edge of darkness. He would've had to pass her on his way in.

"Hey. Hi."

She pressed her shoulders into the wall as her chest inflated. "I just...I needed a moment alone."

"So did I. Too much going on out there."

"Exactly. The silence is..." She detached her back from the wall and stepped forward. "It's nice."

Holy hell, he'd finally found a moment alone with her. And of all possible places, they were alone in the almost-dark, with no one in earshot. No wandering eyes. He would forgo a silent moment if it meant privacy with her.

He couldn't have dreamed it this way.

His hands itched at his sides. He could fantasize all he wanted, but now that the moment was here, boldness was impossible.

"Did you have anything to do with that ad in the program?" she asked.

He didn't have to question what she meant. There was only one ad she'd ask about, and of course he had something to do with it.

"Mmhm" was all he could muster.

Hot damn, Taryn's presence was the incarnation of fate itself. Except he was too much of a scaredy cat to do anything about it. Maybe he'd misinterpreted how she really felt about the ad. Hell, he'd probably overstepped. Hadn't she said she wanted to be alone right now?

Shit.

"I should get back out there," he said.

"Oh. Sure."

"Can I…can I get through?" He'd slipped past her already, but now that he knew she was there, the quarters were too tight to walk by again without asking.

Taryn nodded then pressed her back against the wall to let him pass. He turned sideways and looked downward to squeeze by, sucking in his stomach, sure she'd hear his unstable heartbeat if he attempted a breath.

Not a single hair on his body grazed her — success. Then he was past, no longer at risk of inadvertent touching, regardless of how much he'd dreamed of it.

"Riker," she croaked.

He froze. He angled his shoulder toward her.

In the silence of the wings, he heard three breaths escape her lips. How could she possibly breathe at a moment like this? His chest tightened from the tension — thick and heavy in the dimly lit space around them.

"Taryn."

His eyes lifted up, up, up as his head turned back toward her. Had he even said her name out loud? It had come out so quiet, so soft, he couldn't be sure.

She flattened her palms against the wall.

He caught her gaze before looking away, quickly.

Stop it. Look at her.

He looked back to her at the same moment she reached a hand toward him. She stared unblinking as her fingers found his closest hand and clutched it.

Riker's heart faltered.

He curled his fingers around hers. Then he took two steps, squeezing into the space in front of her. The two inches between their bodies was somehow both an ocean and a thread.

Taryn's breaths were short, butchered with an invisible saber. Her eyelids fluttered as she held eye contact, her pupils dilated, wide-eyed desire emblazoned in them.

Neither said a word. Good thing, because Riker's heart would have exploded out of his chest like confetti if he'd heard her voice in this moment. Especially if she said his name again with that breaking rasp.

He angled his chin down and touched his lips to Taryn's as she gasped.

Though her lips shuddered, she pressed back firmly. Her fingers tightened around his, fingernails threatening to leave creases in his skin.

The world spun around him — around *them* — as Riker lost himself in the kiss.

Just like last time. Hopefully just like next time.

When he pulled away from her lips, he touched his cheek against hers and exhaled into her hair. Her chest heaved against his so hard that his heart rushed to sync up with the beat of hers. Riker snaked his arms around her waist, his palms finding hold on her lower back. A minute passed in silence.

Too many words floated around his mind, accompanied with too many directions from his brain. Anyone else would've told Taryn they liked her. He should've told her how long he'd wished for this, how happy he was that they'd finally found themselves in this position, in the perfect place at the perfect time. He should've pulled back just far enough to kiss her again, to learn everything about her that he'd always imagined knowing.

But no words came out, and not a single muscle moved. He'd stress over all this later, but for now it was enough to just be with Taryn.

It was enough to feel her so close.

She squeezed his fingers, an indicator she was still conscious of what was happening between them. He wasn't sure what her other hand was up to, though he didn't feel it anywhere on him.

Then he remembered, there was something he wanted to share with her over anyone else. Amid the excitement of being with Taryn, he had something else to be excited about, too.

"Taryn, I have to tell you," he spoke softly into her hair.

"Yeah?"

"I said before that I wanted to do voice acting. That I really wanted to get into—"

"Video games," she finished for him.

He pulled away to look at her. "Yes! Video games. So this morning I went to a casting call for a video game voiceover. It's going to be two whole weeks of work this summer."

She blinked twice. "When will you find out if you got the part?"

A smile crept to his lips, overtaking all the muscles in his jaw and cheeks. "Well, that's the thing. They already called me back. I got it!"

"What!" she said, her voice still low, keeping with the ambiance of the wings. "That's amazing."

"Thanks." God, it felt so good to just tell her. To be excited about it with someone other than his sister.

To share the news that he'd finally made strides toward his goal.

And hopefully this backstage interaction meant he was making strides toward Taryn, too. He moved forward again, putting the side of his face against hers.

Taryn touched their temples together. She cleared her throat. "Riker. I..."

He sucked in a breath, anxious to hear where she would take this.

"I didn't go to the overnight tournament because I couldn't get out of bed. I couldn't do anything."

He nudged his nose against her thick hair, unsure how to respond. Was she referring to depression, like him?

She continued. "And it's the same reason I stopped kissing you in Beezy's office. Not because I didn't want to kiss you, but because I couldn't handle all the pain."

"Pain?" he said into her ear, softly. This he'd seen, the way her face sometimes blanched, the way she sometimes froze with her body tensed. He felt her head nod against his.

"My..." She cleared her throat again. "My ovaries. There's a lot of crap going on with them, and sometimes they hurt too much to function. But it's...it's getting a little better."

He pulled away from her hair to face her. Her eyes glistened in the dim lighting, brimming with tears that hadn't spilled over the lashes. Her words made so much sense, in a way he couldn't define. "What can I do?"

She shook her head. "Nothing. I just wanted you to know. I wanted to explain why."

"I wish I'd known. Maybe I could've helped."

Taryn blinked. A tear eked its way out. "That's the thing, though. No one could've helped. There's no cure or anything."

"Then I wish I could've just sat next to you through it. You could've grabbed my hand till it broke and I wouldn't care." He lifted a hand to swipe away her tear with the pad of his thumb. "That's something else we have in common — not being able to get out of bed."

She chuckled, gravelly and weighted. "That's a pretty crappy thing to have in common. Both of us liking girls is a lot more noteworthy."

"So what? We both know what being stuck in bed feels like. Except you're in pain and I…well, my mind stops me from getting up. Like it's this heavy blanket that's either weighing me down or hovering nearby. And it was stopping me from talking to you, but I'm working on it. I'm trying. Those morning texts mean everything to me right now."

A second tear spilled down her cheek, then a third. She blinked three times, but all it did was prompt more tears. He swiped them from her cheeks one at a time.

"It's okay," he said. "We can work through this. Together."

"I'm leaving," she choked out.

A lump the size of Cincinnati welled up in his throat. "What do you mean?"

Taryn pulled her fingers from Riker's and cleared her throat. "I mean, I'm leaving Fir Grove. I'm moving over winter break."

"What?" His eyes flickered up to hers. Strain marks creased her forehead.

"I'm sorry," she continued. "I wish...I wish we could work through all that together. I don't want to leave."

The lump in his throat enlarged. Thankfully, not enough that he couldn't talk. Five minutes ago, words were impossible. Now, there was no time to waste.

"Where are you going?"

"Back to Trippe."

"That's not too far. We could...we could work something out." Except she wouldn't be in Drama anymore, and she wouldn't be in Speech. She wouldn't be the light waiting for him at school.

He gave her a weak smile, though his heart was being crushed by the weight of an elephant. If he hadn't wasted so much time inching up to her over the past few months, they could've moved past the tiptoeing ages ago.

They could have had so much more.

And now they would have nothing except the memory of two world-shattering kisses.

Chapter Thirty-Five

Taryn

The auditorium seat under Taryn was scratchy, even through her dress pants. She'd already competed for the judges at the state qualifying Speech and Debate tournament. Now the only thing left to do was sit through the closing ceremony.

Then the entire season would be over. All of Speech would be over for her. Winter break was just around the corner, and after Christmas she and her mom would pack up and leave Grandma's house.

A man in a suit stood at the microphone on the stage, going on about what qualified a competitor for the state tournament. She'd heard it all from Beezy in advance, already knew she'd have to make the top five to qualify for State in the Oral Interpretation category, based on the number of competitors. An impossible feat after not placing in the top six all year.

Beside her, Riker sat with one leg crossed over the other, his lanky limbs appearing especially long in his dark-blue dress pants. His right hand lay on the armrest, palm down, the pinky hanging over the edge on Taryn's side. Her own hand was palm-up on her left thigh, clutching his pinky between her thumb and forefinger.

It hadn't taken them hours to get to this point. There'd been no buildup at all. As soon as they'd entered the auditorium after lunch, they'd sat down next to each other. His arm had immediately gone for the armrest. Her hand had reached right up to his. No question about whether she should, no internal debate about whether he wanted her to.

And they'd stayed like that.

She side-eyed their hands with her face still toward the man on the stage. The mere image of their fingers touching sent a thrill through her heart—his thin, pale finger clutched between her own tan ones.

"And now," said the man, "it's time to announce the state qualifiers in our first event—Original Oratory."

Taryn looked down the row to Quinn, who looked perfectly kempt in her burgundy blazer and pinned-back hair. Original Oratory was her event, and this was the first year she'd done it. Taryn knew how hard Quinn had practiced this year, knew how badly Quinn wanted to go to State. As she'd only placed a couple times throughout the season, though, her chances were up in the air.

"In sixth place, and our runner-up for the state tournament, is Declan Cassidy, from Dyson High School."

Taryn removed her hand from Riker's to applaud. Down the row, Quinn stood, the customary thing to do in honor of all people placing in her event. The sixth-place winner made his way to the stage, where he accepted a small trophy before taking his position at the edge of the stage.

"In fifth place, and going to the state qualifying tournament, is…"

The announcer did not call Quinn's name. Taryn looked down the row at her, could see the tension etched across her forehead.

The next name called wasn't Quinn's either. Nor was the next.

As the announcer called the second-place name, and as the entire audience stood to clap for the first-place winner, Quinn's name was left out.

Taryn had come to terms with not being a good match for Quinn, but she had no reason to wish ill upon her. She was certain that this would crush Quinn. With everyone now standing, it was impossible to get a look at Quinn's face, but Taryn was sure it hinted at disappointment and dejection — only hinted, though, as Quinn didn't wear her emotions on her sleeve.

Taryn sat down as the clapping faded, a lurch in her gut indicating she, too, was blue that Quinn hadn't placed after trying so hard. But so it went when the competition was this fierce. There had to be at least eighty people in Quinn's event, similar to Taryn's.

Riker reached over the armrest and grabbed Taryn's hand, lacing their fingers together. Her eyes drifted closed, just for a moment, as she relaxed into the touch of his palm against hers.

"Congratulations to you all," the announcer said, swinging his arm wide as if to present the six competitors on stage. Everyone around them clapped again, though Taryn kept her hand where it was. Right where it felt good.

The state qualifiers made their way off the stage as the applause faded. By the microphone, the man in the suit picked up another envelope from a nearby table and opened it.

"Our next category is Humorous Interpretation."

Riker's arm tensed. She squeezed his hand, hoping to send waves of silent encouragement.

"Only the top four in this category will go to the state tournament, so we will announce the top five. If I call your name, please come to the stage." The man cleared his throat. "The fifth-place winner, and the runner-up for the state tournament, is Beatrice Montgomery, from Pleasant View High School."

More applause. Riker pulled his hand from Taryn's so he could stand and clap for the runner-up in his event. He remained standing as they waited for the next name.

"In fourth place, and going to the state tournament, Olivia Whitmore."

Taryn couldn't bear to watch the competitor make her way to the stage and accept her small trophy. Instead, her eyes were locked on Riker's thighs as she kept her head bowed. She hoped beyond all hope that Riker's name would be among the next three winners.

"In third place…"

Taryn scrunched her eyes closed and waited for it.

"Frankie Adams, from Fir Grove High School."

Oh! Taryn opened her eyes and sprung out of her seat to clap as her teammate sidled past her to get out of their row. The tension had made Taryn forget about all her other teammates in this event. Frankie climbed the steps to the stage, accepting her trophy before joining the other two competitors.

Taryn sat back down. Her heart pounded as the announcer read another name that wasn't Riker's.

Which left only one spot.

Her face fell. What were the chances Riker would get first place? Not amazing, with so many competitors. He was really good, almost always placing, but he hadn't gotten first all season.

"...Riker Lucas, from Fir Grove High School!"

Her eyes widened. Around her, their teammates jumped to their feet, hooting and clapping. Taryn looked up to find Riker grinning down at her, his cheekbones high enough to reach the moon. She returned the smile as she stood, joining her teammates with a well-deserved cheer. Riker sidestepped out of the row and made his way down the aisle toward the stage.

He'd done it! He'd really freaking done it! The season might be over for her, but the indomitable Riker Lucas still had a state tournament to kick ass at.

Riker lifted his chin high as he accepted his trophy. She hadn't seen this level of confidence in him since he'd performed that monologue in Drama class.

It felt like a lifetime ago.

She beamed at Riker as he returned to his seat, clutching the base of his trophy in one fist.

"You rock," she said, her smile failing to go away.

"Thanks." He ducked his head, but she could still see the raised cheekbones threatening to fly off his face. Without looking her in the eye, he reached for her hand and pulled it into his lap.

The man in the suit cleared his throat at the microphone. "Our next category is Oral Interpretation.

We'll announce the top six, with the top five qualifying for the state tournament."

Taryn sat up straight. She was prepared to stand, to cheer on whoever made it to the stage in her Prose and Poetry event.

Her hand continued to grip Riker's. No way was she letting go until the last possible second. Not when she could finally touch him without hesitation.

"Our sixth-place competitor, and the runner-up for the state tournament, is...Taryn Platt, from Fir Grove High School."

Her grip tightened. Did they just...?

They did. They called your name. Get your ass up to the stage.

Riker stood and pulled her up with him by the hand. The other teammates in their row and in the row in front of them stood as well, all looking at her, all clapping for her.

For me.

Riker pulled his hand from hers and stepped back against his seat so she could pass him and reach the aisle. She sidestepped, acutely aware of all the eyes on her.

She hadn't made it to the stage all season. All she'd hoped for today were better scores than the previous tournament. And now...

Now she was a runner-up for the state tournament. Now all eyes were on her for once.

Reflex told her to stare at her feet. Logic reminded her to hold her head high, to put her shoulders back and proceed up the aisle. Her strides were so long she felt like she was running to the stage, running to accept an award she never expected.

Discomfort shot through her side as her foot stepped down, then more with the next foot. Weeks ago, this discomfort would have been full-blown pain—impossible-to-move pain. Not anymore. Not with her hormone medication finally kicking in, finally keeping the endometriosis at bay, even if it couldn't cure it.

Keeping it at bay for moments like this, when keeling over in pain was just not an option.

She slowed when she reached the steps, taking them one at a time, careful to not trip up them and ruin her one and only moment on an awards stage. When she reached the top, a second man handed her a small bronze trophy with a curved line of stars on top.

Her heart soared.

The man directed her to the edge of the stage, where she stood and waited for the state qualifiers to stand beside her. If any of them couldn't make it to State, she'd be tasked with taking their place. Unlikely to happen, but…holy shit, the idea of it!

Except I won't even be here. After winter break I'll be back at Trippe, not even a student at Fir Grove.

She shoved that thought down, down, down. She'd figure that out later, if it came to it.

For now, she was on a freaking stage with a freaking Speech trophy.

She'd wish for it no other way.

* * * *

Someone was sitting at the foot of her bed.

Taryn blinked her eyes open, her lids still heavy with sleep.

"Mom?" she groaned.

"It's me," her mom replied, voice appropriately subdued for so early on a Monday morning.

Taryn rubbed her eyes with the heel of her hand and used her other elbow to help her sit up. "What's wrong?" *And please don't tell me you're pulling me out of Fir Grove a few days early.*

"Oh, nothing." Her mom crossed one leg over the other. "I wanted to talk to you about something before you go to school."

"And it had to be…" Taryn yawned. "Now?"

Her mom shrugged. "I want to know what you think about staying with Grandma some of the time, a few days a week."

"You mean after we move out?"

"Yeah."

This line of questioning did not seem worthy for a Monday morning. Taryn reached to the bedside table and grabbed her phone to check the time. Only ten minutes before her alarm would go off.

"That sounds okay, I guess. It would be a lot of driving, though."

"It would. But if you're here enough, we can keep using Grandma's house as your address. That way, you could stay at Fir Grove until you graduate."

Taryn sat bolt upright, no elbow-leaning needed. "What? Are you serious?"

"I already talked it over with your grandma. She says it's fine if the bus keeps dropping you off here after school, and some days I'll pick you up instead. We'll sort it out."

"Yes. Yes, I want that."

"Yeah? We were thinking it'd be good for you to stay in your classes, and you seem to really like the Speech team."

"Yes! I'm in!"

Her mom patted the comforter beside her. "Good, then it's all set."

Taryn collapsed back onto the bed as her mom left the room.

I get to stay! I get to stay I get to stay I get to stay!

Her pulse quickened as she stared at the ceiling, taking it all in. There was so much she still wanted to do, so much she still wanted to say to Riker. About her goals, about her pain, about her fears for the future. And now she could tell it all, could embrace every moment with him.

I don't have to leave!

She grabbed her phone and held it in the air above her face. Her thumbs typed rapidly before she hit "Send."

Taryn: Time to wake up! Turns out I'll be in your hair all the way to graduation, so I hope you're looking forward to one of these texts every school day from now to next May.

Want to see more like this?
Here's a taster for you to enjoy!

Finding Aloha
Jennifer Walker

Excerpt

The garlic from Dad's Caesar salad clings to my breath and burns my eyes as I hide away under this stifling blanket.

Crap. I should've brushed my teeth. *Why didn't I think about brushing my teeth?*

I rack my brain trying to remember where I might have put a pack of gum or a Tic Tac, or God, even one of those disgusting cough drops. But my mind comes up blank.

My chest burns, forcing me to do some of those short, panicky breaths dogs do when they first show up at the vet. It's been forever since I've taken a fresh breath of air. All I want to do is toss these suffocating blankets off me and smooth the frizzy mane my hair has become. But I'm paralyzed, terrified someone will barge in without knocking and my nightly rendezvous with Marcus won't be able to continue.

In one desperate move, I pop my face out of the covers and gulp in air like it's water from an oasis.

Sweet, sweet oxygen!

My brain starts functioning again and has a chance to fantasize about what's about to take place. How thrilling it's going to be to see his face again...to kiss those lips, press my body against his. The deceit... The sneaking out... I'm not going to lie. It makes this all feel so...so...*badass*. And lately, well lately, I've enjoyed a bit of badass.

As if he knows right this second that I'm thinking about him, there's a buzz in the pocket of my jeans, and it sends a deeper buzz through the rest of my body.

Without rustling the covers, I carefully slide my hand under my butt and pry my phone out without allowing my bed to creak and groan. The screen lights up and buzzes again, making me smile with what's written. It's from Marcus.

You coming? I'm already here. Can't wait to see you. Brought a little treat for us too.

He sends an emoji of two people kissing, followed by a leaf emoji. Meaning he's brought a joint, but I giggle because it looks like he's brought us a salad. *Is there a weed emoji?* Probably better he didn't use that anyway, just in case Mom and Dad ever creep on my phone. No one can get in trouble for sneaking out to eat a salad.

I expertly navigate the screen with my thumb as I text him back underneath the covers.

Yeah, I think they're both asleep. Coming now. Can't wait to see you too – and eat salad with you lol.

In one swift movement, I throw the covers off and roll over to sit up. As I stand, I reach around to return my phone to the back pocket of my jeans, but it slips through my hand and lands with a crash on the hardwood floor.

Shit.

I'm not sure whether it's loud enough for my parents to hear. I still my body and hold my breath one more time, listening for any sign of footsteps through the hall.

I'm sleepwalking. That's what I'll tell them. *Yeah, if they ask, I'll just mumble something incoherent about algebra, then wander back to bed, pretending not to remember in the morning.* I might have a tough time explaining why I'm sleeping in jeans and a T-shirt, but whatever. It's not like I can get in trouble for sleepwalking. I mean, how could I get in trouble for something I don't even remember?

I wait for a few more seconds, then exhale a slow and relieved breath, because all is silent other than the faint *sh...sh...sh...*of my dad's CPAP machine in the other room. *Alleluia for sleep apnea!* It has made this whole sneaking out thing way easier. The only downside is that Mom has recently made the spare bedroom on the main floor her own personal refuge. She claimed Dad was just too noisy to sleep beside, which was weird at first. He used to snore louder than a train whistle before the machine, and she didn't seem to have a problem with it then.

But when I started questioning why they were sleeping in separate rooms, it got me thinking about Tamara Lindsay. Poor Tamara Lindsay, who accidentally walked in on her parents in a very compromising position—*position number 69* if we want to get real about it. And now Tamara is damaged for life. Seriously. The details Tamara gave? No one needs to see their parents doing that.

So, I figured *whatever*. If Mom and Dad no longer want to sleep together, it just means that at least I won't ever have to worry about walking in on things Moms and Dads should *not* be allowed to do. What it does mean is that I have to be a little more careful about creeping past Mom's bedroom downstairs.

I crane my head toward my bedroom door and don't hear any footsteps coming up the stairs. I'm positive Mom is asleep by now.

I peer at the clock as I reach down to retrieve my phone.

Twelve-fourteen a.m.

Yeah, they've both got to be asleep for sure.

My jacket is draped over one arm, and I hold my pair of red Converse with my other hand as I inch my way across my room. I open the door soundlessly, grateful that I convinced Dad to fix the creak in it last weekend. After a quick glance across the hall and into the front room, I gently close the door behind me and tiptoe all the way down the stairs, making sure to skip the step third from the bottom because of the groan it makes. My heart gallops like a racehorse the whole way. I'm convinced Mom and Dad are going to barge out of their rooms any second to pounce on me.

But somehow I slide past Mom's bedroom without incident and make it to the back patio door. I don't dare creep out through the garage or the front door. That would basically be suicide. But the patio door is quiet, discreet and leads to a perfect escape route just left of the house. There's a large pine tree there, wedged between the fence and the shed. It creates cover and forms a darkened shadow, despite the glare of the porch light that is always left on. All I need to do is inch my way down the length of the shadow, all the way to the far corner of the yard. The fence is old and needs to be rebuilt, and sharp slivers dig into my bare arms as I slide along it. But I'm eternally thankful for my parents' procrastination in fixing it so my nightly escapades can continue.

Once I reach the end of the yard, I pry loose the third board from the left, the one I wedged back in last night. I lean it against the neighboring boards and squeeze myself through the ten-inch gap in the fence.

Crap, my T-shirt snags on a rough edge of wood as I squeeze through, and I swear under my breath. I just paid full price for it at H&M. *Oh well, this is worth it — totally worth it.*

The entire world belongs to me as I race through the back alley, the glow of streetlights chasing me as I run. There's a crispness in the air — a sure sign of autumn's impending arrival — but that's not the reason for the outbreak of goosebumps all over my arms. Every inch of my skin tingles, and my heart races from exertion and anticipation. I don't slow until I reach the chain link fence enclosing the park of the elementary school down the street.

It's here that I slow to a walk, because, well, it's not like I want *him* thinking I'm this excited. *No, I've got to play it cool.* I let my breathing slow, slip my jacket on as an attempt at camouflaging all those goosebumps and make my way through the gate of the playground.

He sways gently on the tire swing, a beautiful human pendulum with ripped jeans and scruffy blond hair. His sneakers brush the sand with each pass and the chain croaks with his weight. He doesn't see me. He doesn't sense that I'm there. And I love the element of surprise, my growing sense of urgency. I quicken to a run the last few steps, kicking sand up as I go. I reach my arms around him from behind, his delicious boy-smell filling my nostrils as I press my face into his neck.

"Guess who?" I whisper into his ear.

"I hope it's who I think it is or this is gonna be super-awkward." He doesn't turn as he says it, causing me to doubt my confidence just a bit. Then he reaches around smoothly, pulling me onto his lap and swiveling me around so our faces are just inches apart. "Oh, good, just the person I was hoping it would be." And that mischievous smile of his is irresistible once again. I can't help but reach up to pull his lips down to mine, our bodies a jumble of arms and legs jutting from the hanging tire.

Eventually, we untangle our entwined bodies and trade the tire swing for a picnic table. We stretch out and light a joint, the glowing embers twinkling like one of the distant stars hanging in the night sky.

"I remember when I first saw you at the mall that day, at the beginning of summer. You were all shy and quiet, like you didn't even want to be noticed. How could you ever think you'd just blend in?" He nudges my shoulder playfully as he takes a long toke, then passes the joint to me.

I inhale deeply, then roll over onto my back, tilting my face up to the black, velvety canopy of sky. "I don't know, Marcus. I just thought you were into Maggie. Everyone is—and that's fine by me. I mean, she's my best friend for a reason. It's because she's awesome. If I were into girls, I think I'd be after Maggie too." I giggle and pass the joint back to him.

"Yeah, Maggie's great, but...I don't know. You were the one who caught my attention. It's like you don't need to try so hard, like you have a quiet confidence that she doesn't. Not everything needs to revolve around you all the time. What you show the world is the real you. And I, for one, really like it." Marcus leans over to give me a soft kiss on the lips.

"I just can't believe we've only been together for a little over a month. I never thought when I saw you that day, that it would actually turn into something. You were all—I don't know—cute and cool... It just sucks we don't go to the same school. I mean, what's going to happen in a couple of weeks when school starts? How are we going to keep this going?"

"Trust me. We'll find a way..." The words drip off his tongue, slow and sticky like honey, and he leans in to start nibbling my neck. He drapes his right leg over mine and scoots in closer, so our bodies are flush. Then he inches his fingers just under the hem of my T-shirt, so his palm lies flat on my stomach. It sends an electric buzz through my entire body, but nagging thoughts in the back of my mind dull the feeling.

"But seriously, what's our plan? It's our senior year. I'll be super-swamped with the swim club, and you said you're hoping to be captain of your school's hockey team this year. Plus, my parents are totally going to be on top of me when it comes to my grades. They're really pushing for me to get into a good college. I don't know... I just worry that we're going to fizzle out, that this is just a *summer* thing." The word 'summer' comes out sharp and thorny, scratching the back of my throat.

"Relax, Jess. Things have a way of working out. Let's just enjoy the time we have together now and think about the future tomorrow." He continues his trail of kisses, his fingers creeping up to my ribcage. "This has been the best part of summer, and summer's not over yet."

My skin melts wherever his fingers touch, turning me into a swirling palette of watercolor, the tones becoming more vibrant with each of his breaths on my neck, each of his kisses on my lips. I push the nagging feeling of summer's end to the back of my mind and enjoy the pleasures of right now.

Eventually I nudge Marcus away, realizing I've been gone way too long. Sneaking back into the house is always the worst part of the night, and the closer we are to morning, the more likely it is my parents will wake up with the tiniest of noises. Dealing with an intense grilling session about my whereabouts is not how I want this night to end.

"So, I'll see you this week sometime? Maybe you can come by when my parents are at work?" I ask.

"Uh, yeah, sure. Sounds good. I've got nothing going on this week." The indifference in his words stings. He obviously doesn't feel my same sense of urgency. He tugs on his sweatshirt, then tilts his face down to give me one more quick kiss on the mouth. "I know how you get all up in your head about stuff, but let's just try to enjoy the end of the summer, okay? We'll worry about the rest when we need to."

I give him a slight nod and a weak smile, but I don't feel his confidence. The uncertainty of the changing seasons sparks an uncertainty about us. The phrase 'summer fling' flits around in my brain like a frightened sparrow, and I can't seem to catch it and tuck it away.

"Okay, so I'll text you later in the week then." He squeezes my hand as he takes a step backward. "I promise, things will work out. Stop stressing!" he calls, readjusting his cap and shuffling back the opposite way through the field. I feel a stab of hurt about the casualness of his goodbye, but I force my mind to replay every delicious moment prior to that, until the tingling in my body convinces me all's right with the world.

My solo walks home after my secret rendezvous with Marcus always have me feeling giddy and lightheaded, but today's race home feels extra wobbly, due to the slight buzz I got from the joint. I'm lost in my thoughts as I slide the patio door open and have almost made it past the kitchen island when my name slices through the silence.

"Jess, sit down. We need to talk."

Crap, crap, crap! I glance at the clock on the microwave.

Two forty-three a.m.

My brain races through a thousand lies I could come up with to try to squirm out of this situation.

"Uh, sorry, Mom. I had a coffee after dinner last night and I think it caused insomnia. I thought taking a walk in the brisk air might help me to fall back—"

"No, Jess, this isn't about you out in the middle of the night, although we'll get to that. I've had insomnia myself over the last little while, and I just can't take it anymore. I know this isn't the best time for either of us to talk, but I'm not sure I'll have the same confidence if I wait until morning."

I avoid Mom's heavy gaze and brace myself for the lecture of a lifetime. But it doesn't come.

"Jess, please sit down." Her words come out soft and hesitant, almost apologetic.

I double-check the time on the clock in case I've got things all wrong and it's much earlier than I think. But no, it is clearly the middle of the night, and my sly attempt at sneaking back in seems to be the last thing on my mother's mind.

I steal a glance at her and notice, for the first time, her red-rimmed and puffy eyes, and how her ragged robe, cinched tight at the waist, makes her look gaunt, almost child-like. *When did Mom lose so much weight?*

Her hands, pale and thin, tremble so badly that she keeps pressing them together, almost as if in prayer.

I reluctantly shuffle over to the kitchen table and plunk down on one of the chairs, my head swimming, my eyes probably bloodshot. Suddenly, I'm very confused, remnants of the weed pulsing through my veins and making my thoughts patchy, disconnected. The only other time I've seen Mom looking this lost and broken was years ago, when my grandfather died. A flurry of names and faces fly through my head. *Who in my life could have possibly met with a terrible fate? Is it Dad? Is it Gran?*

There's electricity in the air like right before a violent summer storm. I can't help but wonder what kind of damage it's going to cause. I reach my hand out to hers, trying to anchor the two of us to the kitchen table to calm her fraying nerves. Anxiety and trepidation swirl around us.

"Mom, what's going on? You're scaring me."

"Jess…" She breathes my name out with an exhausted sigh. The red rims of her eyes glisten with tears that are ready to spill. She pulls her hand away from mine, immediately creating a space between us.

Oh my God, it's my mom. *My mom.* She's the one who's sick or dying, or whatever this is about. That explains the trembling, the loss of weight, the fact that she's so rail-thin right now that her left hand is even devoid of her wedding ring.

"Mom, what happened? Are you sick? Is it cancer? How long have you known?" I close my eyes tight and hold in a breath, like shuttering a home right before the first surge of a hurricane. It seems that by locking myself down for a moment, I'm better able to brace myself for this impending doom.

"No, Jess, I'm not sick. It's not that. God, no, I'm fine."

The air starts escaping my lungs like a slow leak in a tire. I snap my eyes open because it's going to be okay. *Mom is fine. She's okay.* There's still a question of what the hell is going on, but it can't be worse than that. It surely can't be worse than that.

Mom breathes in like she's about to dive to the bottom of the pool, then spews poison through her mouth, her words burning me to the ground. "I've met someone else—another man." She pauses, looking down at her hands that are folded in her lap, as if they give her the cues for what to say next. Then she looks back up at me. And with her eyes and her words, she causes a black hole to implode my insides. "He and I…well…we're expecting a baby. I'm leaving your father."

The storm finally surges, a tornado of feelings threatening to carry me away.

"What the hell are you talking about?" is all I manage. My throat starts closing up as if the moisture from it has been sponged dry and I've been left with a pasty scum covering the inside of my mouth.

I don't know what she's talking about. *Did I hear things right?* I thought something bad had happened to *someone else*, not to *me*. I was just *consoling* my mother, for God's sake! I'm having a hard time comprehending how the last five minutes have unraveled so disastrously that I find myself begging to go back to the simple horror of being caught sneaking out with a boy.

"I'm sorry, Mom. I know I shouldn't have lied about where I was. I wasn't out for a brisk walk. I was meeting a friend—my boyfriend, actually. His name is Marcus, and you'll really like him, I think. I can bring

him by the house so you and Dad can meet him and —
"

"Jess, I don't care about your lies or being with a boy. Well, not right now at least. We need to talk. What I'm telling you is real, and it's important. Please listen to me."

But the words coming out of her mouth are flat and tinny, like they're being broadcast from an old-fashioned radio. I work to grasp the meaning of what she's saying, but I only catch random phrases, and it's like I'm trying to put together a puzzle without being able to look at the picture on the box.

"We've worked together for a long time and have grown very close over the years."

"Your dad and I have been leading separate lives for a while now, and we both knew this was coming. It would have ended years ago if it weren't for you holding us together."

"The baby wasn't planned, but Robert and I see now what a gift it'll be. It'll allow us all a new start. You'll be a big sister, just like you've always dreamed!"

And that's when the fireballs start spewing from my mouth, like when I get the stomach flu and can't stop puking. Swear words, accusations, questions — they all just shoot out of me faster and louder, until I can't even keep track of what I'm saying.

"What the hell do you mean, Mom? This doesn't make any sense. You're having a *baby*? You've been having an *affair*? Like, with another man? What about Dad? What about *me*?"

"I didn't plan for this, Jess. Your dad and me? Well, we've just sort of drifted apart. It has nothing to do with you. We just want different things out of our marriage right now."

When she mentions Dad, I suddenly remember that he's the other person in this messed-up family. *Where's*

Dad? I suddenly need him urgently, as if his presence might dampen the blow that just hit me.

"Dad? Dad?" I scream at the top of my lungs. Immediately, I see movement on the stairs, like he's been waiting in the wings to be called in. He rushes over to me, dressed in his plaid pajamas and a robe identical to my mother's—a present from me two Christmases ago, when I thought it would be cute for them to be the same, to be a matching pair. I catch a whiff of whiskey on his breath as he tries to embrace me in a hug, and for some reason, this only heightens the anger inside me.

"How long have you known about this?" I push away from him and scowl.

"Jess, calm down and we'll talk this through." He takes a deep breath. "I found out about the affair around a month and a half ago, near the start of the summer. And I was angry...so angry." He wipes the palms of his hands down his face, pulling at the sagging skin as he does. "But your mother and I have been together for almost twenty years, so at first we tried to work things out. We really did try." He meets my gaze with pleading eyes. "But, ultimately, it's not what either of us wants anymore.

"Then last week, when your mother told me about the pregnancy, well..." He takes a deep breath and swallows hard, his face suddenly turning steely. "Obviously, that means we're done for good." It's only now that my dad's voice takes on a razor-sharp edge.

"Your mother wasn't supposed to tell you until tomorrow. She was going to take you out to lunch, where you'd be able to talk things through in a little more detail. But apparently"—he glares at her with an icy stare— "she couldn't wait and decided to spring this on you in the middle of the night. Your mother always did have a knack for the dramatic." Bitter sarcasm drips off every word. "But, now that you know, I suppose it's best if we all sit down and discuss this as a family."

I find his choice of the word *family* a bit sardonic, and I glare angrily at him. He ignores my rigid body language and comes close to me again, attempting to hold me, hug me…but I feel like I'm suffocating in the velvety folds of his robe, and I thrash him away once more.

That's when he moves away from me and goes to stand with *her*.

"Jess, I know this is a lot to take in, especially all of a sudden, in the middle of the night. Your mom and I haven't been happy for a long time. We've grown apart. Did I want this to happen? No. Did I know she'd fallen in love with Robert from payroll? No. But I've also had time to reflect on the fact that I'm not blameless in all of this. And I guess I should've fought a little harder a whole lot earlier on.

"But in truth, neither one of us really wants this anymore. So…yes. Your mom is moving out to be with Robert. And we all need to discuss some options with you. Things are going to change. We think for the better, although we know this initial shock is going to be really hard for you. But you need to know how much we love you. Both of us."

I can't believe my ears. *How on earth can he defend her right now, after what she's just admitted?*

I don't dare glance over at my mother or I run the risk of poking her eyes out. In the back of my mind, I keep thinking that God is punishing me. I knew all the lying and sneaking around would catch up to me, and somehow, I would be punished. I just didn't think it would be like this.

I stand paralyzed in the middle of the kitchen for a few more moments, because really, I don't know where to go. The clock on the microwave now reads nearly three a.m. and I have a hard time believing that my life has completely turned upside-down in less than a half-hour. Less than the equivalent of one single episode of *The Simpsons* has erased the entire world I live in.

I push past my parents and through the front door. I'm so eager to get away from the house that I stumble over my own feet as I race down the driveway and catch myself before completely falling on my face. Then I run. I run and I run and I don't feel my legs reaching or my arms pumping, but I have this crazy idea that if I move fast enough, I'll break away from the nightmare my life has just become.

Several minutes later, I become vaguely aware that the pavement beneath my feet has transformed to silky sand, and I find myself flopping into the rusty tire swing that held so much excitement just a few hours before.

Divorce? A new baby? I plant the toes of my right sneaker in the dimple of wet sand directly beneath the swinging tire and use the rest of my body weight to twist the chain around and around. The tension grows and the tire creeps higher and higher until my toe can't anchor my body any further, spinning me recklessly out of control as the heavy night air whips by around me.

About the Author

Heather DiAngelis produces scholarly publications by day and writes young adult novels by night. If she has enough energy on the weekends, she can be found binge-watching shows with a cat nearby, losing lightsaber battles against her husband and sons, and perpetually wishing for more time. Her stories focus on mental health, "invisible" illnesses and the intersectionality surrounding queer characters, with the hope that teenagers will find themselves in one of her stories.

Heather loves to hear from readers. You can find her contact information, website details and author profile page at https://www.finch-books.com

Sign up for our newsletter and find out about all our romance book releases, eBook sales and promotions, sneak peeks and FREE romance books!

CPSIA information can be obtained
at www.ICGtesting.com
Printed in the USA
JSHW061234170822
29395JS00001B/38